NIGHT CRIME

A Kat Makris Greek Mafia Mystery

ALEX A. KING

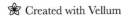 Created with Vellum

For Corinne:
We can play Snakes and Ladders now.

Chapter 1

When I was a kid my father sat me down and told me I could be anything I wanted, except a lawyer or a hooker. By the time I reached high school he'd changed his mind. A prostitute, he said, was at least honest about what they did for money.

Mom covered my ears with her hands. "Mike, are you kidding me? Why are you telling her this bullshit?"

"Mom said 'bullshit'," I cackled. My mom, who almost never cursed.

Dad laughed. "She has heard worse than 'bullshit,' I guarantee it."

"There's nothing wrong with being a lawyer," Mom said

Dad made a sucking sound with his teeth. He cupped his ear. "Do you hear that? That is the sound of a lawyer sucking blood and money."

Mom let go of my ears and got busy doing one of those mom things. Wiping invisible crumbs off the counter or something like that. "There are worse things Kat could do."

"Name one." Dad grinned. He leaned back in his chair, hands behind his head. "I dare you."

She pitched a paper towel at his head. "Cop."

"What is wrong with the police?" Dad asked. "Are you a fugitive on the run because a one-armed man killed your secret first husband?"

Mom pointed at Dad with the Windex bottle. "My problem with law enforcement isn't what they do. Sometimes they go to work and never come home. That's my problem with them. I don't want my daughter going to work and never coming home. Lawyers come home."

As luck, fate, and the universe's other tricksters would have it, Mom never got to see me become a lawyer, probably because I hadn't been studying law. I dropped out of college when she died and went on to become a bill collector. That career ended abruptly when I was twenty-eight and my family—my Greek family who were also Family—knocked me out, stuck me on a private plane, and hauled my snoring, drooling carcass to Greece.

As luck, fate, and the universe's tricksters would also have it, I was attracted to two men with badges. One wore his out in the open; the other kept his hidden, while pretending to be a badass mobster. I'd kissed them both, and both men made my toes curl and my sensible underwear smoke.

Earlier today the man who was blatantly a cop told me to call him if I wanted a good time. He was simple, but we were complicated.

And the other guy?

Strong, silent Xander. Henchman. Bodyguard. Secret agent. The man who brought me hot chocolate and knew when to retie my ponytail. His taste in music was tragic, and he always made me ride in the backseat.

I'd just driven a few hundred kilometers, chasing a hunch—a hunch that Xander could talk.

That hunch had paid off. Now I was standing in front an open hotel door, wondering who I was and what had happened to the old Kat.

Okay: Greece. Greece had happened.

I aimed a finger at Xander, who was missing a shirt. His face was as chiseled as his body, and every part of him that I could see was bronze and smooth. His exterior said he was in his late twenties, early thirties, but his eyes said they'd seen it all, and "it all" was mostly clowns. Although I couldn't see it now, his back was covered in a waterfall of scars.

"Ha! I knew it. You can talk."

He leaned forward so his head was in the hotel's hall-way, raised his eyebrows at Elias, who was waiting a couple of dozen feet away, discreetly watching for trouble. Elias nodded once in acknowledgement. A silent exchange. Typical in every way.

Xander took a step backwards, giving me room. He was expecting me to come inside, but my feet were glued to the floor. Something light flashed in his dark, serious eyes.

"We can do this out here," I said.

"No, we can't."

His voice was deep, rich, warm bordering on scalding. The kind of voice that's buried under a thick blanket of testosterone. The kind of voice that can talk a woman into doing that one thing she won't do with other guys. But Xander wasn't the kind of man who would abuse that power. Rumor had it the man lived like a monk.

"I just wanted to see if you could talk. Now I that I know you can, I should probably go."

"It's late."

I tilted my head. "Is it late or is it early? Is the glass

half full or half empty? These are very important philosophical questions."

"Just get in here." He grabbed my hand and yanked me into the hotel room.

The room was every hotel room ever. Even the swankiest had an air of shabbiness lurking beneath the Egyptian cotton sheets and crown molding. This wasn't the swankiest, but it wasn't bedbug central either. Marble tile floor. Borderline tasteful art of the Parthenon and other Greek architectural wonders. Widescreen television that was currently replaying a basketball game. Balcony with a view of the parking lot.

"But Elias ..." I stammered.

"Can't come in."

"He's my bodyguard."

"Your body is safe with me."

Was that whooshing feeling below my diaphragm disappointment or relief?

"I mean, I can't just leave him in the hallway. It's not nice."

"He's okay with it. That's the job."

"I get that it's the job, but I'm still not used to this life. To me it's bad manners to leave a guy standing in the hallway."

He slowly shook his head with something that might have been exasperation and reached for one of two keycards sitting on the desk. Then he opened the door and vanished for a moment. When he came back, the keycard was gone.

"Elias is across the hall if you need him."

"You paid for two rooms?"

"Yes."

"Is it for your other personality?"

"It's for you."

"You knew I would come?"

"Hoped."

The room came with one chair that was currently snugged up to the desk. Xander pulled it out and offered it to me. Once I was sitting, he leaned his back against the wall and folded his arms.

"You left without saying goodbye," I said.

"There wasn't time."

"Why did you leave?"

"Business."

"NIS or Family. Or something else?"

"Yes."

Frustration welled up inside me. "Which is it?"

The subject changed. "I don't talk because it's easier."

"Easier?"

"To lie."

"To lie that you're a good guy or that you're a bad guy?"

His smile was tight. "Yes."

This conversation was so circular it was making me dizzy. "You're not exactly an open book, are you?"

"More like a classified file."

The questions in my head jockeyed for attention. They all wanted to go first.

"Whose side are you on? I mean really, whose side?"

"I'm assigned to your grandmother. I do whatever she needs me to do, whatever that is."

"She killed your whole family."

Not even a twitch. "Yes and no."

Schrödinger's slaughter, obviously. "How can you not hate her?"

It took him a moment to answer. "What do you know about it?"

"The night your family was killed, you mean?"

He nodded once.

"Uh …" I dredged my memory for the few details I had. "Her family and your family were adversaries. She meant to take out a few key family members, but instead you were the only one who escaped."

He took a deep breath. "That's true and it's not. She didn't kill my family. She killed a whole family of people by mistake, but they weren't my family."

"Are you saying you were adopted?"

"Abducted. Kyria Katerina saved me."

"Saved you and raised you?"

"Yes."

"And then you joined the NIS?"

NIS. The National Intelligence Service. Greece's CIA.

"It was her idea—one I liked. I applied and they recruited me right out of the army."

I blew out a sigh. This was awfully familiar. Dad had also joined the NIS on Grandma's command. She was really into living dangerously. Grandma, I had discovered a couple of days ago, worked for Interpol. Yes, Greece's most notorious mob boss was also a cop. Duality was everywhere.

"But now you're also a henchman?"

"Not everything is what it seems."

"I am," I said.

He laughed. "Maybe that was true before Greece, but now you have layers."

"Like an onion, right?" Just my luck, this was shaping up to be a *Shrek* joke. "What happened to your real family?"

"The Makris family is my real family."

"I meant your birth family."

A smile. Lots of straight, white teeth. Great dental work or good genes? "I knew what you meant."

"You were just being evasive, right?"

"It keeps me alive."

The questions in my head kept on coming, but they had to wait for an ear-popping yawn that worked its way up from my toes to my mouth. The long drive had caught up with me and now it wanted its eight hours of slumber.

Xander pushed away from the wall. "Bed. We can talk more in the morning."

Another yawn forced its way out. Xander couldn't help himself: he yawned next. We laughed. He carefully pulled me up out of the chair, loosened my ponytail, pushed the hair tie into my pocket.

"I love your hair," he said. "It always smells like flowers."

My cheeks flushed. "Shampoo. It's a modern invention."

"No. I think it's you." He buried his nose in my hair and inhaled. "Definitely you."

And then he kissed me.

Chapter 2

Baby Dimitri looked like he would never overcome the grief. The Godfather of the Night and Winter Boots shoved his finger up his left nostril and blasted a runny nose oyster onto the sidewalk with his right.

"Every autumn this happens," he lamented. "The women pack up their breasts and leave my beach until next summer."

Baby Dimitri has the physique of a pipe snake, dresses for Florida in the 1960s, and bathes in Brylcreem. Despite the fact that he's corruption with feet, I like the old guy and he seems to like me.

"Don't you own a bunch of strip clubs?"

"Yes, but it is not the same. Those I have to pay for. On the beach they are free. Everything is better when it is free."

Marika crossed herself. She had a bag of cotton balls in one hand and a wooden statue with a giant wiener in the other, but she managed anyway. Marika is a lot of woman, and she's almost always wrapped in a floral dress. At the

8

moment she was pregnant, so she was slowly evolving from a comfortable love seat to a full-size couch. She's my body-guard, which mostly means she collects a paycheck for waving a gun around while Elias, my real bodyguard, watches out for my hide. I think of her as more of a sidekick and friend. Marika is married to my cousin's cousin's cousin, Takis, one of Grandma's favorite henchmen. Takis doesn't think Marika should be anywhere near a gun, and I'm inclined to agree.

"Amen," she said. "Just like free food. Free food always tastes better."

"Not me," I said. "I prefer things I've paid for, that way I know they're mine."

Baby Dimitri managed a smile. "That is what I like to hear. Come in and buy some boots for winter. I have a new shipment. The newest fashions, or so they tell me. Pay for them and they will be yours."

Baby Dimitri sells shoes and souvenirs in a brightly lit store that sits directly across from the beach. It's a strange mix but it's not his main business. As a Godfather of the Night, Baby Dimitri specializes in nocturnal crimes. Strip clubs. Prostitution. Drugs and fighting rings. I suspect the shop is a funnel, of sorts. Dirty money flows in and comes out smelling like candy.

"Here." Baby Dimitri pulled a pair of boots off the shelf. Black. Wicked heel. Totally practical for traipsing around Greece, with its pockmarked streets and dirt roads. "Thirty-nine is your shoe size yes?"

"How did you know?"

He tapped a knuckle on my head. "This is not the first time you have bought shoes from me."

Less than a month ago I'd bought espadrilles from Baby Dimitri's shop. Then I had the bad luck to be wearing them when the NIS kidnapped me and dumped

9

me in Naples, Italy. My pretty shoes had barely survived the experience.

"Good memory."

I plunked my backside down on a small bench and jammed my feet into the boots. The heel was killer and I could barely walk.

"Takis will not let me wear boots like that," Marika said, eyeing my feet.

I staggered back to the bench and unzipped the boots. "Why not?"

Baby Dimitri laughed. "He is worried you will stab him in a fight with the heels."

Marika's head bobbed. She reached into the bag of cotton balls. "Baby Dimitri is right."

"But he lets you have guns," I said.

She made a face. "I would not say 'lets'."

The godfather handed me a pair of knee-high flats. Now these were more my style. I pulled them on. Perfect.

"Your friend is eating cotton balls," he said.

Marika paused, cotton ball halfway to her mouth. "What?"

My brows took a hike. "Cotton balls, Marika? Really?"

"Cotton balls?" Marika looked at the packet. "I thought it was cotton candy."

"Is it sweet?" I asked her.

"No, but everything tastes different with this pregnancy. I thought maybe these had that fake sugar." We looked at her. Slowly, she put the bag down. "Heh. Next time do not keep them on the shelf with the sweets."

Baby Dimitri shook his head. "You Makris people …" He obviously thought our family tree was missing a few vital forks. Like he could talk. Allegedly, he'd hacked most of the branches off his tree. His only living sibling was a porn star, producer, and director whose teenage son had an uncanny knack for tagging along on my road trips.

I checked out the boots in the mirror. The high heels were sexier but these I could run in if I had to. And lately I'd had to run a lot. Things in the family (and the Family) had calmed down in the past week or so, but most of the time my dad's side of the family tree was a flaming hot mess. Grandma is Greece's most notorious crime boss, although unlike Baby Dimitri she refuses to stoop to exploiting women, so there are no strippers or prostitutes on her payroll. Also, as previously mentioned, she works for Interpol. Grandma says to catch a criminal sometimes you have to be one. I was starting to feel like I needed a flowchart app to keep up with who works for whom. If someone was murdered in the woods, and nobody heard them scream, was that a good thing or a bad thing? I didn't know anymore.

Baby Dimitri made an approving noise. "You like them?"

"I like them." I pulled the boots off and handed them to him, then I glanced around the store. Something, or rather someone, was missing. "Where is Kyrios Laki?"

Laki is Baby Dimitri's decrepit pal and henchman. His teeth (what few he has remaining) are gold and he gets his kicks blowing up stuff.

"His father died, so he went to make bombs to cope with his feelings."

Yikes! "I hope no innocent civilians get hurt."

"These are fake bombs. This one *malakas* who buys ammunition from me has mistaken me for a goat, and now he is trying to fuck me in the *kolos*."

"Should you be telling me this?"

"Why not?" Big shrug. "The bombs are fake. Laki is

making them so they make a *klasimo* sound and blast glitter."

Basically they'd be glitter spurting whoopee cushions.

"Glitter." Marika shuddered and crossed herself. "Glitter was invented by the devil."

Baby Dimitri shot her a disbelieving look. "Your friend is a *vlakas* who eats cotton balls, but she knows glitter."

Vlakas. Stupid. Marika wasn't stupid, she was just Marika.

The shop's windows began to rattle. Low-flying aircraft. Not military—not fast enough. Marika crossed herself and reached for the cotton wool balls again. Baby Dimitri snatched the packet out of her hand and stuffed it behind the counter. Overhead, the plane banked and came back for seconds, lower this time. Any lower and it would be using the narrow waterfront road as a landing strip.

"We should look," Marika said. "What if it crashes and the authorities need eyewitnesses? I would be a good eyewitness. I remember everything."

"She remembers everything except that cotton balls are not sweets," Baby Dimitri muttered. "Go out if you want, but I am staying in here. I do not stay alive by being stupid."

Feet pointed toward the door, Marika shrugged and hoisted her bag higher on her shoulder. "Fine. But do not blame me if you miss being the first to see the plane crash."

The Godfather of the Night and These Cool New Boots shook his hands at the ceiling. "I can see why this one's husband comes to my clubs."

Marika's exit came to a screeching halt. She pivoted dangerously on one heel. Her eyes narrowed to vicious slits. Someone was going to lose a head. Takis would likely lose two.

"What did you say?" Her tone was that of a scorned woman with a bunch of guns in her oversized shoulder bag.

Baby Dimitri opened his mouth, but the words didn't have a shot at making it out.

There was a loud *CRACK*!

Plaster began to rain down from the ceiling. Flecks at first, then chunks, and then the whole roof caved in, dumping a pile of rubble on the shop's floor. A dust cloud enveloped us. In that same moment Elias, my real body-guard, came bolting into the shop. He threw me over his shoulder and raced out, depositing me on the sidewalk, then he went back in for Marika. He pushed her out the door then went back in a third time. He came out dragging Baby Dimitri, who slowly drew a cigarette packet from his shirt pocket. Cigarette balanced on his lip, the old mobster struck a match on the doorframe and touched it the tobacco.

"I think I need a new roof," he said.

———

A CROWD WAS GATHERING, drawn by the drama. It wouldn't be long before the crowd became a throng, maybe even a horde. There's nothing small-town Greeks love more than a gossip, especially when it isn't about them.

The plane had been banking overhead all this time, spinning lazy circles, when suddenly it broke the holding pattern and rocketed away.

"*Gamo tin maimou sou!*" Baby Dimitri swore.

Short story short: he wanted to bump uglies with the pilot's monkey.

"We should call the police," I said.

Baby Dimitri laughed. "For what? Because my roof collapsed?"

"Because there's a good chance your roof didn't just collapse and we both know it. Could be there's an undetonated bomb in there."

The dust slowly settled. Baby Dimitri dropped his cigarette and did the Twist on the stub. "Okay, I am going in."

Elias stopped him. "I will go."

"Is he always this heroic?" the godfather asked me.

"Mostly," I said.

"I have been taking lessons and working out," Elias said, chin up and chest out. "Xander has been teaching me everything he knows."

The bottom fell out of my stomach. Xander was an unresolved issue.

"I would go in too but somebody needs to guard you," Marika said.

Behind her back, Baby Dimitri rolled his eyes.

She whipped around, finger pointed. "I saw that. And do not think I have forgotten what you said about my husband."

"You saw nothing. I am behind you."

Marika touched her eye. "I see everything."

"Have you met her children?" I said. "She sees everything."

"Even things I do not want to see," she muttered.

Elias came back out. His expression was grim.

"We have a problem."

Chapter 3

Baby Dimitri lit another cigarette. "This is a problem, but the good news is that it is not my problem. So if you would collect your problem and get it out of here, that would be good."

The problem was … a kind of jigsaw puzzle. A human jigsaw puzzle. The puzzle pieces were slender, female, and frozen solid. Her plastic-wrapped parts, like everything else in the shop, were covered in a layer of ceiling dust.

My head tilted like Nipper, the RCA Victor dog. "Where's the head? We can't identify her until we find the head."

"Who cares?" Baby Dimitri said. "Just get it out of here."

"She's in your shop. Why would you think she's my problem? I don't know any dead, frozen people. They make really lousy friends."

Elias was rooting around in the rummage, carefully collecting pieces and putting the puzzle together.

"How can he do that?" Marika said. Her skin was green on bronze.

"I grew up on a farm," Elias said. "Meat is meat."

Marika gulped.

I steered her toward the door. "You should go outside and get some fresh air."

"Good idea. I should do that." She hurried outside and immediately upchucked on the sidewalk. Baby Dimitri's face twitched.

Elias held up a human head. Female like the rest of the parts. Long fair hair. "Found it."

"Good." Baby Dimitri lit another cigarette. "Now you can go."

Something wasn't right—something other than the dead woman.

My eyes narrowed to suspicious slits as I watched Baby Dimitri satisfy his oral fixation. "What's going on? Do you know her?"

He shook his head. "Know her? Her head is frozen. How can anyone tell who she is?"

"You got a blow dryer?" Elias wanted to know.

"*Gamo tin Panayia mou!* No, I do not have a blow dryer. Get out of here, all of you."

"There is a microwave out the back," Marika called through the open door.

I looked at her in horror. "We can't microwave her head. It'll cook."

"*Ai sto dialo*," Baby Dimitri said. "Get out!"

"And leave the scene of the crime?"

"What crime? Take the body and there will be no crime, just a roof that needs to be fixed. A roof I have to pay for."

I pulled out my phone and called the cavalry. Not the cops—I called Grandma. She'd know what to do about body parts. If anyone knew dismemberment it was Grandma.

"Someone sent Baby Dimitri a message," I said when she answered.

"No—no message. Not for me," Baby Dimitri said.

Grandma and I both ignored him. "What kind of message?"

"An arm, a leg, a head, a torso, and another arm and leg."

There was a long pause. Then: "Did the head say anything?"

"Not yet, but it might once it thaws out."

The second pause was even longer than the first. "Are all the parts frozen?"

"I think so."

"Stay there."

"Are you sending Xander?"

"No, I am calling the police." She sounded indignant, like calling the police was a no-brainer. Back home it would have been, but I wasn't in Oregon anymore.

In the not-too-far distance there was the sound of imminent sirens.

"I think they already heard the news," I said. "It's not every day body parts fall out of the sky."

There was a noise on Grandma's end, then a voice.

"Maybe it was an eagle," Papou said.

Papou is what the American-Italian Mafia calls a consigliere. From what I've heard, his advice ranges from dodgy to suspicious. He gets from A to B in a wheelchair with a shotgun rack mounted on the back, and he owns a hand-me-down eagle. When I first met Papou he had a death wish, but the eagle is working wonders as a therapy bird; now he only wants to kill other people.

"A whole body?" Grandma said, her voice drier than Greece in summer.

"Maybe a flock of eagles," Papou said cheerfully.

"When the police arrive, follow that body," Grandma told me. "I want to know who it is and why someone is sending Baby Dimitri such a message."

I wanted to ask her if this was mob business or Interpol business, but did it really matter? She'd expect me to follow her orders anyway, and this time I was okay with that. Curiosity had me gripped between its fluffy, seductive paws.

A cop car lurched to a halt in the street outside the shoe shop. It was joined by an ambulance and a howling fire truck. Nobody had called the emergency number, yet here they were, the three benevolent horsemen.

Detective Nikos Melas angled out of the police cruiser. My hormones and heart took a moment to appreciate the view. He was wearing jeans, boots, and a black t-shirt under his leather jacket. He had a gun on his hip and handcuffs in his back pocket. His skin was golden brown and his eyes were the color of good chocolate. I hated to compare people to food but my stomach was growling.

When he saw me he grinned, elevating him from a tough kind of pretty to devastating. "I should have known you would be involved."

"I'm not involved!" I squeaked. A couple of firemen and the paramedics trudged past. "I was just standing here, buying boots."

"New boots, eh?" He looked down at my feet. "Nice." A nod at the building behind me. "What happened to you this time?"

"Would you believe me if I told you a body fell out of the sky, and that it was cut into pieces and frozen?"

He looked up at the sky and ran a hand through his short, black hair. I wasn't sure if he was expecting a second corpse to fall out of the sky or if he was simply amazed that one person could be so unlucky.

"If it were anyone else …"

The firefighters emerged from Baby Dimitri's shop, shaking their heads. They climbed up into their truck and rolled away. The paramedics came back for a stretcher and body bag. Melas watched them tilt and lift the stretcher.

"You could have just carried the pieces out one at a time," Marika said to them.

"This I have to see." At five-ten or thereabouts, Melas wasn't the tallest guy on the planet, but he was taller and therefore faster than me. He exchanged nods with Baby Dimitri and Elias, kissed Marika on both cheeks, then entered the shoe and souvenir store, right behind the paramedics.

"If you break anything you will have to pay," Baby Dimitri called after them.

"Virgin Mary," Melas swore a moment later. He stepped back out. "You were serious," he said to me.

"Would I lie about a dismembered body?"

"Who is it?" He aimed his question at Baby Dimitri.

"*Gamisou*, what makes you think I know?"

Melas hooked a thumb over his shoulder. "It is your shop. Dismembered bodies do not usually randomly fall out of the sky. Would anyone you know want to send you that kind of message?"

I stood there pokerfaced because if even a fraction of what I knew about the Godfather of the Night and Stiletto Heels was true, then he had more enemies than I'd had orgasms in my life—and I'd had a lot of those. Not lately, which was why they were on my mind right now. But in the past? Plenty.

Baby Dimitri's face hardened. "You have mistaken me for someone else. If it is a message, it is a message telling me I need a new roof. When you find who did this, tell them they owe me money. Now take the body and go."

Melas put his hands on his hips. Looked to me like he was this close to arguing with the old mobster. He watched the paramedics ease the stretcher into the ambulance, the dead woman's pieces contained within a black body bag, and changed his mind.

"Time to go," he told me. "Can I call you later?"

"Grandma wants me to come with you."

His face said, No," his mouth said, "Okay." Thanks to one of those right-place- right-time moments he knew Grandma outranked him when it came to law enforcement. Before learning about her superhero identity he was merely outgunned.

"Marika?" I said.

"Forget it," she said, digging through her bag. "I know what kind of things happen in morgues. Zombies, for one."

"I don't think zombies are real," I said.

"Nobody ever thinks zombies are real until suddenly they are dragging one leg and moaning about brains."

I looked at my bodyguard, who was deliberately avoiding eye contact. "Can you take her home, please?"

"Good idea," Marika said. "And let us stop for a little something to eat on the way back, eh? Baby is hungry."

"Keep her away from cotton balls," Baby Dimitri called out as we bustled back to our respective cars.

Melas raised his brows. "Cotton balls?"

"They do look like cotton candy," I said in Marika's defense.

———

"YOU DON'T HAVE to do this," Melas said when we arrived. I had followed him in my yellow VW Beetle.

"Grandma said I have to. And what Grandma wants …"

"I know how that song goes." He looked me up and down, his gaze lingering at chest level before reconnecting with my eyes. "Do you have a jacket?"

"Should I?" It was cooling down, but jackets were still a few weeks away.

Melas shrugged off his leather jacket and held it out for me. Once he'd helped me into it, he zipped it from hip to chin.

I jiggled my arms in the roomy jacket. "Is this necessary?"

"Ask me again in five minutes."

We rode the elevator down to the subterranean level that housed the morgue. The doors opened onto a scene out of a zombie movie, minus the shambling dead. Bodies everywhere, covered with sheets. Some were the pale green standard morgue issue. Others were floral and striped. We stepped out into an Arctic winter.

Melas grabbed my hand, used it as a rudder to steer me between the bodies.

At the best of times, the morgue attendant is a small dog in scrubs. Today he was in scrubs and a winter coat with a furry hood that hid his black hair and made his cheekbones stand out like razor blades. I used to think he was more like a miniature schnauzer, but today he was leaning toward shaky Chihuahua. Either the man was taking coffee intravenously or the pressure of the job was getting to him.

He cycled through the whole range of facial expressions as we approached the front desk.

"Is she here for the receptionist job?"

"We've met before," I said. "I'm Katerina Makris."

"I don't care who you are. All I want to know is if you want a job."

I'd been offered several jobs since I arrived in Greece, all of them various degrees of illegal or just not my thing. Nothing against porn, but I didn't fancy being used as a crème-filled bowling ball in one of Donk's mother's movies, no matter how much she thought my status as Baboulas's granddaughter would boost sales.

"What does it pay?"

"All the brains you can eat, plus we have the best coffeemaker ten euros can buy." He laughed hysterically, then his face clouded over like tears were imminent. "I am kidding about the brains but not the coffeemaker. Unless you like eating dead people … which would be useful, now that I think about it." He waved a hand at all the bodies. "It pays a little."

"I'll think about it," I said, immediately forgetting.

He shifted his attention to Melas. "Tell me you are here to take a body."

"Not yet," Melas said. "We want to see the woman who just came in."

The shaky attendant shook his hands at the ceiling. "Which one?"

"The one that was, uh, in pieces."

"The ice cream woman." He chuckled. "I used to give them all nicknames. Now I have so many dead bodies that I cannot name them all. I save nicknames for the special ones, like your woman. Come."

He scuttled off, knowing we would follow. I wanted to. I really did. But I was frozen through to the bone.

Melas slung his arm around my shoulder. "Come on."

"Aren't you freezing?"

"How can I be cold with you here?"

"Liar."

22

His arm shook. It wasn't just laughter; Melas was a human Popsicle. His goose bumps had goose bumps.

"You can have your jacket back."

"Forget it. If you take it off I will just put you back in it." He said it like he meant it, so I believed him. In a way this was a momentous occasion. It was the first time he'd wanted to put me in clothes. Normally he expressed a healthy and passionate interest in tearing them off.

The morgue was a hoarder's paradise. Bodies everywhere. We turned sideways to ease down the corridor.

"Nobody has money to bury their dead," the morgue guy called out over his shoulder. "So they conveniently forget to pick them up. But the good news is that now we have plenty of food to feed the refugees."

"Gus is joking," Melas assured me.

"Am I? I cannot tell anymore. My body is ninety percent coffee and ten percent ice. I have not felt my *archidia* for weeks. They are up inside me, hugging my kidneys for warmth. But we have to keep it like a refrigerator in here, otherwise the bodies will start to stink like a dead goat in July." His laugh came out like a bark. "I say 'we', but there is no one working here but me."

"Why not?" I said.

With one hand he rubbed his thumb and fingers together. "Money. My boss cries every time she gives me my paycheck. Okay, here is your woman." He peeled back an orange and avocado-colored sheet. The bits of woman who'd fallen through Baby Dimitri's roof had been cobbled back together on a stretcher.

"When you find out who did this to her, I would like to thank them for freezing her because they are saving the government money. Of course, I cannot stitch her back together until she thaws out, so ..."

She'd thawed some since she fell through Baby

Dimitri's roof, but not enough for me to get a good look at her face. Too much frost. Looking at her muscle tone and skin she was maybe in her thirties, although it was hard to say for sure. Corpses really weren't my area of expertise, despite the fact that my Family had created lots of them. And I was pretty sure the Family identified them *before* the killing happened. Her nails were fire engine red with gold glitter accents. Her breasts were … well maybe not the best money could buy, but I had to give her surgeon credit for being able to stuff so much silicone or saline into a teeny tiny space. Airlines all over the world should hire that guy as a consultant, because he really knew how to pack 'em in. She was a blonde—or wanted to be. Only her waxer and colorist knew her original hair color.

"What do you think?" I asked Melas.

He didn't answer. His face was stone. "Can you turn her over?"

Gus paused. "All of her, or one part in particular?"

"Torso," Melas told him.

Gus rolled her—well, part of her—over. Sprawling across her lower back was a tattoo of a man's face. He had a curly helmet of hair and a vaguely familiar smirk.

Squint. "Who is that?" I said.

"David Hasselhoff," Melas said.

I tilted my head. "Really? Why would anyone get a tattoo of David Hasselhoff?"

Gus looked horrified. "Are you kidding me? Hasselhoff is huge in Europe, especially Germany. 'Nobody hassles the Hoff,' " he said in English.

"But a tattoo? Really? And … there?"

Lower back tattoos have all kinds of names, most of them unflattering and sexual in nature. For that special someone who likes to pull out and finish on a piece of art.

24

"She loved David Hasselhoff," Melas said quietly. "She was raised by *Knight Rider* and *Baywatch*."

"You know her? Or is that your cop brain speculating?"

I turned around to look at him but he was already half way out of the room.

"Wait for me!"

I took off after him.

"If you have any sheets you are not using, I could use them," Gus called out. "My mama will not let me take any more of hers."

Chapter 4

Without a word, Melas climbed into his cop car and took off with the siren blaring. I jumped into my Beetle and hit the gas. Keeping up with him wasn't easy, and the speed I was going was probably against the law, but given that I was following a cop I figured I had a free pass.

He took the road up to Mount Pelion, screeching to a halt when the road filled with sheep. Their shepherd was taking his sweet time, doing more texting than herding. I hopped out of my car and jogged up to the police cruiser. The windows were up. Melas was starting straight ahead, jaw cut from a slab of granite.

I rapped my knuckle on the window and made the universal gesture for "roll the freakin' window down."

The window hummed down a few inches, but he didn't speak, didn't look at me.

"Who was she?"

Bells jangled as the sheep moseyed at the speed of molasses.

"I have to see Baboulas."

"Why?" A horrible, freezing cold sensation crept along

my spine and settled in my lower intestines. It stuck a fork in my bladder. "Oh my God, is she one of ours?"

Silence.

"Melas?"

"Yes."

"Who?" I thought about it. Melas knew the family well but he didn't seem especially close to anyone except me. But that wasn't always true. Once upon a time, Melas had smudged groins with one of the family's wives. Their affair had produced a child. Melas had never said who the woman was, and I had never asked. At the time it had seemed safer for everyone involved. "It's her, isn't it?"

The shepherd finally convinced the last of his flock to get off the road. Melas shot away like a rocket, leaving me standing there like a dumbass.

I huffed out a long, frustrated sigh and turned back to the Beetle. While I'd been talking to Melas, a bus had pulled up behind me, followed by a long chain of cars. The bus driver stuck his head out the window. The other drivers followed suit. One at a time they showed me the good ol' one-fingered Greek wave, some of them in pairs.

Just what I needed after the morning I'd had.

I stood on the center line and karate-chopped, two-handed, at my groin, inviting them to suck on something I didn't have. Then I hopped into my car and sped away, feeling satisfied and ashamed. Catholic guilt has got nothing on Greek guilt.

Back at the compound, Melas had pulled up to the guardhouse. He was arguing with the guard. Hands were waving, high and fast. Voices were raised.

I pulled up behind the police cruiser, stuck both pinkies in my mouth and blasted an ear-piercing whistle.

Both men winced.

"What's going on, children?"

"He wants to go in," the guard—one of my cousins—told me.

"So why aren't you letting him in?"

"Orders are orders."

"Who ordered you to not let Detective Melas in?"

"Baboulas said no one is to come in without her permission. That includes this one."

Melas pinned him to the guardhouse wall by the throat. "I need to see Baboulas."

Christ on a crusty crouton. *Greek men.*

I vaulted out of the Beetle, leaving the keys swinging in the ignition. Nobody would dare steal my car—never mind that I'd absconded with a family vehicle or two in my time. I grabbed each man by the middle finger and yanked them backwards; not hard enough to hear a crack but enough to make two grown men cry.

"Step away from the testosterone, boys."

Melas let out a string of curse words; the guard took that as challenge and reeled out his own. Things got pornographic fast. I wasn't sure anything they were spitting out was feasible—not with our current laws of physics and nature, anyway. If they were, they'd be illegal. Greeks can do anything—and I mean *anything*—with farm animals, saints, vegetables, and mothers-in-law.

I yanked harder. "Enough!"

Four knees buckled. Not mine; I felt pretty tough.

"Make it stop," the guard begged.

There was a slow clap from the far side of the massive wrought iron gate that served as the entrance to the family compound. Grandma was watching me terrorize two grown men, smiling at me like I'd gone full-on Moses, parting the Red Sea. Grandma is a weather-beaten Oompa Loompa, whose body is fighting gravity and losing. She keeps her long gray-shot hair trapped in a low-riding bun, and lives in loose black dresses, on account of how my grandfather is dead and that's what Greek widows do. Once they go black they never go back. The gossip would be vicious if they reverted to their old colors.

Grandma raised her fist. "That is how you do it, show them who is the boss."

"I was just breaking up a fight," I said.

"Good work. Now can you explain why you are on the YouTube, telling strangers to suck your *poutsa*?"

I gawked at her. "On YouTube? *Already?*"

"Good news drives a sports car. Bad news uses one of those transporters from *Star Trek*."

"You watch *Star Trek*?"

"I like Worf," she said. "I would like to put him over my knee and—"

"Moving on," I said quickly. "How about that weather we're having? It's very … weather-ish."

She addressed the men. "What is the problem?"

Melas spoke up. "Kyria Katerina, I need to talk to you."

"Talk, Nikos. Talk."

"In private."

"Okay."

"Thea Katerina," the guard said, wincing. "You told me not to let him in."

"And I forgot to tell you I changed my mind."

What had changed was that Melas was in Winkler's kitchen in Germany when Grandma came out as Interpol. Now he knew they were on the same team … more or less; Grandma couldn't fully give up crime because crime was the honey she used to catch flies. Before the big reveal in Germany, Melas thought I was dead and had warned Grandma that eventually he'd be coming for her, which must have triggered the lockout.

I released the fingers. Both men slowly rose, massaging life back into their screaming digits.

"Come, Nikos. Walk with me," Grandma said. "You too, Katerina."

Melas shot me a look like he didn't think my presence was the best idea he'd ever heard, but screw that. I already knew the dead woman was family and his former paramour. They'd had a secret baby together, so someone in the family was halfway to orphaned and didn't know it yet. As a half-orphan myself, my heart ached for that child. Unwanted or not, I tagged along.

Grandma took us to one of the smaller gardens in the courtyard, where she was prepping the plants for the coming winter. She pulled a pair of small clippers from her apron pocket and began clipping her roses, according to some gardening rule I wasn't aware of.

"So what is it?" she said.

Melas looked like he was psyching himself up. "Litsa is dead."

Grandma kept clipping. "George's wife?"

"Yes."

The bottom dropped out of my stomach. Litsa and my cousin George (a second or third cousin, but in Greece cousins are cousins) had three boys, the youngest of whom was the coolest, most adorable kid I'd ever met. Tomas was crazy-smart and knowledge-thirsty, and now he was motherless.

"Litsa," I whispered. "The children."

Then I burst into tears.

Grandma shot me a look, half disapproving, half compassionate. "Act now. Cry later."

"It's nothing," I said, wiping my eyes with the back of my hand. "Just allergies."

Her attention swung back to Melas. "She was the woman who was dropped on Baby Dimitri's shop, yes?"

"Yes."

"Okay. I will let George know." For a moment she looked fifty years older, which wasn't a good thing since she's about nine hundred years old anyway.

"I can tell him," Melas said. His face and shoulders said his heart wasn't in it.

Grandma stopped clipping. "Litsa was family. As the head of my family it is my duty to inform her husband." The clippers went back into the apron. "Do you want to ask questions now, or wait?"

"Somebody will come later."

"Not you?"

"I have to find out who owns that airplane. It could take a while."

"Let me know if you need assistance."

My family—and Greece—was one big desert of shifting sands. Every time I thought I was on steady ground, the terrain wagged its finger at me as if to say, "Don't even think about getting comfortable." Right now the sand was getting sucked out from under me. Grandma wasn't just law enforcement; she was a higher totem on the totem pole than Melas. He knew it and he was starting to turn green under that buttery caramel tan.

Then it hit me. If the dead woman was his former paramour, and the dead woman was Litsa, then one of her boys belonged to Melas.

"I will," he said.

Grandma wiped her hands on her apron, then ambled away in the direction of her shack. It was just Melas and me now. I turned to face him.

"How long ago?"

His forehead scrunched up. "What?"

31

"How long ago were you and Litsa … uh … together?"

"A few."

"So which one of her boys is yours?"

"Does it matter?"

Time for a different approach. "What's your father's name?"

He swallowed. Looked away. "Tomas."

Greeks are big on recycling names. First they use up the paternal grandparents names, followed by the maternal. Litsa and George had three boys, so that meant they'd used up both grandfathers' monikers. It wasn't much of a leap to imagine Litsa being somewhat sentimental and reaching for her lover's father's name.

I let out a long, ragged sigh. "Crap." The word came out in English. It didn't have the same impact in Greek.

His phone chimed. He took a quick look. "I have to go, but we will talk, okay?"

"Okay."

"Katerina …"

"Go," I said. "You have to go when the Bat Phone rings."

"Fire outside of Volos," he said. "Suspected arson. I have to be there."

"I would say Laki did it but he's not in town."

"Good to know. Walk me out?"

A towering wall of silence sprang up between us. I hated it but I didn't have it in me to swing a pickaxe right now. Melas was Tomas's father. That was a lot to take in.

He angled into the cruiser, rolled the window down. "Call you later." Then he performed a U-turn and shot off down the long, winding road, back to the capillary that led to Volos.

It was only mid-morning but the day felt bloated and tight, like someone had shoveled a week's worth of drama into a handful of sunlit hours. I stifled a yawn and went back to the Beetle, figuring I'd do the right thing and park it outside the garage.

My hand reached for the keys but they were no longer dangling from the ignition.

Huh. I poked around in my bag. Nothing.

Keys jangled.

"Looking for these?"

My head shot up to see Hera slouched down in the backseat, my keys swinging from her pointy red fingernail.

Hera is Melas's ex-girlfriend. She makes no secret of the fact that she transferred to the area so they could pick up where they left off. Melas swore he wasn't interested in slumming with his leftovers (my words, not his), and I believed him, but that didn't stop her oozing all over him when she could, and banging Melas lookalikes in his bed when he wasn't home. She's tall, thin, and blonde, with an overabundance of boobs and bitchiness. And I couldn't kill her and hide the body because she worked for the NIS.

"Get out of my car."

"Let me think ... No."

I glanced around. There was no unmarked NIS van in sight. Usually Hera traveled with a small entourage of armed flunkies.

"Where are your servants?"

"Nearby." She helped herself to my front seat and inspected me like I was poop on her overpriced shoe. Well ... boot. Fashionable even on the job, Hera was sporting a pair of knee-high boots with crippling heels. The rest of her was covered in a denim jumpsuit that shouldn't work on anyone but somehow managed to make her look like she fell off the cover of Vogue. Strung over her shoulder, an oversized orange leather bag made a tinkling sound. It was covered in tiny silver buckles. "You look good for someone who is dead."

"What can I say, Grandma hired the best necromancer money can buy."

"I liked you better when you were dead."

"What a coincidence. I'd like you better if you were dead, too."

"That can be arranged."

"Your death? Great."

"I mean yours."

I sighed like she was killing me. "What do you want, Hera?"

"Somebody told me it has been raining body parts around here."

"Why does the NIS care?"

"They don't, but I do. Who was the dead woman and why is Nikos interested?"

"He's a policeman. Policemen are interested in police stuff, like crime."

Her eyes narrowed. Of course she was wearing a perfect daytime smoky eye. When I try the same look it's less "I'm with the band" and more "I got drunk at a bar, and by the way, have you seen my underwear?"

"I don't believe you. I know Nikos like I know myself. He was worried."

I tilted my head, unable to stop myself from shoving the knife in. Normally I'm a decent human being and I try to be kind because you just never know what people have got going on in their lives, but Hera was asking for it.

"Does Melas know about the lookalikes you take back to his place?"

Her eyes narrowed to vicious slits. "Tell him and I will ruin your life."

"Good luck with that, drama queen. Since you'll find

out who died soon enough, I don't see any reason to tell you who she was. Now get out of my car."

She sat back and folded her arms. "No."

"Fine." I fired off a text message, then leaned back in the driver's seat, closed my eyes, and waited for the show to begin.

"What are you doing?" Hera sounded uneasy—which was apparently a first for her, given that she was easier to get into than an open window.

"Waiting."

"For what?"

"You'll find out."

All hell broke loose. A human whirlwind came blasting through the tunnel that lead to the courtyard, broom whirling above its head, gun in the hand that wasn't spinning the broom.

"Where is she?" Marika hollered.

I stood up in my car and waved. "Yoo-hoo!" I looked down at Hera. "I guess someone is still bitter that you dumped her in Naples, while she was pregnant. I can't say I blame her. She did wind up imprisoned in a sea cave. She and her unborn child almost died, you know."

Marika fired.

BANG!

The bullet whizzed overhead and buried itself in a tree.

"Tell your friend I am going to slap her!" Hera leaped out of the Beetle and bolted for the trees.

Marika screeched to a halt beside me. "The only reason I did not get her is because she is so skinny."

I wasn't sure that was the reason, but Marika was armed with a broom and a gun and she only really had the skill to work one of them, so I didn't feel like contradicting her was in my best interests.

"I wish she'd get on her broom and fly back to her coven."

"She reminds me of vampire. Probably if we want her to stay gone we will have to cut off her head, burn her body, and bury her remains at a crossroads." Marika stuck the gun in her apron and tucked the broom under one arm. "It is a good thing you texted me when you did. I was going to call you. I heard a rumor that the dead woman from Baby Dimitri's shop was Litsa, but that cannot be true."

Fewer than fifteen minutes had passed since Melas gave Grandma the bad news, and already Marika knew.

"Where did you hear that?"

"One of the cousins overheard Baboulas talking to George, and that cousin told another cousin, and that cousin told another cousin, and then my boys overheard it and told me."

"Aren't your boys at school?"

"They have cell phones so Takis and I can track them."

Terrible thoughts rolled over me. If Marika's boys knew, then chances were good Litsa's kids knew. I barely knew the older boys but suddenly I had to find Tomas. He had a thirty-year-old intellect in a teeny, tiny body.

"I need to get to the school." The words wobbled out on shaky legs.

Marika clutched her chest and gasped. "So it is true!"

"According to Melas it is. Did you know she had a tattoo?"

"David Hasselhoff," Marika said. "She loves him more than chocolate. Can you believe such a thing? Who loves anything more than chocolate? Monsters, that is who. I will come with you, just in case Hera shows up again."

We took off toward the local elementary school.

"Know what classroom Tomas is in?" I asked Marika

when we pulled up outside the school. I'd visited a couple of area schools looking for Dad and neither of them was as nice as this elementary school and the building down the street that housed grades seven through twelve. The Greek government didn't like coughing up funds for things like education, so I knew Grandma had funneled some of her cash in this direction. The school was small, c-shaped, with a courtyard filled with colorful and deadly (by American standards) playground equipment. Fresh paint. Durable landscaping that wasn't an eyesore.

"He will not be there right now anyway."

We'd arrived during the ten-minute gap between lessons, and the kids were putting the playground to good use. Marika was right.

I took a deep breath and surged toward the teachers assigned to making sure playtime didn't devolve into mortal combat. I spotted a couple of Marika's kids swinging from the monkey bars, proving that mankind—at least this branch of it—evolved from apes. If there was a missing link, I'd discovered it here in Greece.

The teachers were sipping frappes. They didn't look surprised to see us.

"Marika, is it true?" one of them asked. Both women. One young, one approaching retirement age, but both plainly the types of teachers small children adore and hold up as a gold standard for the rest of their lives.

Marika eyed them suspiciously. "Which thing? Because if you are asking about Litsa, then yes it is true. If it is a different thing, I cannot say."

All three women crossed themselves. Not me. God and I have a shaky relationship. If I crossed myself, He'd probably throw an impromptu hailstorm at this patch of Greece.

"Do the children know?" I asked them. "Where is Tomas?"

"He's in the classroom," the younger teacher said. "He often prefers to stay inside to complete a puzzle or write a story."

She pointed the way, and while Marika stayed behind to gossip, I trotted over to find Litsa and Melas's son.

The classroom was empty. I went back to the teachers and Marika.

"He's not there," I said. We stared out at the playground. No Tomas. His brothers were hunched over a cellphone with two of Marika's boys. They were hooting and hollering.

Marika launched into mama-mode. "What are you doing, eh? I give you a *kinito* to bring to school in case you need to contact me, and what do you do? You play on the YouTube, watching videos."

"But it is Baba's YouTube channel," one of her boys said. "We're subscribers."

"Give me that phone—now." Marika's hand snapped out, palm up. Scowling, her boys gave her the phone. Litsa's two looked less sure, poor babies.

Marika held up the phone and hit the little triangle. The video buffered for a moment, then started over. We watched me dishing out obscene hand gestures on Pelion's main road, inviting the string of backed-up traffic on Mount Pelion's road to suck on a frank I didn't have stashed in my flower-dotted underwear. The video already had ten thousands thumbs up. Marika shooed the children away and we clicked on the next video and watched as an airplane circled the beach. Then the door opened and a couple of off-screen someones heaved a pile of plastic-wrapped body parts out the hatch and onto Baby Dimitri's shoe shop. A few seconds later, the camera moved and

Elias charged out of the shop, with me draped over his shoulder.

Marika made an approving noise. "In hindsight this is a good action movie. Maybe I can move from being a bodyguard to starring in action movies. Lots of action stars are former bodyguards."

I grabbed my own phone and called Takis.

"What do you want?" he snapped.

"I'm going to kill you in your sleep, or while you're awake. I'm not feeling picky right now."

"Are you bleeding again?" He cackled at his own non-joke. "What are you talking about?"

"Your YouTube channel—again!"

"What about it?"

"You can't put this stuff on it! Litsa's children—and yours—are standing around the school playground, watching their mother's body parts get tossed out of an airplane!"

Silence.

"Takis?" I said.

Marika's head swiveled in my direction. "Is that my worthless husband? Tell him no *tiganites* for him—ever again!"

"I thought you were angry about the other video," Takis said.

"You mean the one of me making rude gestures?"

"I have to go. I have a thing."

"Is your thing a strip club? Because for the record Marika knows. Baby Dimitri told her."

"*Gamo tin*—"

I listened for a moment then ended the call. The conversation had devolved into a tangle of bizarre sexual acts involving a clown, lunchmeat, and my mom. Mom was dead so that was extra-disturbing.

I called Grandma. "Did you know Takis still has that YouTube channel?"

"How do you think I saw the video of you so quickly? I am a subscriber."

I walked away with the phone, out of the kids' earshot.

"Then did you also see the video of Litsa's parts falling out of the sky? Because her children did."

"*Gamo tin Panayia mou*, I am going to kill Takis," she said, and ended the call.

"Grandma is going to kill your husband," I told Marika.

"She says that all the time and then she never does. Maybe today will be different."

Now that the YouTube drama was over and Takis's demise was uncertain, I refocused. Two of Litsa's boys were standing in front of me, but the littlest was still missing.

I crouched down in front of Tomas's brothers, then stood back up again because I felt silly. On my knees they were taller than me. "Do you know where your brother is?"

"Is it true about Mama?" the eldest asked. He was the spitting image of his father. The middle boy was his mother but with smaller boobs and what was probably her natural hair color.

Marika dabbed her eyes with a tissue. "Allergies."

"I think it would be best if Thea Marika and I take you home, okay?"

They nodded, far more subdued than normal. Most of the time Litsa's three boys seemed like twelve monkeys.

"But first we have to find Tomas," I said. "Where is he?"

"He ran away," one of the brothers said.

"Ran away? Where did he go?"

They looked at each and shrugged.

I rubbed my forehead and tried to think. Where would I go if I was Tomas?

The teachers rounded up all the students and together we scoured the school. No Tomas. So I bundled the boys and Marika into the Beetle. Marika's boys begged to come with us, but their mother wasn't taking any of their crap.

We drove back to the compound in silence. When Mom died it was ages before I could handle sound that wasn't Dad. We moved about like ghosts. I'd dropped out of college, so I had nowhere to go, nothing to do. Today I had a toe back in that silent space again.

Back at the compound, Grandma was waiting with George. What role he played in the family business I wasn't sure, but it was bound to be something dodgy. I watched his eyes do the counting and come up one short.

"Tomas?" he asked.

"We don't know," I said. "He wasn't at school."

Grandma pulled out her phone. With one call she launched a manhunt. Every eye in the area would be searching for one small five-year-old boy who was anything but average. Knowing Tomas he'd locked himself in a puzzle box and no one would ever be able to figure out the combination. I had my own ideas about where he'd gone, so I excused myself and walked into a broom closet.

The closet wasn't a closet. A panel opened and I stepped down onto an escalator that carried me to a secret subterranean level that connected to Grandma's bunker via one super-secret door that I'd discovered a few days ago.

I opened the first metal door and immediately found myself in the outer dungeon that was (as far as I knew) window dressing. Old timey cells. Straw on the cold stone floor. Wooden buckets that could be a drinking receptacle, could be a makeshift toilet, if you had no standards and really needed to go. This place was straight out of the bowels of a medieval castle, and it was unoccupied.

I rapped on a second steel door. After a long pause the door flew open. Monobrow peered out at me.

"Katerina? I thought you preferred to come in the back door."

"I guess I'm not as Greek as I thought I was." The joke sailed over his head. "Have you seen Tomas?"

"The little one?"

"Has he been here?"

His chin went up-down. "*Tst.* Why?"

I told him about Litsa, about the body parts, about the Baby Dimitri connection that didn't seem to be a connection.

"Baby Dimitri does not like to get his hands dirty. Look at them sometime. They are soft, weak. That is why he has that one with the gold teeth."

"You know Laki?"

He made a face. "By reputation. Your grandmother likes to tell stories."

"Does she spend a lot of time down here?"

Shrug. "Some. It is good to have someone to be old with, but do not tell her I said that. As for your boy, I have not seen him. But he seems to have connected with you, so I would not be surprised if he finds you."

Mentally, I ran through the list of possibilities and came up empty. This was Tomas's home. He'd been born here, raised here. Which meant probably he had a list of hiding places longer than his leg.

Gnawing on my lip like an overzealous beaver, I thanked Monobrow.

"If you are truly grateful, I could use a little *loukoumia* the next time you are down this way, especially if that is today."

I crossed my heart and hoped to die but left out the part about sticking a needle in my eye, because even though Grandma was secretly law enforcement, the people around her still got excited about pain and torture. I exited via the super-secret tunnel in the movie set dungeon and made my way around to the front gates, hoping to run into Tomas.

No sign of him.

My heart hurt. For him. For his brothers. For Litsa's husband and family. I thought about calling Melas to check for updates but he was struggling with his own Litsa-related baggage. What would happen with Tomas now, once he was found? It wasn't like Melas could march in and claim his child. Didn't matter that Grandma was secretly one of the goodish guys, I didn't think the Family would tolerate the indiscretion and, in their minds, betrayal on Melas's part. He'd vanish, then one day someone would plough into a speed bump and discover his bits and broken pieces.

The hunt was underway. Men were up on the compound's rooftops, armed with the best binoculars money could buy. Others were traipsing around the property, radiating outwards toward the school. These people had been born and raised here. They'd been little boys once, discovering the mountain's nooks and crannies. The mountain didn't have secrets from them. The family wives were tearing into the compound itself. No mattress went unturned.

I called Grandma. "Is anyone looking in Makria?"

"Stavros and Elias."

I ended the call, fired up the Beetle and zipped up to Makria, which was less than a kilometer up the road.

Did I think Tomas was there?

That was a big, fat nope.

But then I wasn't looking for Tomas—not directly. These were desperate times, which meant they called for desperate, maybe even suicidal measures. I parked in the small parking lot outside the village because Makria is a no-car zone. The roads are too narrow and it scares the sheep and goats often found wandering around the cobbled streets.

Then I did the unthinkable.

I walked along the main street, stopping every five seconds to greet someone. Nobody seemed all that surprised that I wasn't really dead. But then they knew Grandma and her mysterious ways. Whatever she was up to, they figured she had it under control.

Melas's parents lived in a neat, white house with brown shutters and a garden contained in dozens of bright red pots. Dried gourds hung from the trees, some painted red, some in their original neutral colors. In the yard a woman was showing invisible debris the business end of a broom. She was a bird of a woman with a pointy nose and helmet hair. Once upon a time she'd worked for Grandma, pulling fingernails and whatever else torturers do for kicks. These days she terrorizes her children, and occasionally me.

"Kyria Mela?"

"You do not have to yell. I can hear you just fine."

It was pointless arguing that I'd just used my most polite inside voice, because I knew something her husband didn't: Kyria Mela kept a box of her old tools in a secret cubbyhole in her fancy entertaining room floor. I liked my fingernails where they were, thank you very much.

"What are you doing?"

That was me being all Greek. Greeks don't ask how you are; they want to know what you're doing. What you do is gossip-worthy. How you feel about it isn't.

"What does it look like I am doing?"

"Painting the walls."

She stopped sweeping. Her face was grim but light danced in her eyes. Probably she was fantasizing about my screams.

"You are looking for the missing boy, yes?"

"How did you know?"

She walked over and tapped me on the forehead with her finger. "Telephone."

"Oh."

"Not everything is woo-woo." She did alarmingly good spirit fingers. "First get the loaf of bread from my husband, then I will look at your cup to see where the boy is. That is why you are here, no?"

"I'm kind of in a hurry."

"So am I. It is nearly lunchtime and if you wait much longer the bread will be gone. You would not like me when the bread is all gone."

I wasn't sure I liked her, with or without bread. "Kyrios Melas doesn't keep a loaf for you?" Seemed to me that would be suicidal behavior on his part.

"Tomas likes to keep me on my toes. He always has."

My stomach seized up again at the mention of the name Kyrios Melas shared with the missing five-year-old boy.

"One loaf of bread. On my way."

I hopped right to it, but before I could take a step Kyria Mela stopped me.

"Is it true about the woman? Was she chopped into little pieces and tossed out of a plane?"

"I wouldn't say little pieces. Just the six obvious ones."

She tilted her head. The helmet of hair moved with it, but maintained its tidy position. "It gets easier, yes?"

"What does?"

"Talking about death."

ALEX A. KING

I shook my head, American-style. "My mother died when I was eighteen. I can't help measuring every subsequent death against that. Compared to losing her they are all easy, even when they're horrific."

"My mother passed when I was young, too. Her death made me hard."

"Not me," I said. "It just made me sad."

———

THE MELAS FAMILY'S bakery was down the street and around the corner, much like every other business in the village. Even though I'd never been inside the tiny bakery Kyrios Melas was single-handedly responsible for the amount of drool I produced every time I stepped into Makria during the early hours. Greek bakeries of the bread-producing kind normally close at noon—in the smaller villages, anyway—because lunch is the main meal of the day.

The door was propped open with a rock. In the window, a cat was flaunting its yoga skills, one back leg in the air.

I stepped up and into a furnace. The bakery was dim, cramped, and there wasn't a loaf of bread in sight. I had a sinking feeling Kyria Mela would blame me for this unfortunate development.

"Oh my God, I'm going to die."

"Relax," a deep, male voice said. "There is more bread in the oven, eh? Helena will not kill you—not today, anyway."

My eyes slowly adjusted. Kyrios Melas was behind the counter, resting in a rainbow-striped deckchair.

"Good to know. We haven't met yet, Kyrios Melas. I'm Katerina Makris."

"With an S. I know. My son and wife talk and talk and talk about you."

"They talk that much, huh?"

He laughed. "Greeks love to talk. Conversation is life."

"You say conversation, I say gossip."

His entire body shook.

Detective Melas was his father's son. Same bones. Same strong jaw and broad shoulders. Warm, dark eyes looked down at me as he stood and braced his hands on the counter, which was a massive butcher's block. They were different, too. Melas had a swimmer's physique. His father looked like he'd sink in the pool. To call him large would be like saying Everest is a hill.

"You learn fast," he said. "I have something that belongs to you. Come. Look."

I scooted around the butcher's block, and there on the floor was a mama cat and five kittens. On his knees, watching the kittens step on each other's heads was Tomas.

The knots in my shoulders unraveled. Not wanting to freak the little guy out, I crouched down quietly instead of throwing my arms around him.

"Cute kittens," I said in a low voice.

Tomas grinned at me. "Want to see something else cool, Thea Katerina?"

"Always."

He stuck a finger in his mouth and wiggled a tooth.

"You're right, that is cool. In the United States, if you put your tooth under the pillow at bedtime, the tooth fairy comes and swaps the tooth for money."

"We throw our teeth on the roof for good luck," Tomas told me.

"So my father used to tell me when I was a girl."

As a child I'd preferred the tooth fairy because money

is money, but as a grownup I liked the idea of an extra dose of good luck.

I messaged Grandma to let her know she could call off the manhunt.

"Have you had lunch?" I asked Tomas.

He did the up-down chin thing. "I was at school and I really wanted to see the kittens again."

"So you left?"

"Did you know cats are blind when they're born?"

I did, but I let him have his moment in the sun. "I do now."

"Their mothers take good care of them, so it doesn't matter that they can't see. Not like rabbit mothers. They only come back to the burrow to feed their babies, then they leave again."

What I knew about rabbits was limited their hunger for carrots. I'd never had pets growing up because Dad said he was allergic to everything with four feet. But I didn't think this was about animals. As a mother, Litsa was ... not negligent, exactly. More like absent. When Tomas had a dentist appointment, he'd asked me to take him because his mother couldn't. Her kids ran wild and unsupervised. Unlike Marika's clan, who ran wild but usually supervised.

"Do you like ice cream?"

Tomas nodded. His attention was on the mama cat, who was cleaning her kittens, one fuzzy bundle at a time.

I held out my hand. He took it cheerfully enough.

"Do not forget the bread," Kyrios Melas said. Heat blasted into the shop as he yanked the oven door open and poked around inside with a hook on a long stick. He stuck a long-handled paddle inside and pulled it back out with a golden, high-domed loaf in a bread pan. With a welder's protective gloves, he shook the loaf onto a pile of paper and wrapped it into a neat bundle.

"Tell my wife I added a cat hair especially for her," he said, winking at me. "There is a prize if she can find it."

My mouth opened and words were about to come out when the foul stench of expensive perfume drowned out the aroma of hot bread. I'd know that stink anywhere.

"I will take that," Hera said, snatching the bread out of my hands.

"If you bathed once in a while you wouldn't have to wear so much perfume," I said.

Her eyes narrowed to hateful slits.

"Sorry," I said, not sorry at all. "I was just channeling Marika. Anyone shoot at you lately?"

She stormed out of the bakery with the bread.

I eyed Kyrios Melas, who was trying not to laugh. "I think I'm going to need another loaf."

Chapter 5

No second loaf necessary. According to Kyrios Melas, Hera had been pulling this same stunt on a regular basis lately, showing up to take bread to the woman she wanted to be her mother-in-law. Because she'd decided the way to Melas's heart wasn't through his heart, now she was trying to hook him via his mother.

If Hera was smart she'd see that her efforts were moot. Kyria Mela already loved her. Melas thought she was a dirty skank.

Okay, maybe I was exaggerating.

That didn't stop me moping past the Melas family's street (which was everyone in Makria's street) with my head down and Tomas's hand clutched in mine.

"What's wrong, Thea Katerina?"

"Nothing," I said. "I'm trying to decide what flavor of ice cream I want."

"Oh. I thought you were trying to decide who you like more: Detective Melas or Theo Xander."

My brain spluttered. "Neither. I mean, I like them both, but not like that."

Except exactly like that.

Both men made the earth move when they kissed me, which was a problem for a one-man-at-a-time woman like me. Melas had made his intentions clear—he wanted to date me, or at least take me to bed on a regular basis. Whereas Xander was still a blank page. In a blank book. With no title. And Xander was MIA, for God only knows how long.

We trotted out to the parking lot where Stavros and Elias were waiting.

"There he is!" Stavros said, grinning.

Tomas giggled and ran to Stavros, who scooped him up and threw him into the air like he weighed nothing. Stavros is my cousin, although I wasn't exactly sure how. Greek families are like that. He's a big-bellied bear with mange, and although he has a penchant for porn that leans toward farm animals, he wants nothing more than to settle down with a good woman—or any woman—and be a stay-at-home dad.

"Baboulas asked us to bring you back to the compound," Elias told me.

"We're on our way to get ice cream."

Stavros brightened up. "I have ice cream—homemade."

"You made ice cream?" I asked.

"Three flavors," Stavros said. "Elias bought me an ice cream maker."

"I've always wanted an ice cream maker," I said.

Stavros sighed happily. "Me too."

Tomas went back to holding my hand. He looked up at me. "Can I ride back with you, Thea Katerina?"

"You bet," I said.

Stavros picked him up and deposited him in my backseat. No booster seats, but car seat laws are something that exist in countries that aren't Greece. The cops don't care unless you're using your newborn as a hood ornament. Probably even that is negotiable.

I called Melas. He answered on the second ring.

"What would happen if you saw a driver using their child as a hood ornament?"

"Please tell me this is a joke."

"Uh … never mind." I ended the call and stuffed my phone back in my bag.

———

FIVE MINUTES later we were rolling through the compound gates. Litsa's grieving husband was waiting. A war was happening on his face. On the one hand he was a stone-cold killer. On the other he was a passionate Greek, and there's nothing Greeks are more passionate about than their kids.

Okay, maybe politics.

And sports.

And things like whose mother makes the best *skordalia* (garlic sauce), and which *kafeneio* makes the best coffee.

Greeks are passionate about a lot of things, including their children.

George waited, arms folded.

George wasn't alone. Grandma was wearing her frowny face. Her frowny face was her usual face. That's the one she put on, even when it was just us in her kitchen. She had a smiley face, too, but that one was downright scary.

"He looks mad," Tomas said to me.

"He's not mad, he was worried. And now he's relieved you're okay."

"I am always okay." He climbed over the front seat and plunked himself down in my lap. "I'm super smart, but that doesn't mean I don't need a hug. I really like hugs." He threw his arms around my neck, his arms like persistent little vines.

I hugged him back because my heart is a big, mushy, sentimental lump. "I like hugs, too."

With his arms coiled around me, I got out of the Beetle carefully, trying not to dislodge the boy. I didn't have a lot of experience with kids, but I knew dropping them was a bad idea. I carried him to his father and waited for Tomas to reach for George.

Nothing.

"Tomas?" I said.

"I want to stay here," he said into my hair. "Can I stay here?"

"In the driveway?"

"He means with you," Grandma said, spelling it out for the slow woman. "The boy wants to stay with you."

"He cannot stay with her," George said. "No offense, Katerina."

"None taken." He was right: Tomas couldn't stay with me, especially not around my neck. I'm not really a scarf person; not unless it's winter, and it definitely wasn't winter yet. "You have to go with your *baba*."

"No!"

"Come," George said. "I need to talk to you. It is important."

"I already know," Tomas said.

"What do you know?"

"Mama was chopped into little pieces and someone threw her out of a plane. I saw it on YouTube."

Grandma and Tomas's father crossed themselves.

I looked at Grandma. "Did Takis take the YouTube video down?"

"Yes, but it is too late."

A gasp slid out of me. "You killed him?"

She gave me a disbelieving look. "No. I made him take down the video but on the internet all the interesting videos get a virus and spread all over the place."

"You mean they go viral."

She shrugged. "I say Yiannis, you say Yiannakis."

It took me a moment. Some Greek sayings don't flow the way they should once I translate them into English in my head—something that happens almost instantaneously now. Yiannis and Yiannakis (John and Johnny) was the Greek version of po-tay-to and po-tah-to.

Tomas raised his head and looked at me with those big, brown eyes. "Thea Katerina, can we get ice cream now?"

My eyes cut to his father, who nodded. He seemed a whopping ten years older overnight. Having your spouse murdered will do that to a person.

"Absolutely," I told Tomas.

Stavros brightened. "I have ice cream, remember."

"I think I'd like to get him away from here for a while, if that's okay."

Everyone else shrugged, which was basically a yes.

"Does he need a booster seat?" I asked his father.

Confusion clouded George's eyes. "A what?"

So that was a "no" then. Greece.

"Never mind. I'll bring him to you later."

He nodded slowly, like his head was a rock.

My phone buzzed. Marika was on the other end.

"Did somebody say ice cream?"

My mouth dropped open. When I recovered I said, "How did you know?"

"I have ears in the back of my head, as well as eyes. Wait there. I am coming, too."

Thirty seconds later, Marika came bustling through the tunnel. She'd swapped her flowery dress for black, which we'd all be doing soon. The women, anyway. Men get off easy with their black armbands. The whole family had just come out of mourning for my fake death, so nobody would be happy about going back to black. I owned a couple of black tops and one black dress that I'd bought for my first Greek funeral, one of Dad's old buddies who'd faked his own death. That same friend died for real in the family compound's swimming pool. Well ... he was murdered. Not exactly the same thing as dying.

The Beetle listed as Marika helped herself to the passenger seat. She turned around in the seat to look at the little guy.

"I bet I can eat more ice cream than you," she said.

He giggled.

"Do not waste time going to a *periptero*," she told me. "Go to a *zacharoplastio*."

"Any reason?"

A *periptero* is a newspaper stand. They sell (surprise, surprise) newspapers, magazines, and an assortment of things science says will kill you sooner or later. They also sell the kind of ice cream that comes prepackaged—none of that scooped stuff.

"Today I need one scoop of everything," she explained.

I eyed her. "Everything?"

"Everything."

"I want one scoop of everything, too," Tomas said.

Marika gave the little guy a mock stern look. "Where will you put all that ice cream?"

He patted his belly. "In here."

"I bet you twenty euros I can eat more."

Tomas's expression was thoughtful. "I don't have twenty euros."

"You have two hands, yes?"

"Marika," I said, "you can't make him do housework."

She laughed. "I cannot even get my boys to help with the housework. But I have something I could use Tomas's help with."

He brightened up. "Is it a puzzle? I helped Thea Katerina with a puzzle."

True story. And the puzzle in question had been a box with a bloody surprise inside.

"Best puzzle solver in Greece," I said, firing up the engine. I turned the Beetle around and began the slow crawl along the winding dirt road. Elias followed close behind.

"It is like a puzzle," Marika said.

"What is it?" I asked her.

"A safe."

I raised an eyebrow. "A real safe?"

"A real safe that I cannot open on my own."

That lone cat hair in my DNA asserted itself. "Whose safe?"

"A safe that has appeared in my bedroom, under my bed. I asked Takis and he told me to mind my own business."

"And you let him live?"

"Only until I kill him."

"For what it's worth, pretty much anyone in this family can help you dispose of his body when you're done. We're known for it. I bet we could put him in a bridge or a speed bump."

"Greece does not really do infrastructure anymore," she said. "Too poor."

"You can't put a corpse in concrete," Tomas said. "Well, you can, but it is not a good idea. The structural integrity would be compromised."

I glanced in the rearview mirror. "How old are you again? Forty?"

He giggled.

I kept stealing little looks at him, trying to see the Melas in him. But either it wasn't there or I was lousy at spotting family resemblances.

Marika gave me directions to a *zacharoplasteio* near the Volos promenade. Sorcery happened, or maybe I had a guardian angel that finally put down the crack pipe, and a couple of parking spots opened up right outside the confectionary shop. We all jumped out and barreled into the store.

A *zacharoplasteio* is heaven on earth. Basically it's a bakery, but for sweet things only—no salt allowed. This one sold big cakes, little cakes, *baklava* and all its cousins, *loukoumia*, candy, pastries, and twenty flavors of ice cream.

I'd be lying if I said my eyes didn't light up. At almost thirty, I was the kid in the literal candy store.

Marika bustled up to the counter. "Two bowls of ice cream with one scoop of every flavor."

The girl behind the counter had fake eyebrows and a real mustache. The eyebrows rose so fast, hard, and high that when they came back down again they'd left behind grey ghosts.

"A bowl?"

Marika held up two fingers. "Two bowls."

"We do not have cups that big."

"How big are your cups?"

The girl pointed to three pink containers: One scoop. Two scoops. Three.

"Those are too small," Marika said. "You would think nobody ever came in here wanting to try every flavor."

"You are the first," the girl said.

Marika gave her the stink eye.

"But," the girl said, "I suppose we should order some bigger cups, just in case."

"Great idea. You should do that. But what about today?"

"I could give you seven cups with three scoops in each cup."

"Fourteen," Marika said, "because my little friend here wants a scoop of every flavor, too."

The girl looked at me like I was the one with ice cream issues.

"I just want two scoops in one cup," I said lamely.

Maybe her head believed me but her face didn't.

"Or a cone," I said. "The other scoops are for Tomas."

Her gaze cut to Tomas. "How is all that ice cream supposed to fit in such a small person?"

Marika's scowl turned into a sunbeam. "She thinks I am thin. Did you hear that?"

Smart girl, she ignored that one and asked me what flavors I wanted.

"*Kaimaki*," Marika said. "Katerina wants a scoop of *kaimaki* and a scoop of *loukoumi* ice cream."

"There's *loukoumi* ice cream?" I asked.

The girl pointed to a pale pink confection speckled with tiny nuggets of *loukoumi*.

"I don't know," I said. I love *loukoumi* but I was in the mood for good old-fashioned vanilla and chocolate. You can never go wrong with either. They're like basic black: they go with everything.

"She will have the *kaimaki* and *loukoumi*," Marika said in her mom voice.

Alrighty then, that's what I was having.

We carried a tray with all the cups to one of the small

tables set up outside under a gaudy pink and yellow-stripped awning. Elias sat with us; he'd refused the ice cream. Said all that sugar was too distracting.

Marika separated her treasure from ours with a napkin wall. "Nobody touch my ice cream."

"Wouldn't dream of it," I said.

"I don't want the boy cheating." She winked at Tomas, who was grinning.

Kaimaki ice cream turned out to be stretchy. Delicious, yes, but stretchy and slightly chewy, like the waistband in old underpants. Not that I've ever eaten old underpants, but I imagined it was a lot like this, but less sweet. I wasn't complaining. Sugar was sugar.

Tomas got up out of his seat, a curious expression on his face.

"Where are you going?" I said.

"I heard a cat."

"We have cats at the compound you can play with."

"This one sounded hurt."

Injured animal. I couldn't help myself. "Let's go check it out together. Marika, don't eat our ice cream."

"Would I do that?"

I cast a glance at her increasing pile of empty ice cream cups. Tomas and I would have to work fast.

"We'll be right back."

"Go—I will guard the ice cream."

I turned to Elias. "Stay here and guard the ice cream. We're just going around the corner."

"Katerina …"

"We'll just be a second. It's a public place—a very public place. We'll be fine."

"I don't like it," he said.

"Injured cat. Got to go."

Elias looked at Marika, who was attacking the ice cream like it was an invading force. Ice cream didn't stand a chance. He nodded but he wasn't happy.

Tomas grabbed my hand, pulled me to the corner, where a produce store was closing up for the afternoon. We crept around it, into a narrow alley that definitely wasn't very public. The buildings had their backs turned to dingy space. No dumpsters, just a row of garbage cans that used to be silver colored. Like every alley ever, it smelled like old urine and older food. The doors were mismatched. The street had been constructed one store, one business at a time, with decades between them in some cases.

"When we find the cat, crouch down and hold your finger out like this." His index finger pointed. "Cats think it's another cat nose and they come over to sniff it."

"And that works?"

"Almost always. Mama taught me that." His voice hitched at the end.

I crouched down to his eye level. "Tomas ..."

"I heard it again. Listen."

My ears did their thing and they did it badly. "I don't hear it."

"Come. I have to save it."

He pulled me along until we reached an open door. The doorframe was cracked and the paint had been sloughed off with time and salt from the harbor that was almost within spitting distance. Inside, dusty wooden crates everywhere. Clean floor. There was something else hanging in still air. A mixture of perfume and cologne maybe. Somebody had bathed recently.

"Tomas, are you sure there's a cat? Because I don't hear a cat."

"There's a cat. I heard it."

If there's one thing I've learned since being drugged and tossed on a private plane to Greece, it's that old, decrepit buildings are a primo place for bad guys to hide. Greece has a lot of structures with broken bones and battered faces. Earthquakes, extreme heat followed by withering winters, and lack of public funding because Greece spent it all on dodgy bankers and overly generous pensions for people who didn't need pensions in their forties, meant nobody had money to fix stuff. So stuff sat around, waiting on bad guys and kids to show them a good time.

At least this old place didn't have an olive factory in its past. It didn't have a cat in its present either, I'd bet on it.

So what was making the noise Tomas was hearing?

"Can you still hear it?"

He pointed. "Over there."

Over there didn't look promising. Mostly it looked dark, foreboding, and exactly like the kind of place a serial killer would hang out, waiting for some kid to wander in with his stupid cousin-ish person, who should know better.

"We should get Elias," I said.

Tomas took off.

Naturally I bolted after him, despite the warning klaxon in my head. The boy's mother had been chopped into pieces and tossed out of a plane, so I was jumpier than ever.

"Elias," I yelled over my shoulder. There was zero chance he could hear me from here but yelling made me feel proactive.

Tomas vanished through a second doorway inside the building. A dark doorway.

"Tomas? Stop! Come back right now."

Silence. Then there was low scuffle and a small plop.

Desperate times called for desperate measures. I turned on the flashlight app on my phone and tossed it into the room. My body followed, performing an erratic and enthusiastic rendition of the windmill. Somebody yelped as my hand slapped them across the face, twice. Somebody much taller than Tomas. Somebody male.

"Why is she hitting me? There wasn't supposed to be hitting."

"There wasn't supposed to be anybody but the kid," a second voice said, also male.

Men in black. I caught flashes of them as I zipped around the room. Men in black right down to the balaclavas. Cowards.

"Grab the boy," one of them barked.

"No!" I kicked him in the shins. "No grabbing. Tomas —run! Go get Elias!"

Tomas took off out of the room.

"*Ai sto dialo!*"

A charming little epithet that meant "go to the devil."

"Get her phone, *malakas*. Stomp on it."

There was a metallic and plastic crunch and the room went dark.

"That was my new phone!" My windmill met a wall. "Ow!"

"Stop her! She is doing the windmill!"

"I can't. We did not train against the windmill."

A balaclava-clad meathead grabbed my hands, wrenched them behind my back. Something cool and plastic touched my skin and tightened. The bastard had zip-tied my wrists.

He crouched down.

And now he'd zip-tied my ankles.

"If I was the kind of person who killed people, I would totally kill you!" I yelled.

"Where is the boy? We have to get the boy!"

Footsteps. Two sets, headed this way.

"In here," I shouted.

A hand struck my face, then it fell away.

Light poured into the room, framing Elias and Marika. Elias had a gun and his phone, and Marika had a plastic spoon and a tub of ice cream. Some kind of berries, by the looks of it.

"I knew it," Marika said. "I knew you two should not have gone off on your own. Who are these two *archidia*?"

Balls. She called them balls.

One of the balls said, "Why is the fat one here? Nobody was supposed to be here except the boy. You said nobody else would be able to hear the sound."

"Tell me you did not call me fat," Marika said in a dangerous voice. "I am pregnant."

"Are you carrying them in your *kolos*?" one of the men said.

As she shoveled ice cream, Marika eyes were sharpening knives.

I jumped around so I could get a look at the men in black. "For the record, the balaclavas are stupid."

"They are not stupid if you can't identify us."

As much as I hated to admit it, he had a point.

"Shut up or he'll shoot you," I said, nodding at Elias. He had his phone out, calling in the troops.

"I would shoot you but I do not want to put my ice cream down." Marika looked at the container in her hand. "Come to think of it, maybe I should. I do not feel so good."

"How much have you had?" I asked her.

"She finished hers," Elias said, "so she went in for more."

I gave her an admonishing look. "Marika!"

"I was doing that girl a favor, if you think about it. Maybe she works on commission." She groaned. "I think I am going to be sick. Probably the baby does not like this flavor."

"I am sure that is it." Elias winked at me. I smothered a smile.

"*Gamo tin Panayia mou*," the biggest of the two balaclava guys said. "What is wrong with you people?"

"They're crazy. I think they're crazy," the smaller one said.

Marika braced herself in the doorway. Her skin was pale and greenish.

"Tomas?" I called out. "Are you okay?"

"I'm okay," he said. "I'm collecting things while you decide what to do about the kidnappers."

I hopped backwards in a tight, inconvenient line so I could see everyone at the same time. "Why are you trying to take Tomas?"

The smaller one shrugged. "Orders."

"Do not tell them anything," his pal said.

"I wasn't going to."

"It sounded a lot like you were telling her."

"I wasn't!"

"I am definitely going to be sick," Marika said.

The Balaclava Boys scooted sideways but Elias was there with his gun. "Neither of you moves or I will shoot."

"We have guns, too," said the big guy.

"Yes, but I am holding mine, and if you reach for yours I will shoot you."

Marika gagged. I jumped sideways just in time. She opened her mouth and a torrent of liquid ice cream shot out and sprayed the Balaclava Boys.

"Her aim is excellent," Elias said.

The big guy wrenched something flat and round off his

belt, threw it down on the ground. Smoke began to fill the room.

A thick, acrid cloud poked me in the eyes and stuck its fingers up my nose. Tears and snot ran down my face and I couldn't do dick about it, on account of how I was trussed up like a bundle of computer cables. This was it. I was going to choke to death on my own snot.

A small hand found mine. "Thea Katerina? Come."

I hopped alongside him. Before I knew it, Tomas had led me outside to where the air was fresh and not trying to make me puke or cry.

"Wait there," he said. "I am going to get the others."

Want to know how much muscle control it takes not to topple over? A lot. Coughing and sneezing, I hopped backwards until my back was against the wall. Somewhere close by an engine roared and tires screeched.

Tomas brought Marika out next. Under all the tears, she was furious.

"You cannot do that to a pregnant woman! What if my baby is deformed now, eh?" She wiped the tears away from her eyes. "Katerina?"

"Are you okay?"

"Do I look okay?"

"I meant the vomiting."

"Oh. That. I feel better now. Much better, no thanks to those two *archidia*. As soon as they come out I am going to make them eat wood."

Tomas was back with Elias, who was coughing and spluttering like a steam train. Now that my eyes were drying up, I could see the boy was wearing a gas mask.

I coughed and reigned in a sneeze. "Where did you get a gas mask?"

"From the van."

"What van?"

He pointed to a roller door two buildings down. "In there."

I hopped away from the wall and fell. "Can somebody help a woman out here? Anyone got scissors? A knife? Nail clippers." These days I kept a multitool in my bag, but I couldn't reach it on account of these stupid restraints.

"Relax," Marika said, rifling in her bag. "I can shoot them off."

"No! No shooting."

"Just give me a moment to stop crying. I can do it."

Yikes! No way. I wanted to keep my arms and legs. Plus I'd already been shot this month. I kept hopping—in the opposite direction.

"Knife," Elias said, fumbling through his pockets.

My hop changed directions. Elias's eyes were streaming, and he was going to cough a lung onto the warm concrete any moment now.

"Give the knife to Tomas," I suggested.

Marika gasped. "You cannot give a knife to a child!"

Tomas reached into his pocket and whipped out a Swiss Army knife. "I got this for my birthday," he said, flipping the blade out like a stone-cold expert. "It wasn't that sharp at first, but then Theo Takis taught me how to hone the blade."

"I am going to kill him," Marika muttered.

Tomas sliced through the plastic straps. I rubbed my wrists, wriggled my ankles, gave Tomas a quick hug, and raced over to the roller door. It was raised. I peered into the gloom.

Empty. The vehicle I'd heard must have been the van leaving. Damn it.

"The kidnappers, did you see them?"

"They had masks over their face things," Tomas said.

Of course they did. Of *course*.

Tires spun. Engines roared. The alley filled up with black cars.

Grandma's cavalry had arrived.

"All this action has made me hungry for more ice cream," Marika said.

Chapter 6

Grandma wasn't happy. No one was happy.

Scratch that; Aunt Rita was happy.

"I spent this morning with my boys," she mouthed. I gave her two thumbs up and hoped it didn't mean anything obscene in Greek.

Back before she was a woman, Aunt Rita was a man. As a man she'd been married twice and had several sons. She still had sons but now she was fabulous. (Today she was a 1970s babe with Farrah Fawcett hair, spangled hot pants, and knee-high socks.) The downside was that the first wife rarely let Aunt Rita see her boys.

We were gathered in Grandma's kitchen and breathing space was limited, even with the windows and doors open.

"Why do I have to sit outside?" Papou said.

"Because you have an eagle on each shoulder and I do not want bird *kaka* all over my clean house," Grandma told him.

Grandma's clean house was a shack, a hovel, a short architectural step up from a condemned rat hole. Worse: the dump was a family heirloom. Whoever controlled the family business was required to live in the pigpen to keep them humble. Grandma was like the genie from Aladdin: she had phenomenal comic powers in an itty, shitty living space.

"Only one of them can *kaka.*" Papou said. "The other one's *kolos* is stitched up."

"Do I look like I care?" Grandma said. "One bird is too many birds."

"You know what you are?" Papou didn't wait for an answer. "You are prejudiced against avian Greeks."

"One of my sons is my daughter and I have an old *malakas* for an advisor. Tell me again how prejudiced I am."

"He's complaining about being outside. Ha! Try being stuck in the bathroom."

That was Dad. Now that he was alive and well he was in Grandma's doghouse for not letting her know he was okay sooner. He was in the bathroom—the bathroom without a toilet. That was located outside, in a legitimate, old-fashioned outhouse.

"You are there because you are full of *skata,*" Grandma said.

"I'm just happy I get to sit close to the food," I said from my position wedged up against the kitchen counter. I was inches away from a stack of powdered *kourabiethes*. I could smell the sugar and almonds through the glass dome. I wanted to eat, not be stuck in this grim meeting.

"Touch the food and I will cut off your fingers," Grandma said.

Maybe she meant it, maybe she didn't, but I wasn't taking any chances.

The rest of the kitchen was filled with various family members, including Takis, Stavros, Elias, and Marika. It was a first for her, and she was practically humming with excitement. Grandma was behind the counter with me, grinding dozens of garlic cloves into paste with a mortar and pestle.

"Tell me again how it happened," Grandma said.

One at a time, Marika, Elias, and I told our stories again while Grandma and the rest of the room listened.

"The van," she said to Tomas, who was sitting on the kitchen table, "what did it look like?"

"White Mercedes Benz. 2016 model." Then he reeled off a string of letters and numbers.

Everyone stared at him.

"I remember things," he said.

"Michail," Grandma barked.

"On it," Dad said.

Thirty seconds later: "The plates belong to a rental place in Volos."

Grandma looked at me. "Would you recognize these two *malakes* if you saw them again?"

"They were wearing balaclavas," I said.

"Is that a yes or a no?"

Tomas raised his hand. "I would."

"You are three," Takis said. "How could you recognize two grown men in balaclavas?"

"Five," Tomas said. "And I would recognize them because I've seen them before, when they weren't wearing the balaclavas."

We all gawked at him.

"Where did you see them?" Grandma asked, oh-so casually.

"At my school."

"And what were they doing there?"

"Watching."

Marika gasped and crossed herself. "Virgin Mary, they want to sell our children into a sex slavery ring."

Grandma stopped mixing. She grabbed a wooden

spoon and pointed the business end at Marika. "You: *skasmos* or get out." The spoon moved to Tomas. "When did you see them?"

"This morning."

"Have you seen them anywhere else, any other time?"

He shrugged.

"What did they look like without their balaclavas?"

"Tan. Both men have dark brown eyes and one—the tall one—has a little mustache and hair on his chin, but not a beard. The other has those big nostrils, like caves. If you looked up you'd be able to see his boogers. You know those artists who work for the police? If you get one of those I can tell them what to draw. I'm good at lots of things but my drawing skills are like a regular five-year-old."

We stared at him. We did that a lot. There was a lot of brain in that little body. Who did he get it from? Who had been the family prodigy, Litsa or Melas?

"We will get you an artist, no problem." Grandma put the spoon down and went back to mixing. "For now, you will stay in the compound. No sneaking out, eh?" There was a twinkle in her eye when she looked at him. "And I will be assigning bodyguards. Xander will be back tonight, and then he will be watching over you."

Organs that didn't normally flutter fluttered, like my liver. And my kidneys. My kidneys, because they remembered the late-night, non-stop drive to Athens. My liver didn't have an excuse. As for that organ in my chest … hearts are basically chickens. They're not too bright and they have a thing for peckers. Right now mine was doing a one-legged tap dance.

What did it all mean?

God only knew—and God and I don't talk. We have issues.

"I want to stay with Thea Katerina," Tomas said.

His father was standing in the corner opposite me. His jaw was clenched and his eyes were hidden behind dark glasses. He nodded once.

Grandma kept mixing. "Katerina?"

"No problem." I grinned at Tomas. Nothing about any of this was happy, but I figure he needed to see I was on his team.

There was a noise outside, then Papou said, "Re, *malaka*, who let you in? Does anybody smell bacon? Because I smell bacon."

Then I heard Melas laugh. "If you were a man I would tell you to eat *skata*."

"I am more of a man than you will ever be. My Greek underpants are older than you."

Insults are how Greek men—maybe all men—give compliments. To make things tricky, insults are also how they insult someone.

"You kiss your bird with that mouth?"

"Your mother likes it."

"Let me call her and ask."

Fear snuck into Papou's voice. "Forget I said anything, eh?"

"Forget what?" Melas said.

There was a small stretch of silence, then Papou yelled, but from further away this time. "*Gamo tin mana's sou mouni!*"

Still laughing and shaking his head, Melas yanked open the screen door.

Grandma raised a sharp, dangerous eyebrow. "What did you to do him, Nikos?"

"Cuffed him to the fence." He nodded to Tomas. "I hear you had a problem."

"The problem is already solved," Grandma told him.

"Anything I can do?" His eyes were on me as he spoke.

"How was the fire?" I asked him.

"Hot." The way he looked at me it was obvious he thought the fire wasn't the only hot thing around. I focused on the floor before a blush showed up.

"There have been a lot of fires lately," Grandma said. "Nikos, I need a police artist."

"We have someone," he said.

"Who?" I asked.

"Pappas' wife," he told me.

"Irini?" I liked Irini. She made a wicked ouzito, which is like a mojito but with a wicked ouzo kick.

"Go get her," Grandma said. "The sooner we do this, the better. First we find out who tried to kidnap the boy, then we find out who killed Litsa."

Nobody disagreed. They liked their limbs where they were.

———

POLICE SERGEANT PAPPAS is a barrel with a human head stuck to the top. In my head I call him Stained Shirt because I've never seen the man without lunch on his clothes. At first I figured he was the culprit, then I saw Irini eating while she ironed his shirts. Irini, his wife, belongs on top of a Christmas tree. She's a tiny, blonde, green-eyed fairy with no concept of personal space. Today was no different. She threw her arms around me and squeezed until my ribs began to creak. Irini is also Hera's sister, but only one of them got the psycho bitch gene.

"I am so glad you are not dead! At your funeral I begged God not to take you, and—look!—here you are. My prayer worked."

"You know I wasn't really dead, right?"

She squeezed harder. "God works in mysterious ways."

In Greece more than anywhere, it seemed like. "This is Tomas," I said.

Irini ended the bone-crushing hug and dropped into a crouch in front of Tomas, who had a death-grip on my hand. Everyone wanted to squeeze the stuffing out of me. Greece was like that.

"What a handsome little man," Irini gushed. Then she fake-spat on him. "*Ptou-ptou.*"

Spitting for real is a serious Greek insult. Fake-spitting is what Greeks use to chase away the evil eye because there's nothing the evil eye hates more than being fake-spat on. The evil eye floats around, waiting on cute babies and attractive or accomplished people to receive a compliment, then it tackles its target and turns their life to crap, unless the compliment-giver quickly fake-spits.

"I'm five," Tomas told her earnestly, "and my mother is dead, so I'm halfway to being an orphan."

Irini burst into tears. She hugged Tomas to her. "You poor little lamb."

The poor little lamb reached up and patted her on the head. "I'm sad but I'm coping okay," he said. "Now, anyway. In a few years I'll probably need therapy. Thea Katerina is taking care of me today."

The tiny blonde pulled away, wiping her eyes. "You are an angel," she told me. "I am so glad we are friends."

Were we friends? I couldn't really say. One night we did too much drinking together, and we both hated her sister, so I guess it was friendship or something like it. I like Irini and she likes me, that's all I know.

She reached into her bag and pulled out a sketchpad and a packet of pencils.

"Look what I've got," she said. "Do you like drawing?"

"It's okay, but I prefer puzzles," Tomas said.

"Well … think of what we are going to do as a puzzle, okay?"

Tomas nodded solemnly. "Okay."

———

AN HOUR and five *koulourakia* apiece later, we were in the conservatory, looking at two sketches. Irini had serious talent. She'd waved her magic pencil a few times and turned two living, breathing creeps into two two-dimensional creeps.

She wrinkled her nose at the pictures. "They look familiar …"

They really did. Both men looked like Melas—if Melas was a sleaze-ball.

"Melas," I said.

She slapped her forehead. "Nikos."

"They can't both look like Melas, can they?"

We both looked at Tomas, who was working on his sixth *koulouraki*.

"That's what I saw," he said.

Somehow that didn't seem right. "Melas was watching you?"

His head bobbed. "Uh huh."

"But Melas wasn't one of the balaclava guys," I said.

He shrugged. "All I did was tell Kyria Irini what I saw. That's what I saw."

On the way out, Irini issued an invitation for me to drop by and drink coffee with her any time I liked. One of these days I'd take her up on her offer. She was peppy and fun. I needed some pep and fun. Plus I genuinely liked her. It's hard not to like the human equivalent of sunshine and puppies.

Tomas and I schlepped back to Grandma's shack, stopping on the way to dish out hugs and pets to the various assortment of animals loitering around the courtyard. The family kept cats and dogs. I have a goat who thinks he's a dog and doesn't have a name. I also have a cow, gifted to me by a penitent call center employee in India. She—the cow, not the call center employee—was living on the family farm now, spending her days eating grass and definitely not being ground into burgers.

Grandma was waiting, not for us, but for her bread that was baking in the oven.

"Normal people buy their bread at the bakery," I said.

"Normal people are *vlakes*," Grandma said.

I couldn't disagree; I was related to some of them.

"We have sketches."

She waved me over. "Show me."

One at a time, I handed her Irini's sketches. Grandma's forehead dug a few more ditches as she pinned her eyebrows to her hairline.

"That is Nikos."

"I know."

"And this one is Nikos, but maybe fatter in the face and meaner in the eyes."

"I know that, too."

She looked past me. "Tomas, go and wait outside with Elias and Stavros for a moment, okay?"

He jumped up. "So you can talk about me?"

"Yes," she said bluntly.

"Okay."

Off he trotted. He opened and closed the screen door gently.

Grandma watched him go. "That one will either be the best of us or the worst."

"The best, I think."

She grunted. "Optimist. So. Either the artist got it wrong or the boy did."

"He's five," I said.

A Greek five is younger than an American five. Five in Greece is four. You start being one-year-old the moment you're born. Maybe you're thinking they're trying to get a jumpstart on the legal drinking age. Nope. Greece has no legal drinking age. You can't buy liquor in a bar until you're eighteen—a Greek eighteen—but no one cares if you swagger out of kindergarten, swilling retsina out of a bottle.

"Five, yes, but he is a Makris. Probably the artist got it wrong."

"Maybe." I sidled up to the wood-burning oven and breathed deep. "What happens now?"

"For now, the boy stays with you. He does not want to stay with George."

"Okay."

She eyeballed me. "I did not think you would agree."

"Why wouldn't I? It makes sense—logistically, I mean. But there's nowhere for him to sleep in here …"

"A room is being fixed for you as we speak. Xander is coming back tonight, so he will need his room back. You and Tomas will be next door. Xander will be watching you at night. During the day you will have Elias and Stavros. It will be good to have Xander back, yes? I miss that boy. It is not the same without him here."

Blood rushed to my cheeks—the ones on my face. Hopefully in the gloom Grandma wouldn't notice. Deflect, Kat. Deflect.

"What about Marika? Are you putting her on body-guard duty too?"

Grandma snorted. "Are you changing the subject? Because it sounds to me like you are changing the subject."

"Who, me?" I glanced at the watch I wasn't wearing. "Wow, I have to go and do a thing."

"Go, go. As long as the thing you need to do is in the compound. I want you here if the boy is with you."

"As a matter of fact, it is."

There wasn't a thing. The thing was me getting out of the kitchen before the conversation turned to Xander.

I trotted out to where Stavros and Elias were busy entertaining Tomas.

"Let's roll," I said.

Three puzzled sets of eyes landed on me.

"It's an American thing," I explained. "Let's go."

"Baboulas says you are not to leave the compound," Stavros told me.

"She says that a lot," I said, "but we're not leaving the compound."

"Where are we going?"

"I don't know." I looked at the massive pool, the pets, the courtyard with its leafy alcoves. "Is there anything fun to do here?"

They looked at me.

"I mean, is there anything more fun to do than escaping?"

"You can't leave," Elias said. "Baboulas said so."

"I know, but something happens in my brain when she tells me I can't go anywhere. It's like I immediately want to do the opposite thing."

"I heard that," Grandma said from behind me. "Fine, go wherever you need to go. But you take Stavros and Elias. Do you hear me?"

"Wow," I said, "it's magic. Now I don't want to go anywhere. Anyone else up for a swim?"

"Good choice," Grandma said dryly. "You should do that."

————

BY THE TIME we were done with our swim, I had a new phone with everything put back the way it had been before the dumbass wannabe kidnappers stomped on my old-new phone. Oooh, and look: I had a new call. I didn't recognize the number but a quick Google told me it originated at the hospital.

Who did I know at the hospital?

Nobody.

Good thing they left a message.

"I am looking for the woman who was here with Detective Melas. Be here tomorrow morning at nine. Wear comfortable shoes. Or uncomfortable shoes. Or no shoes, if you like. I don't care, as long as you show up. Oh—this is Gus Zentefis from the morgue. Do not forget to bring a coat. And sheets. I need sheets."

Weird guy. I wondered why he wanted me at the morgue. Maybe he knew something else about Litsa, other than her identity.

With Tomas glued to my side, I went back to Grandma's place. She was at the kitchen table, talking to my dead grandfather.

I crouched down and looked at the olive oil can my grandfather's ashes lived in. Years ago, someone had taped a post-mortem photo to the can. The nice thing was that Granddad didn't look dead. His eyes were closed but he could have been napping. Greeks napped a lot so it wasn't a stretch. Dead Granddad was wearing a suit that was his and hair that wasn't. "Hi, Granddad. Sorry I never got to meet you." I straightened up then got busy hunting for something to eat. Those *koulouraki* hadn't stuck with me. They were like Chinese food: a few laps of the pool and they'd left my stomach and gone to settle down on my hips for the impending winter.

"Do you want something to eat?" I asked Grandma and Tomas.

"I'm always hungry," Tomas said.

Grandma sat the can on the windowsill and shooed me toward the kitchen table. "You want food, I will fix you food. What do you want, eh?"

Since I'd discovered that Grandma's cancer was in remission and she was one of the goodish guys, she seemed stronger, so I didn't mind her flapping around the kitchen. She was territorial and I was likely to lose an arm or my head if I tried to seize control of the kitchen.

"Anything that isn't gross."

"Gross," she muttered. "In my day we ate what our elders put in front of us. Sometimes it was *skata*, but we ate it, otherwise we had to go foraging for berries and bugs."

Tomas and I gawked at her.

"No bugs," I said. "Please no bugs."

"I will make fish."

Fish was fine. Fish was good. Fish I could do. In the meantime, I had a burning question.

"What did Granddad do?"

Grandma arched her eyebrows in my direction. "Do?"

"He was Greek Orthodox, right?"

"What else would he be?"

I made a face. "I was just wondering."

She pulled ingredients out of the refrigerator and cupboards. "Just ask your question, Katerina. Better to be direct, except when it is better to be indirect."

Okay … "Why didn't you bury my grandfather? Cremation is a huge sin in the Greek Orthodox Church. It used to be against the law in this country."

"The law changed."

"Yeah, but he's been dead for years. It used to be you couldn't even get a cremation done in this country, unless you had access to the equipment." I thought about it a moment and slapped my forehead. "Jiminy Cricket, did you have the equipment? Wait—don't tell me. I don't want to know if you did a home cremation."

Grandma rolled her eyes. "I took his body to Bulgaria because it was his wish to be cremated. Your grandfather was a visionary. He could see a time when Greece would run out of places to put the dead to rest, permanently. For people who did not have the funds, anyway. He did not want to contribute to the problem."

"So you didn't cremate him because he did something terrible and you wanted to condemn his soul for all eternity?"

Grandma's shoulders shook. She was laughing at me.

"Why would I do that?"

"Because … you're Baboulas?"

Her gaze slid sideways. "Not in front of the boy, eh?"

"I already know everything," Tomas said.

"I doubt that," Grandma muttered. She dipped the fish in flour, slapped it into a sizzling pan. The kitchen filled up with garlic-scented smoke. "Open the window."

I leaped across the table, shoved the window open. My elbow bumped against Granddad. For a long, terrible moment during which I was completely paralyzed, the olive oil can wobbled back and forth. Then it performed a somersault and crash-landed on the ground. Outside.

"Please tell me that was not your grandfather," Grandma said.

"Lying isn't really my thing."

Grandma crossed herself. She produced a Dustbuster and handed it to me across the counter.

My eyes widened. "You want me to vacuum him?"

"Go."

I took the Dustbuster and scurried out to the back of the shack. The container was on the ground, leaking ashes. Some had sprayed out during the fall. Grandma's gardenias were covered in a thin grey blanket of Granddad.

"Crispy critter Christ, I'm going to hell."

Grandma's voice wafted out the window. "Greeks do not go to hell."

"Greeks don't go to hell," I muttered.

"I heard that," she called out. "Maybe they will make an exception for you. There is a first time for everything."

The mini vacuum made a small racket as I sucked Granddad out of the gardenias.

"It does not have to be too perfect," Grandma called out. "Gardenias love acid."

There was laughter behind me, the hooting and hollering kind. "What are you doing, Katerina?" Takis said. "Practicing to be a good wife?"

There was a primal scream from a distance away. "I heard that!" Marika hollered from their apartment balcony.

Takis' gaunt face looked spooked. "I do not know how she does it. That woman has ears like a dog." He paused for a moment, then lowered his voice. "I figured she would have heard that, too."

My phone rang. It was Marika. "Tell that *malakas* I heard him just fine, but my throat is sore from yelling the first time."

I ended the call. "She heard you."

"That woman …" He jerked his chin toward the ashes. "What is with the vacuuming, eh?"

I slapped the Dustbuster into his hand and set the plant upright.

"Granddad."

He dropped the vacuum. *"Gamo tin Panayia mou …"*

"It's just ashes. You handle dead people all the time." When it came to arts and crafts, some people scrapbooked. Takis made dead people.

"Ashes are different. Ashes are creepy."

I snatched the vacuum, grabbed the olive oil can, and headed back inside. "Did you want something?"

"I wanted to make fun of you. Does that count?"

"No."

He laughed and trotted off to do whatever it is henchmen do whenever they're not henchman-ing.

Inside, Grandma was spooning *skordalia*—garlic and bread sauce—onto two plates, then she heaped on crispy fried fish. Small, crunchy, fish. With open eyes.

My stomach started to rock and roll. "They're looking me at me."

Grandma stabbed one of the fish with a fork. She picked it up, made eye contact. "Are you looking at her?" She put the fish back down. "The fish is dead. The fish is not looking at you. Eat the fish, Katerina."

I ate with my eyes closed.

———

GRANDMA HAD my things moved to the apartment next to Xander's. Now I had my own kitchenette, indoor plumbing, and tasteful furnishings. Some of Tomas's things were there, too. Clothing. A puzzle book. His iPad, with a full complement of games and apps for kids way older than five.

At bedtime, I tucked him in. Poor George. How was he coping with two boys, no wife, and a little boy who—at the moment, anyway—wanted to cling to me?

"Stay with me, Thea Katerina."

"I'm right here."

"You won't leave, will you?"

"See that bed over there?" I pointed to the second queen in the room.

He nodded.

"That's where I'll be."

"Can I sleep with you?"

My heart ached. "Do you hog the bed?"

"No."

"Steal the covers?"

"No."

"Okay. The most important question. Do you snore?"

He giggled. "No, but I can if you want me to."

I laughed and patted the bed that was designated as mine. "Come on over."

He rocketed out of his bed and burrowed down in mine. It didn't bother me in the least. It was kind of nice, actually. Not the circumstances—but having Tomas around was … nice. I could see being a mother someday, if I ever met a man who wasn't bosom buddies with crime.

Tomas snuggled up to my side. Within minutes his eyelids drooped and body relaxed. I lay on the bed, new phone in hand, and swiped around my favorite apps and sites. Facebook was filled with my old friends doing normal things. Family picnics. Fun runs—which was a misnomer if ever I'd heard one. Children they'd made. Good times they were having. I was "friends" with a bunch of my Greek family but they didn't post much. I didn't post much either. What could I say? Sometimes I uploaded a picture of Greece, a view of the water, but my real life and my online footprint didn't really intersect.

Next I skipped over to the Crooked Noses Message Board, a forum for organized crime nerds and aficionados. My murder had been a big deal on the board, and I was an even bigger deal now that I was really alive. Some posters decided it had been an elaborate scheme devised by Grandma to keep me safe from her enemies, which was pretty much everyone. Others figured I'd staged the shooting myself, which was ridiculous. I'd been shot and I'd been fake-shot, and they both hurt. Pain isn't really my thing. I could never go all *Fifty Shades of Grey* and be on the receiving end of a thrashing.

Yeah, I was a big deal on the board but I wasn't the only one. Litsa's murder, dismemberment, and subsequent flying lesson was the new, hot topic. Ten pages and counting. Everybody had a theory. Litsa knew too much and Grandma had her killed. Litsa was a leak and a snitch. Litsa was having an affair. On and on. Winkler's arrest hadn't made the news—not as an arrest anyway. The German godmother, and Grandma's sister, had mysteriously vanished; only maybe not so mysteriously, some suggested. Nudge nudge. Wink wink. Someone even posited that my fake murder and Winkler's disappearance were connected. Grandma made me vanish so I could pop up in Germany and snuff Winkler and my Uncle Kostas, who had also gone up in smoke.

The somebody jumped in—a poster with this one lonely little post—and wrote, regarding Litsa:

I know her. She used to be a stripper in Volos.

Chapter 7

The good thing about most of the family living at the compound is that I couldn't walk twenty feet without tripping over a relative. This was also the bad thing. Sometimes, like tonight, it was also the lucky thing.

When I went out to get some air, I spotted a familiar figure by the pool, head and neck wilted over a tumbler of cloudy ouzo.

"George?"

Tomas's father looked up at me through red-rimmed eyes. "Katerina, sit."

It was the least I could do for the newly minted widower. On some level I felt responsible for his misery, which was nuts. But feelings are not logic's biggest fans.

"I'm not going to ask how you are."

"You can ask. I want you to. Everyone else is asking what I am doing."

"How are you?"

"Better than you would think for a man who just lost his wife. But if I am being honest I lost Litsa a long time ago. Maybe I never had her."

What was I supposed to say to that? The usual Greek post-death platitudes didn't seem fitting. "When was the last time you saw her?"

"Two days ago. She said she was going to visit her sister in Athens. She visited her sister a lot." He took a long slug of the ouzo. "Litsa did not have a sister. Stupid *putana*. And now she is dead."

Why beat around the bush? "Did you do it?"

"Kill her? No. Sometimes I wanted to but it was nice having someone to do my laundry and cook my dinner."

"Practical."

"Very."

"Any idea who might have wanted her dead?"

He laughed into his drink. "A shorter list would be people who wanted her to live."

"Could I have that list?"

"Did you want to kill her?"

"No."

"There you go. That is your list."

Wow. Short list. I hoped the list of people who wanted me to stay alive was longer.

"If you don't mind me asking, what do you know about Litsa's life before you met her?"

"Are you a policeman?"

I looked at him, surprised. "Not that I know of, and I feel like I'd probably know if I was."

"Then why all the questions? Litsa was no good. Let her rot."

———

I WOKE UP AFTER MIDNIGHT, according to the phone in my hand. There was drool on my cheek—mine. And somebody besides Tomas was in the room with us.

The compound is safe—well, mostly safe; there have been exceptions—but my heart flopped around, desperately seeking an exit. My heart is a dumbass. My brain wasn't too far behind it; that big, pink-grey lump was firing off messages to my limbs, telling me to get up and be proactively violent.

I jumped up and pitched my phone at the dark, scary corner of the room.

No crash. Just the soft slap of my fast phone being caught by a faster hand.

"Who's there?"

The chair in the corner creaked. Someone stood. A tall, broad body stepped into the less dark patch. I knew that shape.

Xander was home.

Chapter 8

"You're back."

Wordlessly, he held out my phone. I reached up and took it from him.

"So we're back to this now, the not talking thing?"

Nothing.

"Seriously?"

More nothing. He was so good at it.

"You're in the wrong business. With your skills you should have pursued a life of mime."

With all these shadows I couldn't be sure, but it's possible his lips made something like a smile.

"So what are you doing here?"

He moved to the side of the bed, pointed to the night-stand. I sat my phone down and flopped back onto the pillows—but carefully, so I wouldn't disturb the little guy. Xander pulled the covers up and tucked me back in until I felt like a snuggly burrito.

Then he went back to the shadows, to his seat in the corner.

———

AFTER THE KISS in Xander's hotel room nothing had happened. My toes had curled and I'd gotten all hot, bothered, and damp for nothing. Me and my ego limped back to the room across the hall. Elias had the door open and waiting.

"Something wrong, boss?"

"Nothing. Everything."

"I used to have days like that."

"What changed?"

"I tried to assassinate you, then Baboulas hired me as your bodyguard."

I'd flopped down on one of the beds. "Maybe I need a job."

"Or maybe you need to find love." He looked pointedly at the door.

"Xander is no good for me. He just told me so."

Elias looked me up and down, then he ruffled my hair. "Since when do you listen to anyone?"

"Hey, I listen."

"When they are saying something you like?"

"No—when they're saying something logical."

"And was Xander being logical?"

"Mostly he was being evasive."

He raised his eyebrows in what I interpreted as a challenge. Damn him, he was right. Jumping off the bed wasn't happening on account of how I'd just spent hours hunched in the driver's seat, so I rolled off the bed and let go of my dignity while Elias helped me up.

"Just do it," he said, channeling Nike.

What "it" was I wasn't sure, but I had an idea. I just hoped I remember how to do "it." I rearranged my hair, straightened my shirt, brushed my teeth, then marched across the hallway to Xander's door.

The door opened. Xander was there, still missing his shirt. I ducked under his arm before he could protest. He closed the door with a look of resignation on his face.

"You don't listen, do you?"

"You're slow," I said. "Elias and I already had this conversation."

"And?"

"Elias thinks there should be more kissing."

Xander smiled one of those smiles that sucked the wind out of my lungs and whacked me behind the knees. "Elias or you?"

"Does it matter?"

"I don't want to kiss Elias."

He didn't wait for my comeback, and once he slid his hand under my shirt I no longer had one anyway. His kiss was long and deep. Lots of tongue and heat.

For the second time that night, he pulled away first.

"I'm not a good man," he said.

"If you say so."

"Stick around I'll break your heart."

"Okay." My fingers roamed the length of his back, tracing those scars. "Can we get back to the kissing now?"

"No. I just told you I'm not one of the good guys."

Crap. "I thought that would be an in-the-future problem, not a tonight thing."

"Go back to your room. I'll meet you downstairs for breakfast in the morning."

I snatched my hands away from his body, folded them tight around me.

"You're serious?"

"I'm doing you a favor." He opened the door again.

Gave me a bad boy smile. "Don't think I don't want you to stay. I do."

"And you believe you're one of the bad guys? I don't think so."

He kissed me again, gently and sweetly. In hindsight it tasted like goodbye.

"Get some sleep," he said.

Against my hormones' wishes, I went to bed. The next morning, breakfast came and went without Xander.

He'd checked out.

The *asshat*.

Chapter 9

Tomas and Xander were gone the next morning, but there was a note under the door from Elias and Stavros, saying that Tomas was having breakfast at Stavros' apartment. Stavros had left a basket of baked goods on the kitchen counter, which officially made him my favorite cousin. So what if he liked weird porn and was basically a mangy bear from the neck down? Nobody is perfect.

I had just enough time to throw myself into the shower, scramble into jeans and a fitted black t-shirt, and select something from the goody basket, using the time-honored tradition of *eenie, meanie, miney, mo*. Not prepared for a Greek winter, seeing as how I'd never experienced one before, I found myself coatless and unprepared for the morgue. So on the way out I grabbed the blanket off the end of the bed and trotted out to find my yellow Beetle waiting outside the garage.

The cousin whose job it was to keep the vehicles in tiptop shape was around the side, smoking a cigarette. As soon as he spotted me, he dropped the cigarette and hid it under his shoe.

"Katerina!"

"Didn't see anything. Don't care anyway."

He eyed the blanket over my shoulder. "Sleepover?"

"Morgue."

"Americans are strange."

"Not as strange as Greeks."

"Baboulas said you would be going out this morning. Your car is ready."

"She's letting me leave alone?"

He laughed like I'd said something *h-i-l-a-r-i-o-u-s*. "Alone? You are dreaming again. Someone will be here in a moment."

Somebody turned out to be Elias. He jogged over wearing the Xander wannabe outfit all the guys in the family were wearing these days. Black cargo pants, black military boots, black t-shirts.

"Tomas is helping Marika bake. Stavros and one of the other cousins are with them," he said before I could ask.

"You mean he's cracking that safe for her."

He grinned at me. "Where are we going, Boss?"

"Morgue."

"You take me to all the best places."

I eyed his t-shirt. "If you have a winter coat, now would be the time to grab it."

He was back five minutes later with two heavy coats, both black.

"One should be fine," I told him.

"One for me, one for you. I noticed you do not have one."

Was there something in my eye? "Thanks. You're the best bodyguard a mobster's granddaughter could have."

He winked, and then he jumped into the black compact parked behind the Beetle.

After a quick jaunt to the morgue to see what was

bugging Gus Zentefis, my big plan was zip down to the waterfront to look up a sort of friend-like person. That comment on the Crooked Noses forum had me thinking about Litsa and who she'd been before she married into the Makris family. If Litsa really had been a stripper, Penka would know. Then I could branch out from there.

Did Melas know?

My mind raked up the random flakes of crazy in my head into one sloppy pile, because that's what minds do when they have more questions than answers and they have no job to keep them occupied during the daylight hours. Maybe, my brain decided, Melas met Litsa while she on the pole. My brain pitched a movie reel at me: Melas swiping his credit card between Litsa's glitter-splattered butt cheeks.

Ugh. Stupid brain.

I pulled into the Volos hospital and found two parking places together so Elias could park alongside me. As early as it was the hospital wasn't busy. We rode the elevator down to the morgue level. The doors opened in the lobby. The cold slapped me in the face. Elias's coat was big and warm but this fake winter was a real groper.

"You want to share the blanket?" I said to him.

"Keep it." He nodded to the bodies packed in like this was Tetris, with bodies. "Backlog?"

"More like nowhere to put them. People die and no one comes to pick them up."

From deep inside the morgue there was a cheer, followed by rubber slapping the marble tiles.

Gus scampered into the lobby, grinning. Today he was less shaky Chihuahua, more cheerful Pomeranian. "You came! Okay, do you know how to make coffee? It is never as good when I make it. The receptionist …" he counted on his fingers "… five receptionists ago made the best coffee. I call her sometimes to ask for the secret but she always hangs up on me. All I want is her coffee recipe."

Elias raised his hand. "I make good coffee."

Who knew? Not me. "You do?"

"Stavros taught me to make the perfect cup. He has one of those fancy coffee machines that makes foam."

"Ours isn't fancy," Gus said sadly. "Wait—who are you?"

"We're conjoined twins," I said as Elias ducked into the reception area, where an el cheapo coffee machine was waiting.

"I don't suppose you have any *koulourakia*?" Gus said hopefully.

"What did you want to see me about?"

His face broke out into one of those grins that hurts if you keep it up too long. "You start your new job today. Congratulations!"

Wait—what? "New job?"

"You need a job, and I have one."

"But I'm not qualified!" And I wasn't looking for a job —was I?

"Dead people do not seem to bother you, which means you are completely qualified, and you look like a woman who knows where to get inexpensive sheets. I really need sheets." He cast a longing glance at the blanket wrapped around my head and shoulders, like a hood.

"Dead people totally bother me, especially when they're dead people I know."

His face fell. "Oh."

On the far side of the reception counter, the coffee was beginning to drip. I reached into my pocket and pulled out the cellophane wrapped muffin Stavros left in my room. It looked like peach, with white chocolate chips. I really like peaches and white chocolate chips.

"i can't work for you, but I can share this muffin."

"You would do that for me?"

"It's just a muffin."

He wiped his eyes with the back of his hand. "Not to me."

Elias carried three mugs of coffee over. It was good. It was hot. It didn't put a dent in the permafrost setting up shop in my bones. I ripped the muffin in half and gave one half each to Elias and Gus. Elias tried to split his share with me but I wasn't having it. It was because of me that he was one giant goose-bump.

Gus sighed into his coffee. "Why can't you work for me? You have muffins. I like muffins."

"Because I have a job." I thought about it a moment. "Okay, I had a job and I don't have it now because Grandma probably burned down my place of employment and broke my boss's legs."

He pointed at me. "A-ha! So you do need a job."

"No? Yes. I'm not sure."

Good ol' Gus was on a roll. "It pays money. Not much, but I think the money is real. Given who you are, the hospital will be too scared not to pay you."

Oh boy. "What would I—I mean, what are the duties?"

"Sit at the front desk and yell at anyone who wants to bring a body in. Be nice to anyone who wants to take a body with them, even if it is not their body to take."

"Maybe you need to advertise: *Free body to good home*."

He clicked his fingers. "Great idea. Can you take care of that?"

"I was joking!"

"That is no joke."

The elevator dinged. The doors opened. A hospital orderly wheeled a body out, which wasn't easy given the space issue. It looked like a necrophiliac hoarder's place in here.

Gus elbowed me. "Do it."

One deep breath later I'd summoned up my inner Spartan. My inner Spartan had washboard abs, a pointy spear, and a minor speech impediment like that Scottish guy screaming about Sparta when he was clearly Glaswegian.

"You can't bring that in here," I said. "I'm really sorry, but you just can't."

On a scale from doormat to Spartan that was more of a grumpy squirrel.

The orderly looked up. "Oh, okay." Then he turned around and got back into the elevator without the body.

"That went well," Elias said.

"That is what they do when I tell them the same thing," Gus said sadly.

"This *is* the morgue," I said.

"I know." He did puppy dog eyes. I hate it when guys do puppy dog eyes. He wasn't even cute but he did effective puppy dog eyes.

"Christ on a cookie." I stood. "Okay. Give me a moment."

I jogged over to the stairs, not because I wanted the exercise but because movement meant warmth. By the time I reached the top step, sweat was trying to punch through my crispy ice coating.

The elevator dinged and the orderly hurried out.

Oh no, he didn't. He was the reason I wound up on the receiving end of puppy dog eyes.

My hand snapped out. My fingers hooked themselves into the pink shell of his ear.

"Ow!" he howled. "What is wrong with you?"

"You just made me commit to a job I don't want," I

muttered.

"What?"

Twisting his ear, I steered him back toward the elevator. "Get in."

"Why?" He stared at me in the polished steel interior. "You are the woman from the morgue."

"That's right, and you left something behind."

"You mean a body?"

"Yes, I mean a body."

"But it is the morgue! That is where the bodies go."

"Ordinarily I'd agree with you, but this is Greece, where everything seems to be topsy-turvy—or whatever the Greek word for topsy-turvy is."

The elevator dinged. We got out.

"Okay." I pointed to the corpse he'd left behind. "Please collect your belongings and leave."

"But—"

"You can bring him or her back when you have a written statement from the family that they're willing to collect the body in a timely manner. Tell them if they won't agree, you'll stick their loved one in a taxicab and send it to their home."

"I cannot—"

"Oooooh, please don't use that word. My grandmother doesn't like that word and just now I realized I don't like it either. There is no can't—there is only can."

Head down, he wheeled his cargo onto the elevator. The elevator pinged. The doors closed.

I sagged against the wall, and suddenly I realized I wasn't cold. Probably I was about to drop dead from hypothermia.

Elias and Gus were staring at me, openmouthed.

"What?"

Gus grinned. "I knew you were the right one for the

job! If you come here every day and do what you just did, you will be making my job three hundred percent easier."

The elevator pinged again. The doors opened, revealing a different orderly, wheeling a different corpse.

"Don't even think about it," I barked.

He pressed the button. The doors closed.

"I love you," Gus said, stars in his eyes. "Please say you'll be back again tomorrow, and all the days after that."

————

THE MORGUE CLOSED for three hours every afternoon, which meant a long lunch was the only job perk. On the way along the coast, I stopped for three souvlakia. I handed one to a grateful Elias, who was still shivering.

"Tomorrow I am bringing a sleeping bag," he said.

"You don't have to come."

"My job is to go where you go." He held up the souvlaki. "Besides, you buy lunch—good lunch."

Souvlaki number three stayed in the bag until I snugged the Beetle up to the curb outside an abandoned brick and stucco house that sat directly across from the beach. The tourist crowd had thinned out. All that were left now were the handful of folks who'd bought off-season plane tickets, and the occasional crazy Greek who didn't head home to sleep off what was left of the heat.

Penka was on her shaded stoop, scowling at the world. The Bulgarian woman is one of Baby Dimitri's drug dealers, except she sells prescription drugs, which are much classier than the regular kind. That makes her less of a criminal and more of an easy-going pharmacist, she says. Her customers wear nice clothes and hold good jobs, and they need regular pick-me-ups or put-me-downs so that they can keep those nice clothes and good jobs. High quality clothes and jobs are apparently stressful. As usual, Penka had ignored the number of servings on her clothing labels and was trying to stretch a dress made for one over a body built for two. The green lycra number looked exhausted.

She eyed the plastic sack in my hand. "Is that a souvlaki? Because a souvlaki would go a long way toward fixing my bad mood."

I handed her the bag. "What's wrong?"

"Have you seen this beach?" She tore in to the paper and foil. "Empty. How can I blend in when the beach is this deserted?"

Some people blend. Penka wasn't one of those people. She was oil—bright, colorful oil—on water.

"There're still some people."

"You see people. I see that my regular clients won't come here now because someone might see them."

"What do you normally do in winter?"

"I go to church a lot."

"People buy drugs in church?"

"You have no idea," she said darkly.

"So why don't you go to church now?"

"I am waiting for Baby Dimitri to call about a new shipment. There is no point going to church to sell lots of drugs if I do not have lots of drugs to sell."

That made sense. "Speaking of Baby Dimitri, did you hear about the woman who was tossed out of a plane and onto his shop?"

"I heard about it. Everybody heard about it. Baby Dimitri is not a happy man. He has all the money in the world but he is cheap. And now he is a cheap man who has to pay money to fix his roof."

"He doesn't have insurance?"

"He *is* insurance."

She had a point. "The woman was Litsa Makri. She was married to one of my cousins."

"Never met her. Never heard of her. Did I say I never heard of her? I meant it."

"So you never heard of her and you never met her?"

"That's what I said."

"Huh. Because I heard a little rumor that Litsa used to be a stripper in Volos. And I know you know everyone who matters, so I figure you probably heard of a woman with a great big tattoo of Tom Cruise on her lower back."

"David Hasselhoff," she said, correcting me.

"A-ha!" I pointed. "You did know her."

"It was in the newspaper."

"No, it wasn't," Elias said.

"Give me a minute to think of a different excuse," Penka said. She rifled around in her medical bag and pulled out a sleeve of Ambien. "You want to take a little nap while I think? It is free for people who do not ask me too many questions."

"Just tell me," I said. "Don't make me work for it. I've had to be the bad guy all morning, and I don't really want to be the bad guy on my lunch break."

"You got a job? What does Baboulas have you doing? Wet work?" Her eyes narrowed. "You are not selling classy drugs, are you?"

"I'm not working for Grandma. I accidentally scored a job working at the Volos Hospital's morgue."

"And I thought my job was bad," she said. "Okay, okay, but do not tell anyone I told you this, okay? Especially not Baby Dimitri. He's already angry at me about the money."

Being dead had had unfortunate side effects. One of those was that my bank believed I was dead for real. When I reached out to their call center they'd accused me of trying to steal my own identity, so I'd had to find money elsewhere. Penka had raided Baby Dimitri's store stash, then we faked a robbery.

"I gave it all back!"

"I know that. You know that. But Baby Dimitri is an old man. Old people collect grudges like little children collect trading cards and those plastic figurines shaped like food. People like Baby Dimitri tend to their grudges carefully, and then one day—pop—you don't wake up in the morning because he had you killed in your sleep."

"Cross my heart and hope to die," I said, "and I really don't want to die again anytime soon, so you know my word is good."

"Okay. Litsa used to work for Baby Dimitri. She used to work at one of his strip clubs in Volos. It was a long time ago and that club is gone now."

"What happened to it?"

"Fire. Fire happened to it."

"Arson?"

She made a face. "Arson, Laki, same thing."

"Why?"

"I know some things, but I don't know that. Probably it was time to start paying taxes on the building or something, so it was cheaper to burn it to the ground."

Probably Penka was right. Tax evasion is Greece's national sport. They'll tell you their hearts belong to football (or soccer, as we call it back home) and basketball, but they'll tell you loudly and proudly how they avoided writing the government a check that year. Baby Dimitri struck me as a guy who enjoyed cashing checks more than he enjoyed writing them, so I wouldn't be surprised if the fire was a dodge.

"So if Litsa used to work for Baby Dimitri, why would someone kidnap her, chop her into pieces, and throw her out of a plane directly over his shoe shop."

"He sells souvenirs, too," Penka said. "I cannot believe he sells that *kaka* to tourists. It's not even made in Greece."

"Nobody dropped her on his roof because he sells shoes and statues with chin-skimming sausages."

Penka shrugged. "I told you what I know. Maybe you should talk to Baby Dimitri."

"Maybe pigs could fly."

"Is that an American expression? I like it. If you talk to Baby Dimitri, do not tell him I told you. I don't want to wake up dead."

I left her to her lunch and zipped down to Baby Dimitri's shop.

Closed. No chairs outside. There was a sign on the door saying that the shop would be open when it was open. I left the car at the curb, cupped my hands, peered through the dusty window. Good thing it hadn't rained because the roof was still on the floor.

"You were here when it happened, yes?"

I saw her reflection in the glass beside me. Her short hair was the red of a violent murder scene, and her lids were heavy with lashes too long and fringed to be her own. She was in her late thirties but her eyes said she seen a lot, and most of it she'd seen while her knees and looking up at a man's marble bag.

Baby Dimitri half-sister and Donk's mother.

"I was here," I said.

"A lucky thing you did not get hurt."

"Nobody got hurt, thankfully."

She crossed herself. Not that I was an expert, but it looked to me like she had sincerity issues when it came to God.

"Thank the Virgin Mary." She gave me a sly look. "If you had not been inside when that woman through the roof, I would have wondered if your family was responsible."

"Why would they drop a body on Baby Dimitri's shop?"

"Why wouldn't they? My brother is a cheap *malakas*. I bet you the reason there is nobody here fixing his roof is because he will not pay for anybody reputable." She fixed a crimson smile on her face. "And now that we are talking about money, have you reconsidered coming to work for me? I could make you a star in the industry."

When it came to careers, my dad had two no-nos. Me; I had a list as long as my leg. Near the top somewhere, between *stripper* and *canine bikini waxer*, was *porn star*. Maybe I'd feel differently if I was starving and homeless, but I'd had a good breakfast, and I knew an equally delicious lunch was in my near future.

"I don't think so," I said.

She shrugged prettily. "That is too bad, because I really like money. Call me if you change your mind."

"I won't," I said.

Her laugh was real enough. "I like a woman who knows what she does not want." Then she sauntered around the corner on heels that could murder a man and vanished out of sight. A minute later she zipped away in a sporty black coupe.

Duh. I slapped my forehead. Baby Dimitri's sister had been standing right here. I should have asked her where I could find the old gangster.

I jumped back into the Beetle and called Grandma. "Where would I find Baby Dimitri if he wasn't at his shoe shop? One of his clubs?"

"At his house. Dimitri never goes to his clubs, because he is cheap."

Funny, his sister had said the same thing. "Wouldn't he

get stuff for free?"

"Somebody still has to pay for free things, and in his clubs that is him. Why are you asking me this? You better not be thinking about going to his house."

"Who, me? Definitely not. Where did you say he lives?"

An exasperated sigh leaked out of my only living grandparent. "I did not say, but I will tell you because if I do not tell you then you will just call someone else and ask."

"It's like you know me," I said.

She gave me an address, and when that didn't show up on my phone she gave me directions that mostly involved turning left or right at a pile of donkey bones and following a dirt road until it was more gravel than dirt. After my recent jaunt around this village, first to the high school, then to the home of one of Dad's old school buddies, the place was starting to feel familiar. The Beetle edged up the narrow street where Jimmy Pants used to live, metal fences inches away from the side mirrors. Traffic was strictly one way. Things got dicey for a moment when a decrepit pile of rags and a fisherman's hat wanted to come down while we were going up. He had a donkey, a face that was mostly mustache, and he was convinced he had the right of way.

Elias jumped out of the black car and squeezed past the Beetle. "I will help him see the light."

"Just as long as the light isn't the flash from your gun."

He grinned at me and slogged up the hill.

Words were exchanged. Hands waved. Then Donkey Guy backed up.

"What did you say?" I asked Elias as squeezed his way back to his car.

Bigger grin. "We like the same football team."

I rolled my eyes. It figured that sportsball would be

involved.

Up ahead and around a corner, the road turned to dirt. A sepia cloud shot out behind me, enveloping Elias's black car. As many dirt roads as Greece had, Grandma had to spend a fortune on keeping the fleet clean.

Baby Dimitri lived in a glass house, which didn't seem smart when I considered how much gravel was spread around his property. One good tire spin and his mansion would be a shattered heap. Everything that wasn't glass was a white column. The only green thing around was a wisp of pathetic grass at the edge of the property. Basically the place was hospice care for good taste. Baby Dimitri had clearly been inspired by Las Vegas.

Like Grandma, Baby Dimitri had security. Two armed guards met us at the gate.

Did I mention Baby Dimitri had a wall? A big wall. A lot like Grandma's actually. People who kill other people like walls. The outside of the wall was laced with wire. Thanks to Jurassic Park and its sequels I knew the fence was electric.

"Cool razor wire. Has anyone ever peed on that fence and lived?" I asked the guards.

The Godfather of the Night ran a tight, military procedure, which was a little bit surprising, considering how casual he was at his shop. His security wore military green. No patchy camouflage bits, just that dull solid green that makes me look like puking is one slimy mouthful of okra away. Grandma's security guards had a guardhouse and guns. Baby Dimitri's place was set up like a prison.

"Who are you and what do you want?"

"Is Baby Dimitri home?"

"Who is asking?"

I looked around. "Me?"

He sighed. Someone was losing patience fast.

"Your name."

"Katerina Makris."

"With an S?"

"Yes."

He leaped aside like his butt was on fire and waved us through.

"Somebody has connections," Elias said when we parked out front of the glass monstrosity.

"That would be me."

He snorted.

Baby Dimitri met us at the door in his robe and slippers. Underneath the robe he was wearing his regular day clothes, slacks with a razor sharp crease and a short-sleeved button-down, rolled to the biceps, no doubt. A few wisps of hair had escaped the oil slick and were standing at attention.

"Katerina Makris-with-an-s, the shop is closed today. But if you want to buy shoes, I can have one of my men take you to my warehouse."

He shuffled back inside and slammed the door.

I knocked.

The door opened again, just a sliver this time. He was reduced to a watery eye.

"What?"

"I have questions."

"Of course you have questions. You are Greek. All we have are questions. Do what everyone else does around here: make up your own answers."

"Are you wallowing? You're wallowing, aren't you?"

Somehow he managed to make a face with one eye. "I am relaxing until my roof is fixed."

"When will that be?"

"When the contractor shows up."

Which could be today, tomorrow, or next year. Greece

runs on Greek time. It's the least precise form of time in the universe. The only thing more nebulous is mist.

"I know whose body fell through your roof."

"Congratulations." He went to shut the door again but Elias's foot was in the way. Sometimes having a bodyguard is awesome.

"Her name was Litsa—Litsa Makri. A little birdie told me she used to work for you."

"Lots of people used to work for me."

"I was wondering if maybe she made any enemies on the job."

"What—are you a policeman now? Why do you care?"

Funny, George had asked the same question. "I'm just curious, that's all."

"Go be curious somewhere else. I do not have answers for you. If she worked for me it was a long time ago. Plenty of time between then and now to meet someone who wanted to chop her up and throw her out of a plane."

"But they dropped her on your building. Don't you think that's strange?"

"You know what I think? I think it is inconvenient because now I have to close my shop for who knows how long before the lazy *malakas* I hired to do the job shows up."

"You can't, you know, convince him?"

He laughed. "How? With free shoes? It is like you think I am a gangster, Katerina Makris-with-an-s."

I looked around at his property, wondering how Melas would squeeze the old mobster. As a bill collector I had certain skills, but they were mostly limited to garden variety good manners. Putting the squeeze on someone wasn't my thing. This morning, at the morgue, that wasn't my usual MO. "I love your gardens. I bet maintenance is a real pain."

He grunted. "You know what it costs to employ a gardener? Gravel is cheap."

"You know you have lots of windows, right?"

"If my enemies come for me I want to see them approaching."

"I thought you were just a simple shoe salesman."

"People get angry when their shoes do not fit properly."

"You're not going to tell me anything, are you?"

"Tell you what? I know nothing. But if you see my nephew, tell him I am looking for him, eh?"

I promised to pass the message along, then I blew out a long frustrated sigh as Elias and I crunched across the gravel, back to our cars.

We had an hour to kill before lunch was over, so Elias made some calls to figure out where Litsa's former place of employment used to be. It wasn't there now, but maybe I'd get a flash of inspiration.

"Why don't you let the police do what they do?" he asked.

"Because I have reasons," I said. "I just don't know what they are yet."

"Good enough," Elias said and got back into his car.

He had a point—a good one. Why wasn't I letting the police do what the police do?

Maybe because now that I'd found Dad there was a hole inside me and I wanted to stuff it full of meaning. Litsa had been murdered, and she'd left behind children, including the coolest little guy around. A kid who happened to be the son of one of two guys I wouldn't mind seeing naked.

No, this wasn't about Melas.

Maybe it was my Greek genes asserting themselves.

There was a mystery here and I was desperate to figure out whodunit, and why.

The old strip club and its charred bones were long gone. In its place now was a coffee shop. One of the newer, Americanized places that made fancy coffees and offered three kinds of milk: cow, goat, and sheep. Cooler weather meant the locals were hanging around longer, and the place where they all seemed to be hanging out was here, at Cafe Americano.

Elias and I weren't the only sightseers. Detective Melas's car was hugging the curb. He was slouched behind the wheel, staring at the building.

Oh God, was he still in love with Litsa? Is that what this was about?

I got out of the Beetle and jogged over to the police cruiser.

Melas jumped. His face was tight, tense. It softened some when he realized it was me rapping on his window with my knuckle.

He rolled the window down. "What are you doing here?"

"What are *you* doing here?"

"My job."

"Oh. I'm not doing that."

He flashed me one of his devastatingly gorgeous grins. Really, those things should be illegal. Stare too long and a woman could lose her underwear.

"You don't have a job, thanks to Baboulas," he said.

"Wrong. So wrong."

His forehead bunched up. "Are you leaving Greece?"

As the Magic 8-Ball I had when I was a kid would say: "Reply hazy, try again." I swore I'd leave Greece when I found Dad, but now that I'd found him—or he'd found me —the one-way trip to the airport wasn't happening. I wanted to go home, I really did; and I would, I swear. But not today.

"I have a job—here. Apparently. One sort of fell into my lap."

He thought about it for a moment, and then he laughed. "You're working at the morgue."

"I see dead people."

"Has Gus released Litsa's remains?"

"Not yet."

He was unreadable. "You never said what you are doing here."

"I heard a rumor."

"It wasn't a rumor. Litsa used to work here when this place was still a strip club. But she left her job a long time before she married your cousin."

"So why are you here?"

He gave me a half smile. "Trying to shake something loose. As far as I can tell, she didn't have any enemies. She was a devoted wife and a good mother."

I snorted.

He seized on that. "What?"

"Good wife and mother? She was sleeping with you, right? Years ago, sure, but she was married."

"Okay …"

"And a good mother? You should talk to her children—only not right now because they're hurting. But one day, you should definitely talk to them. Tomas compared her to … I don't remember what animal, but it was one that dumps its young pretty quickly after birth. So maybe you're not digging hard enough. If she wasn't a great wife and she wasn't exactly a present mother, what was she doing with her time? Maybe whatever she was doing got her killed."

"Not now, Katerina."

"Are you even considering the possibility?"

"You want to know what I'm considering? That Baboulas had her killed."

"Why would Grandma do that?"

"Why do you think?"

I gnawed on it a moment. "Was Litsa cooperating with law enforcement? Because that wouldn't make sense. Grandma is law enforcement. She's as law enforcement as it gets."

"Not law enforcement."

"Then who?"

"Think harder."

Math happened—slowly. "You think Litsa was talking to other crime families?"

He shrugged. His phone chirped. He glanced at it quickly then said, "Another fire. I have to go. You want to get something to eat later?"

"You mean tonight?"

"Or sooner."

"Can't. The family is in mourning."

"So come to my place." There went that wicked smile again. "Wear something sexy. I'll pick you up after dark. Your reputation will be safe with me."

Somehow I doubted that.

———

BACK AT THE MORGUE, Gus was pacing and it wasn't just the cold to blame.

"She was here—I know it. There is never any space here, and now I have a space where there is not supposed to be a space."

"What happened?"

"Somebody stole a body. Not that I am not grateful—I

113

am—but now the police are going to make me eat wood."

My intestines looped around themselves and tied a loose bow. "Who?"

"The Hasselhoff woman—your cousin's wife."

And that loose bow tightened into a knot.

"Maybe someone in the family picked her up."

He did the up-down chin thing. "Your family always fills out the proper paperwork."

I called to check anyway.

Grandma met my question with silence. Lots of thick, dark, heavy silence. That couldn't be good.

"So that's a 'no' then? Nobody in the family claimed Litsa's body?"

"We always fill out the proper paperwork."

"That's what Gus said."

I ended the call.

"Okay …" I looked around. The morgue had security cameras mounted to the lobby ceiling. "All we have to do is get security to run the tape—right?"

"Fake. We cannot afford real security cameras. Until today, nobody ever stole a body."

"Do the police know yet?"

"Not yet. Detective Melas likes you, you should call him."

"No, no, no. You call him."

"You are the receptionist. It is part of the job."

He had a point. I hated that he had a point. "Maybe I could just text him."

"Great idea. That way neither of us will have to hear him yelling."

With great trepidation, I texted Melas.

Almost immediately, a message appeared on my phone's screen.

Be right there.

Chapter 10

Fewer than ten minutes later, Melas arrived, dressed for winter. He was wearing his usual boots and jeans, but now he was wearing them with a black beanie, a puffy jacket, and leather gloves.

"Will someone tell me how a whole person worth of body parts marched out of here?"

Gus did a little head wobble while he considered the possibilities. "If it were me I would put the pieces in garbage bags and carry them out. All the difficult work was already done. The deceased was not a large woman, and some of the pieces were small enough that a child could carry the bags. That is how I would do it: with children."

Melas stared at him. "That was a rhetorical question."

"You could have mentioned that. I had to comb through several scenarios, many of them disturbing. I already have nightmares. The things I see …" Gus shuddered.

Melas rubbed his forehead. His shoulders were riding high and tight. "I cannot even think of an expletive right now."

"Something with goats, donkeys, the Virgin Mary, and some of your dead relatives?" I suggested.

There were footsteps on the stairs. We had company. Hopefully not company with a corpse.

"Goats, donkeys, the Virgin Mary, and dead people? Sounds like a party," Takis said, rubbing his hands together. He jogged down the remaining stairs. "*Gamo tin Panayia mou*, it is colder than my wife's—"

"Don't you dare say it," I said.

He did two palms up. "What? I was going to say it is colder than her frappe. Marika makes a good frappe. Where was the body?" Takis was one of the few people on the planet who didn't have to turn sideways to scoot between the sea of stretchers and bodies.

"What are you doing here?" I asked him.

"Baboulas sent me. She said Litsa is missing. Where was she?"

"Out the back," Gus said.

"Show me."

Gus led the way. I went to follow and he made a *tst* sound.

"What if someone tries to leave another body, eh? You need to stay here to make sure that does not happen."

———

THEY DIDN'T STAY for long. There was no reason to. Whoever had stolen the body hadn't left evidence apart from an empty locker.

"They even took the sheet," Gus said sadly. "What kind of person steals sheets?"

Melas kissed me on the forehead on the way out. "See you tonight?"

"You know where to find me. I'll be in front of Grandma's oven, thawing out."

He grinned and then he was gone.

Instead of buzzing off, Takis stuck around to annoy me. "Why are you seeing Melas tonight?"

"We're going to carve pumpkins. I figure we'll start with your head."

"You should ask him to show you his *poutsa*. After, you will be in a much better mood."

My hands roosted on my hips. "Is that why Marika's always cranky?"

Takis cackled. "You must be bleeding again."

"Be nice to her," Gus said. "I cannot afford to lose another receptionist."

———

GRANDMA WAS in her garden when I emerged after some low key primping for my date with Melas. Just because her house was a dump, didn't mean her garden had to suck, too. Grandma has a green thumb, eight green fingers, and possibly green blood. Not me. Black fingers of death, all ten of them.

Hose in hand, she stared at my outfit.

"Something wrong?"

"Is that what you are wearing?"

"I'm wearing it, aren't I?"

Jeans. Fitted black shirt. My new black boots. Hair scraped into a high ponytail. I looked cute.

"You are wearing that on a date with a man?"

"It's just Melas."

She poked the air with her finger. "Do not move."

It's always a shock to see old people use modern technology. Not only could Grandma text, she could text better, faster, and with fewer typos than me.

"Who are you texting?"

"Your mouth is moving," she said. "I told you not to move."

"I didn't realize talking counted."

"Everything that is moving counts." She dropped her phone into her apron pocket. "Rita will be here in a moment."

My eyes narrowed. "Why?"

"Because you cannot go out with a man dressed like that, even if that man is Nikos."

My eyes rolled in their sockets. "So you don't mind me going on a date with Melas?"

"It could be worse. It could be that Papagalos character."

I gawked at her. Papagalos—Parrot—was her choice. She had expected me to marry the man. Then there was the creep who hired Donk, Baby Dimitri's teenage nephew to assassinate me. Not to mention—although here I was mentioning it—one of Winkler's "children," who also tried to kill me. I could, and had, done so much worse. At least I liked Melas, and he liked me back.

I opened my mouth to protest. Grandma cut me off with a bunch of words.

"Here comes your aunt—look."

Sure enough, Aunt Rita was rushing into the yard, a manic glint in her eye. It was the look of a woman who lived for makeovers. She had an armful of dresses (all black because we were a family in mourning) and a train case in her hand. She meant business—and business was me.

"I love makeovers," she said, looking me up and down. "You're already beautiful, even in casual wear, but let me work a little magic, eh? Nikos's pants will fall straight off."

"No—no falling pants," Grandma said. "Everybody keeps their pants on."

"Don't worry," I said, "Elias will be there. He'll make sure everyone's pants stay up and on."

"Elias is with Stavros. They are watching Tomas this evening. Xander will be going with you tonight."

"Xander is coming on my date?"

This wasn't good. This wasn't good at all. I liked Melas. I liked Xander. This was a recipe for bad feelings and instances where I said and did ridiculous things.

"Not on your date, just near it," Grandma said.

Oh. Well. That made everything better … except totally not.

"Melas is a policeman. Do I really need a bodyguard?"

"Nikos is a policeman, yes, but police do most of their work after the crime has already happened."

While the verbal dissent was happening, Aunt Rita attacked my face with fluffy brushes and pots of magical ingredients. The lipstick skating over my lips was fire truck red. Not that I'm prejudiced against red, but it has a tendency to light up my face like a STOP sign.

The dress was next. She'd brought dozens, all black, and held them up against me, one by one. Aunt Rita cycled through her facial expressions, until a smile showed up.

"This one is perfect, my doll."

"Perfect?" I looked at the scrap of black fabric in her hand. "Is it a swimsuit?"

"Spandex," she said. "This dress will change your life."

"Will I magically be back on my couch, eating Doritos out of the bag and watching Netflix?"

She laughed and patted my powdered cheek. "If I had twenty nieces, you would still be my favorite. Nikos will not be able to resist you."

"That hasn't exactly been a problem," I muttered.

Aunt Rita yanked up my shirt and tugged the dress down over my head, then she indicated for me to lose the jeans. I pulled the dress, what there was of it, into place.

My aunt made a disapproving sound. "No underwear. You cannot wear underwear with that dress."

"Yes, underwear," Grandma said. "Nobody is taking off their underwear tonight."

"Do not tell her I sleep naked," Aunt Rita whispered.

"I heard that," Grandma said.

"You heard nothing, Mama."

I left the jeans and kept the underwear. Panty lines or no panty lines, I liked the feeling of having my butt covered. Besides, I liked this underwear; it had cats.

"Mirror?" I asked.

"No mirror," Aunt Rita said. "Trust me, you look like a goddess—one of the attractive ones."

I looked at Grandma. If anyone would tell me the truth about my outfit it would be my grandmother.

"Nikos will like it, but keep it on, eh?"

My phone jangled. Melas was on his way.

"Go, go, have a good time," Grandma said. "But not too good a time, otherwise I will have to bury Nikos in a shallow grave, and I do not want to have to bury Nikos in a shallow grave because I like the boy and he comes from a good family. And remember, we are in mourning. Do not let anyone see you having fun, otherwise I will have to have their tongues cut out."

Xander appeared outside Grandma's gate. He didn't look happy; he didn't look anything except big and fore-boding, like the monolith in *2001: A Space Odyssey*. He was in his big and foreboding uniform: black cargo pants, military boots, a black t-shirt that had a death grip on his chest and biceps. It was dark out but he was wearing sunglasses, possibly because his mother ingested a Corey Hart cassette while she was pregnant with him. His expression gave away nothing, and neither did his mouth.

"If Nikos touches her, cut off his hands," Grandma said to him. There was no winking involved, so I was pretty sure she was serious. Turns out it's no less scarier hearing threats from a high-ranking law enforcement officer than it is a crime lord. Grandma was partly terrifying, no matter which hat she wore.

Xander followed me out of the yard. His legs were longer but he stayed behind me. What was his problem? Okay, what was his problem besides the fact that I was going on a date with Melas?

Hey, he'd sent me away then bailed before breakfast. He didn't get to complain, even silently.

I stopped, turned around. "Are you watching my butt?"

He grabbed my arm and spun me around until we were moving in the same direction again.

"You probably wish I was out of this dress and in something decent, like a Snuggie. Do you have those here? They're a cross between a sleeping bag and a blanket."

He yanked me into the tunnel and we stopped. His mouth got up close and personal with my ear.

"Out of that dress?" he whispered. "The dress is sexy —you're sexy—but you're every bit as beautiful in jeans or shorts or crawling across your grandmother's yard, trying to avoid anyone who might see you sneaking to the outhouse. I don't know what a Snuggie is, but you'd look good in or out of one."

My face went up in embarrassment-tinted flames. "Newsflash: I pee inside now, like normal people."

"I like you wherever you go. Now quit talking to me, unless you're at peace with me not responding."

"I'm at peace," I said, smoothing down my dress so that it covered more than just my top and tail. The dress was pretty—pretty uncomfortable. How was I supposed to be myself on a date in this dress?

Melas was at the front gate, arguing with the guard about something that sounded like sports. He was wearing dark gray slacks and a white button-down shirt, rolled to the elbow, revealing a lot of strong, tanned forearm.

I wolf-whistled. His head snapped around and he did this thing where he dragged his gaze from my freshly floofed hair to my high heels, spending an exorbitant amount of time inspecting the chest zone.

"Katerina?" He sounded bewildered.

"I was attacked by a fairy godmother on the way out."

"Huh?" Was that drool on his chin? I think it was drool.

I waved at my dress and face. "Aunt Rita was here."

His gaze snapped to Xander, who was behind me. I was currently the spandex filling in the world's most uncomfortable sandwich.

"Xander," Melas said, doing one of those overly effusive male greetings. Xander didn't say anything of course, but I felt the air shift as he ponied up a reluctant nod.

Melas went to open the police cruiser's door, but Xander was already there, holding the door open for me, and waiting until I was safely tucked inside. Melas's jaw was hard, frustrated. He scooted around to the driver's side, but Xander beat him to it again and held his door open.

Testosterone flooded the air.

Oh boy. I hoped they wouldn't fight—especially not over me.

The tension snapped when Melas yanked his door shut and turned the key. Xander jumped on his motorcycle. He followed us to Melas's house, a refurbished firehouse that still had the pole. Melas had cuffed me to it once, then the monster ate moussaka in front of me.

Who does that? Psychopaths, that's who.

Melas's jaw stayed rock hard. The day hadn't been a good one for him. Litsa and he were no longer a thing but that didn't mean he was happy she was dead or that her body was stolen goods.

"You okay?"

He reached over and cupped my knee. Warmth spread up my leg and crawled up under my underwear's elastic. "Long day. Fires are cropping up all over the place."

"Arson?"

"Has to be. Targets are all abandoned buildings."

"Any common denominators?"

"Apart from being abandoned? No."

Greece was dotted with old rebar and concrete bones. For a time there was a building boom, then people ran out of cash part way through the building process, wiped their hands, and walked away muttering, "Building? What building? *Malaka*, you are imagining things."

"Any suspects?"

"Teenagers, maybe. When I was that age we used to party in old buildings." Here came another one of those devastating smiles; this one was a whole lot of wicked.

"You were the bad boy. Of course you were."

"Ask my mother, I was good."

I snorted. "Greek mothers think their sons are all the second coming of Christ."

He squeezed my knee. "We are."

"What does the fire marshal think?"

"What fire marshal? He quit two years ago after the government tried to pay him in anything he could haul away from a fire."

So much for that. The conversation came to a stop

because we were at Melas's place. He lived in an older residential street—although, like most streets around here, zoning was for places with town planners, not Greek villagers who occasionally built things to perpetuate grudges. There was adequate street lighting, and the roads and sidewalks were cracked, but at least they weren't dirt. The houses were cared for in a way that suggested there wasn't a lot of money but there was an abundance of elbow grease. No lawns. Gardens confined to red pots, the pattern broken by the occasional terra-cotta.

Across the street, I saw the curtains twitch. Melas had his own Greek security system. His neighbor had a direct line of sight to his bedroom … if she craned her neck and pressed her nose to the upstairs window.

The door opened a crack and witchy nose poked out. Kyria Kalliope had a face like a paper bag that had been used for forty years' worth of school lunches.

"You, girl. Come here."

"I'll be right back," I told Melas.

"Do not keep me waiting too long."

I hobbled over, tugging at my dress. The crack in the door widened.

"I remember you," Kyria Kalliope said. "Last time you had more clothes on."

"This outfit wasn't my idea."

"The man you are with … is that the real one or one of the replicas?"

She was referring to the parade of Melas lookalikes Hera brought over when Melas wasn't home. Hera was trying to recreate their love story, one impostor penis at a time.

"The real one."

Two beady eyes scanned Melas from a distance. "It is

hard to tell because the replicas are good. You can barely tell the difference, especially when they are naked."

"I wonder where she finds them?"

"Eventually most men walk past her street corner," she said, then she winked at me. "I will not watch tonight, okay? Okay, maybe I will look out the upstairs window, but I will not wear my glasses."

"Do you wear glasses?"

She looked at a spot past my shoulder. "What is that?"

I turned around to look. Kyria Kalliope's door clicked shut.

Great. I hoofed it back to Melas, who was leaning against his car, looking equal parts amused and curious.

"What did she want?"

"She thought I was selling Girl Scout cookies."

He grinned. "Americans …"

Xander stayed outside. He planted himself in the shadows across the street where he had a clear view of all traffic coming and going. Like most Greek residential streets, this one was narrow and clogged when you threw in two cars, or one car, one donkey, and a moped. Most of the traffic moved on foot as people went to and from their houses, often weighed down with large, bulbous water bottles and mesh bags filled with groceries.

Melas took me around the back, ushered me into his lair. I liked what he'd done with the place—what little he'd done with the place. Melas lived simply. The furniture was masculine, the surfaces were clean, the floor plan was as open as open gets. The downstairs contained his living room, dining room, and kitchen. Upstairs, Melas had a combination bedroom and office. Only the bathroom was walled off from the rest of the space.

To cover up my nervousness, I said, "What's for dinner?"

He grinned. "Moussaka."

My eyes narrowed. "Did you cook it yourself?"

"Baby, I like you too much to let you eat my cooking."

"So ... you bought the moussaka?"

"Mama made it for us."

My heart curled up in the fetal position. "Your mother knows we're having dinner?"

"She knows I'm eating dinner like I do every day, and she knows I can eat a lot." He patted his flat stomach.

"So that's a no?"

"Do you tell your mother everything?"

"I don't tell her anything, mostly because she's dead."

Blood packed its bags and fled his face, leaving him pale. "My Virgin Mary, I forgot." He laughed in a tight, bitter way. "Sorry. I wanted tonight to be fun and I'm messing up."

I threw him a lifeline. "Don't worry about it. You want to talk about messing up? I let my aunt dress me and do my makeup."

His gaze turned hot and got hotter and darker as he inspected me again. "I am glad she did. You look good."

Yowza. "Normally I'd thank you and move on, but I feel like a Thanksgiving turkey, all dressed up and nowhere to go except the dinner table. I don't feel like me."

"So take off the dress."

I laughed nervously. "I'd settle for taking off these shoes."

"Kick them off," he said. He went upstairs and came back with a pair of slippers. His obviously, because they were way too big, but I didn't care. I made a happy sound as I shucked the heels for the slippers. Going barefoot in Greece is a huge faux pas. Going shoeless screams, "I'm too poor to wear shoes." So everyone wears shoes, inside and out, to deflect gossip.

Melas bustled around the kitchen while I leaned against the butcher's block island. His mother's moussaka came in a large ceramic dish, which he placed in the oven.

"I'm impressed," I said. "No microwave."

"If it was just me I would use the microwave. Wine?"

The wine was red and wet and dry. Two sips later, the warmth began to spread over me. I was caring less and less about the dress.

"Any idea who killed Litsa yet?" I asked.

"Lots of ideas. No answers."

"Any luck finding out who stole her body?"

He selected a serrated knife and began carving up a loaf of what I guessed was his father's bread. "None. The hospital has cameras but they don't work."

"Austerity measures?"

"They cut funding where they can. Security is not normally a big deal at Greek hospitals. Most people do not steal patients."

"Or body parts," I murmured. "I can't believe there's not one old Greek woman, whose whole purpose in life it is to watch people come and go from the hospital. Sick people go in, then they come out …"

"Most of the time."

"… And in between there are visitors and deliveries and gifts. Seems to me like that would be an endless source of entertainment to some Greek widows whose children and grandchildren don't visit often enough. If there was a woman like that, I bet she saw someone hauling garbage bags."

"Garbage bags," he said flatly.

Boy, for a cop he sure had a weak constitution.

"That's how Gus said he would do it, and with children."

"I know, I was there."

He finished hacking up the bread, and then he dumped it all in a Ziploc bag. Then he grabbed a couple of Tupperware wannabe containers out of the cupboard, yanked the moussaka out of the oven, and quickly dropped a generous slab into each container. He gathered forks, napkins, drinks and put everything in a plastic bag.

"Going somewhere?" I asked him.

"We are," he said. "I think you are onto something with the eyewitness angle."

"And we have to do this now?"

"The sooner the better." He kissed me on the forehead then grabbed his keys. "You want to come with me?"

"In this dress?"

There was a knock at the door.

Melas opened the door. Xander was there, holding a backpack. He held it out. Melas went to take it but Xander pushed past him and handed it to me, then he was gone again.

I looked inside. The bag contained my original outfit, my new boots, a hairbrush, and ponytail tie.

Melas eyed it sadly. "I like the dress."

I liked the dress too, just not on me. "Can I change somewhere?"

"Upstairs."

"I'm sorry."

He smiled. "I am never sorry about spending time with you, and I would like to spend more with you tonight. So get changed. I will be waiting right here."

Five minutes later I was myself again. My hair was defluffed and caught up in a ponytail. My feet were happy in comfortable boots.

We hit the road. I was all too aware of the food in the bag at my feet. I wanted to eat and I wanted to eat now.

"That poor moussaka," I said. "Going cold in a plastic container."

"It is just as good cold, I promise."

Melas parked at the hospital. We got out of his car and made a beeline for the front doors. It was early evening and visiting hours were over, but there were smatterings of people everywhere. Some looked set in for the long winter ahead, with their worldly treasures in bags. Others were huddled together, passing lighters around, lighting up cigarettes. At the curb, a pair of dilapidated pickup trucks held scores of Romany men, women, and children in mismatched clothing. Most people looked like they were in the process of coming or going.

"There," I said, nodding to a couple of antiques dressed in black. They were under the shelter of the ambulance bay, clucking at the world.

"Greek security system," Melas said, and we headed on over.

From their puckered mouths I could tell the women were living life toothless. They looked Melas up and down, then they shoved me under the microscope.

"You," the one on the left said. "I know you."

The old crow on the right elbowed her. "How do you know her?"

"How should I know? All I know is that I know her."

"You have the memory of a dead fish."

"At least I do not smell like a dead fish." Left waved her fossilized hand in front of her nose. "No wonder your husband killed himself."

"He did not kill himself," Right told me. "He had the cancer. But her husband? He killed himself. He went fishing every day until one day he was eaten by a giant squid. The creature spat his bones and his hat onto the beach when it was finished"

"He was a fisherman," Left explained.

Melas's full lips were a single thin white line. He was suppressing a laugh.

"I was wondering if you ladies could help me," he said.

They looked up him and down.

"With what?" Left said.

"What about her?" Right said. "Does she need help, too?"

"What she needs is a souvlaki," Left said.

Was that a metaphor? I couldn't tell.

Right gave Melas a gummy grin. "He looks like he has a good souvlaki."

Melas whipped out his badge, showed it to them. They stared at it for a moment, toothless mouths making sucking sounds.

"*Po-po*, my eyes are not what they used to be," Left said.

"Nothing is what it used to be," Right told her. "Have you seen my breasts?"

"Not since they migrated to your knees."

Melas's jaw twitched, so I jumped in. "You both look like you pay attention to the details, so we believe that you and only you can help us."

"She is flattering us," Right said in a singsong voice.

"*Skasmos*—it is working," Left said. "Okay, girl, tell me what you need."

"Were you here between the hours of twelve and four this afternoon?"

Left answered. "We are always here during the day, even in the middle of summer. Why?"

"Did you see anything unusual?"

"This is a hospital, almost everything we see is unusual. That is why we come here: for the entertainment. Two winters ago we saw a man whose *archidia* were the size of a dog."

"Two big dogs," Right said.

Melas stepped in. "A body was stolen from the morgue today."

Right shrugged. "Bodies come, bodies go."

"More bodies come than go," Left said.

"This one was unusual," Melas said.

They looked from him, to me, and back again. "Unusual how?" they said together.

"She was … she was in pieces," he said.

Left crossed herself. "Pieces!"

Right crossed herself, too. "Was it a suicide?"

Left rolled her eyes. "How can a person cut themselves up, eh? You are a *vlakas*."

"If you saw anything it would be a big help," I said.

Left's eyes narrowed into cunning slits. "How will you reward us for that help?"

"I won't arrest you for loitering," Melas said.

Right grimaced. "That is helpful."

Left crossed herself again. "We did not see anyone taking a body in pieces."

"Maybe some …" I glanced at Melas, who was refrigerator-white under his overactive melanin "…small children staggered out carrying those big black plastic garbage bags?"

"Children … no. We saw bags, yes?" Left elbowed Right.

"We saw bags, and we said to each other, 'I bet there is something bad in those bags.' Nobody walks around carrying big garbage in the middle of the day."

"Garbage men. Garbage men walk around with big garbage bags," Left said.

"These were not garbage men. They looked like soldiers, but their clothes were black. And they had masks on their faces."

"Balaclavas?" I said.

"Those woolly things? Yes. Very strange for September."

"Were there two of them?"

They nodded enthusiastically.

"Two men," Right said, "and they were driving a white van, like kidnappers. That is how we knew they were up to no good."

"The van," Left said, nodding. "That was a criminal's van."

"I don't suppose you saw the license plate," Melas said.

"We don't need it," I said. "We already have the plate. The van was a Mercedes and the plates are registered to a rental place here in Volos."

Melas looked at me. Hard. "You have the plates?"

"I guess you weren't at Grandma's for that part."

His expression morphed into exasperation. When he spoke it was in a lower voice. He aimed it at me. "Why would these guys take Litsa's body?"

"Maybe they dropped her out of the plane by accident so they had to get her back."

"Nobody throws body parts out of a plane by accident."

"I wouldn't know. This is all so new to me. Nobody in my old life ever got cut up and thrown out of a plane—or out of anything. My friends and I did get thrown out of the movies once, when we were fifteen, but that's not exactly the same thing." My voice trailed off. The old women and Melas were gawking at me.

"For what?" Melas wanted to know.

"We were *fifteen*," I explained. "There was candy involved, and popcorn, and maybe some throwing. But bodies out of planes and stealing corpses? New. All new."

Left and Right cackled. "You know," Left said, "You look like one of them."

She was talking to Melas, which was a lucky thing. Being mistaken for a man wasn't on my bucket list.

"You said they were wearing balaclavas," Melas said.

"At first, but when they got back to the van, the one who was not driving pulled off his funny mask, and underneath he looked like you."

"It was not me," Melas said.

Left shrugged off his denial. "Do you have a brother? Could be he is in the body-stealing business."

The universe grabbed a cast iron skillet and whacked me over the head.

"Oh crap," I said in English.

Chapter 11

Melas let out the long, ragged, utterly frustrated sigh of a man who has had just about enough. He dropped his fork into the plastic container, his moussaka mostly untouched.

We were sitting on a ledge in the local park that sat directly across from the crystalline gulf. The trees were dense, but here on the edge I had the waterfront lights keep me from missing my mouth with the fork. Nobody wanted an eating malfunction while they were on a date-ish thing.

"So a couple of men in black tried to abduct you and Tomas, and then these same men stole Litsa's body?"

"I don't think they were trying to grab me—just Tomas. I just happened to be there."

"And these men looked like me?"

"We assumed Tomas had it wrong because he's just a little kid, but we should have realized he's not *just* a little kid."

"Why did you not tell me any of this?"

"You were busy with the fires."

"Not that busy."

134

"You've got a personal stake in this. How focused and impartial can you be?"

"I am a professional."

"Professionalism can only take you so far."

He leaned back, away from me, arms folded in the defensive position. "So who are these guys, are you going to talk?"

"You'll be mad if I tell you who they are."

He shook the bag containing the food at me. "*Bougatsa* for dessert. Tell me …"

"I don't know what *bougatsa* is, only that I want it."

"Custard wrapped in phyllo. You definitely want my *bougatsa*."

He was right, I did want his *bougatsa*, and I wanted it bad. I pushed the moussaka aside. "Give it to me now."

"*Tst.* Tell me about the men first. If you do not tell me, you are obstructing justice. I could lock you up for at least a few hours before Baboulas springs you out."

"Are you threatening me while we're on a date? Because I'm sure that's not how dates are supposed to go. Although I have been on some strange dates …"

"And I want to hear about them, but not right now."

"Fine. Okay." I took a deep breath and prepared to drop Hera in the quicksand. "I think they work for Hera. At the very least she knows them."

"Hera? How do you figure?"

"She has a thing for men who look like you."

"A thing? What kind of thing?"

I gave him a long, meaningful look, like, *How dense are you? What do you think a thing is?*

Realization dawned. "How do you know?"

"Because I saw her with one of them. You know, she's good at choosing them, because he really had Marika and me fooled."

His eyes narrowed. He laid the trap, and silly me, I was too distracted by the idea of *bougatsa* to realize. Science is right: sugar is dangerous.

"Where was this?"

"At your place."

He folded his arms. "At my place?"

"Outside your place, really."

"What were they doing outside my house?"

Bougatsa. Bougatsa. Bougatsa. Would you believe me if I said they were trying to sell religious paraphernalia?"

His face said no—no, he wouldn't believe me.

He popped the lid of the plastic container holding the *bougatsa*, waved it under my nose. I closed my eyes. The Borg knew what they were talking about: resistance was futile. The words tumbled out of my mouth.

"Hera takes men back to your place when you're not home. For sex. Kyria Kalliope across the street has a fantastic view into your bedroom."

"*Gamo tin Panayia mou,*" he swore. "How long have you known?"

"Since, uh …" I did the mental math "… since just after I got back from Naples."

"Is there anything else you're not telling me that I should know? Is my house bugged? Is someone tailing me? Is Hera taking her lovers to meet my mother and take over my life?"

Ahoy! Dilemma straight ahead. Grandma's subterranean control room had a wall filled with screens, each with a direct feed from a particular location. My grandmother had her fingers in a lot of pies, and she had eyes in almost as many. One of those pies was the police station where Melas worked. I couldn't betray Grandma, but lying to Melas didn't feel right either.

What would Xander do?

I looked across the street to the church butted up to the Volos harbor. Xander was waiting in the church's shadow, watching us, watching the street for signs of trouble. Well, trouble was here, and I was in it.

Xander would do what Xander did best. Well, one of the things Xander did best. He'd keep his mouth shut. So that's what I would do too—for now, anyway. Melas and I weren't a couple. Even our date had taken a professional turn, and now we were eating moussaka in a park, discussing how his ex was boning lookalikes in his bed. Grandma was Grandma. Blood. Family. And now that I knew she wasn't strictly a criminal, everything she did had a newer, pinker aura.

I did the only thing I could do with a clean conscience: I stuffed a forkful of moussaka into my mouth and shook my head.

"Hera would not do this," Melas said. "She had no reason to steal Litsa's body and kidnap Tomas."

I put down my fork and swallowed. "You do know Hera is psycho, right? Screwing guys who look like you, and in your bed, isn't normal."

"But theft and kidnapping?"

"And maybe murder."

"Hera did not kill Litsa."

"That you know of."

"I know Hera."

Yes, he did. But I knew Hera, too, and she was an asshole. "I'm not saying she did it. I'm saying she might know who is responsible and why."

"I will talk to her."

"The sooner the better."

Melas, the big jerk, whisked away the moussaka, the bread, and my fork. He didn't need to take the knife because there was no knife. Asking for a knife in a

Greek restaurant or home is like asking for a fork in Chinatown. Greeks use chunks of bread to coax food onto a fork. Then—bonus!—they eat the food-soaked bread.

"Tonight," he said, his voice warm and velvet smooth, "we are on a date. This is not the date I hoped it would be, but it is still a date, and there is no room for Hera on our date."

Hera wouldn't agree. In fact, I was surprised she hadn't rocked up with Jaws of Life to pry us apart.

"Oh," I said.

"You want to go for a walk?"

"A walk?" Disappointment sharpened a shiv and stuck me like a pig. There was *bougatsa* and it still wasn't in my mouth.

"Why not? It is one of the last perfect evenings we will have before winter and before they stop closing off the street at night."

His phone chirped. Melas's lips clamped together as he glanced at the screen.

"Another fire?"

"Another fire," he said. "I have to take you home."

"This wasn't how I imagined this date going."

His voice was low, warm, suggestive. "What did you imagine?"

Fewer clothes. Lots of kissing. "More *bougatsa*," I said. "A whole lot more."

———

MELAS WALKED me back to Grandma's yard. The firing squad was waiting: Grandma, Aunt Rita, and Papou with his two eagles. Yiorgos the eagle was pecking its stuffed brother's glass eye.

"Where did you go? What did you do?" Grandma wanted to know.

Aunt Rita looked me up and down. "And where is your dress?"

"Xander has the dress. Our date took a strange turn so I changed clothes."

Grandma looked to Melas, who cleared his throat. "Katerina had an excellent idea. I wanted to follow up immediately. Which reminds me, I have to go." He pecked —pecked!—me on the cheek and took off.

Everybody looked at me.

"If you had kept the dress on that would have been more than a peck," Aunt Rita said.

"More like a poke," Papou said.

Grandma shot them both with her killer stink eye. "There will be no poking, but I am surprised there was not more kissing."

Dad emerged from Grandma's dilapidated shack. He had an Amstel Light in one hand and a plate of feta, olives, and bread in the other. "If he pokes her I will cut off his *poutsa* and then I will give it to Papou as a necklace." He winked at me. Melas's wiener was safe from Dad, as long as he didn't hurt me.

"Try," Papou said, "and I will make you eat wood."

"I have done it before," Dad said.

The valleys on Papou's face deepened. "I thought that necklace was made of chili peppers."

"*Poutsas*," Dad said casually. "Sheep *poutsas*."

"Where did you get that many sheep *poutsas*?"

Was it my imagination or did Papou sound impressed?

"I won them in a card game," Dad said, offering me his plate. I helped myself to a small cube of feta and an olive. Greek feta was a million percent better than the stuff Dad bought at home.

"Where did Nikos have to go in such a big hurry anyway?" Grandma asked.

"Another fire."

"Another one … *po-po*. Rita, ask the Google where the fire is."

Thumbs flying, Aunt Rita did Grandma's bidding. "Agria. This one is an old house on the waterfront."

Agria is a local village that's technically part of Volos now.

"What was this strange turn your date took?" my aunt asked.

I told them what I knew about the thieves. "Hera has issues." I explained in as little detail as possible what I knew about Hera's obsession.

"And he thinks Hera took Litsa's body?" Grandma asked.

"Melas doesn't think so."

Grandma and Dad exchanged glances. Neither of them said anything, which made me wonder if Papou and Aunt Rita knew about their crime-fighting alter egos.

"Hera is crazy," Grandma said, "but what would she want with Litsa's body?"

That was a good question. If Hera had a motive I couldn't see it from here.

My phone rang. Baby Dimitri was on the other end.

"Katerina Makris-with-an-s, my sister just called me crying and crying. She is looking for that worthless nephew of mine. Is he with you?"

I hadn't seen him for days. Which was weird, now that I thought about it. The skinny teenager had a way of popping up in the strangest places—Portland and Naples; my backseat; the family compound. He was always following me for one reason or another.

When was the last time I'd seen Donk? I scoured my memory.

Here. I saw him here at the compound. He said he was dating someone in the Family, but whom could he be dating? Apart from Grandma, Aunt Rita, and me, every woman in the family had grafted themselves onto the family tree via marriage. But that hadn't stopped Litsa, had it? Maybe she wasn't the only one with fidelity issues.

"I'll call you if I see him," I told Baby Dimitri and hung up.

Everyone was looking at me.

"Grandma," I said, "I need to roll the tapes."

———

AUNT RITA and I assumed the position. The concrete pad lowered us into Grandma's underground bunker and we stepped off into the control room. The lights were on. The screens were playing non-stop reality TV, the actors completely unaware they were being watched. Aunt Rita sat in the captain's chair and got busy wiggling the mouse and tapping on a keyboard.

"Watch the main screen with me and we will find the boy and figure out where he was going and who he was doing."

She typed in a range of numbers until we reached the right day. There I was with Melas, leaning against the cop car's grille, looking like dog poop. My arm was bandaged and my hair could be be described as brushed with an egg beater. And there was Donk, his efforts to sneak up on me thwarted by his baptism in cologne. There was no sound but there didn't need to be; I remembered the conversation well. Donk told me he was dating someone in the family, and I made a crack about how, if he were lucky, he wouldn't wind up wearing concrete boots. He vanished through the front gate, then his performance was over—on this screen, anyway.

"Good," Aunt Rita said. "Perfect. Now I know what I am looking for." She waved her magic mouse, and a new feed popped up on the middle screen. Donk continued through the courtyard and disappeared into the stairwell in the far left corner. Aunt Rita clicked again and Donk exited the stairwell and loped along the hallway. He stopped at a door, knocked, then he vanished into the apartment.

Crunchy Christ, I knew whose apartment that was.

"That's George and Litsa's apartment. Maybe he was babysitting their boys."

"Babysitting? More like she was using his face as a chair." Aunt Rita crossed herself. "If anything happened to that boy, it will be war. Baby Dimitri does not like anyone killing his family members except himself."

"Litsa? Really? He was seeing Litsa?"

I rubbed my forehead. This wasn't good. Litsa was dead; Melas facsimiles were trying to abduct Tomas; and Donk was missing.

"What's the connection?" I said.

"I do not know. I never had much to do with Litsa. She was too fake. Did you see those implants? They were like big water balloons shoved under her shirt. Terrible work. Cheap."

Aunt Rita knew implants so I trusted her word.

"What else do you know about Litsa?"

"Years ago she was one of Baby Dimitri's strippers."

"And now his nephew, who was maybe bumping goodies with her, is missing."

She made a face. "I do not like it. It smells like old fish. And old fish smells disgusting, which is how this smells.

"How long did he stay?"

She clicked again and time sped up. An hour later, Donk exited Litsa's apartment and disappeared into the stairwell.

"That woman was a criminal," Aunt Rita said, disgusted. "We are criminals, yes, but there are levels. She was one of the lower levels."

I couldn't disagree. I couldn't agree either, given that Grandma wasn't a full-blown criminal.

What now?

I raided the bunker's pantry for ION chocolate with almonds. Aunt Rita and I took turns snapping squares off the block.

"I can eat all this chocolate because I still have a man's metabolism," Aunt Rita said.

Sometimes I wished I had a man's metabolism, too.

Thinking cap on. Thinking snack in—into my mouth, that is. Baby Dimitri would have called Donk's phone, and his mother definitely called Donk's phone, hunting for him. But I hadn't called his phone. Could be he'd pick up for a friend. Well, a friend-like person. Okay, an acquaintance he didn't hate.

I dialed his number. Voicemail. One message later, I ended the call and flopped down in one of the control room's swivel chairs.

"What if the kidnappers have got Donk?" I asked my aunt.

"Why would they take him?"

"I don't know. Wrong place, wrong time? They tried to grab me because I was there with Tomas."

"A crime of opportunity, you think?"

"Donk does have a way of showing up where he's not supposed to be."

"It is late," my aunt said, "and I have to start getting all this makeup off." She kissed me on both cheeks and hugged me tight, then she left the way we'd come down.

Not me. I raided the pantry for a box of *loukoumia*, grabbed the lock picks I kept in my cross body bag, and jimmied the lock separating the bunker from the dungeon.

Monobrow opened the door from his side. "You are late," he said.

"Late for what?"

He relieved me of the *loukoumia*. The guy had an addiction.

"Who knows? Only you know."

"Is this one of those riddle things?" I narrowed my eyes at him. "You're not going to start going, 'Gollum, Gollum,' and arguing with yourself, are you?"

He held up the box of *loukoumia* and chuckled. "Now that I think about it, these are precious to me, and my feet used to be hairy. Get in here. How can I help you this evening? You want to escape again, maybe? Does Katerina have you under house arrest again?"

"I'm thinking."

He grinned. "Does it hurt?"

My eyes narrowed. "I can see why you were Makria's only homeless person with that sense of humor."

He laughed. "Sit, sit. Tell me what you are thinking about. Do you want coffee? Tea? A little retsina?"

"Do you have any retsina?"

"Of course. Your grandmother is not a monster. Okay, she is a bit of a monster, but she is a civilized monster." He let himself out of his plush cell and vanished down the hallway. There was the sound of a kitchen cupboard opening, then he reappeared with two open bottles. He gave me one, then sat in his swivel chair and watched me thoughtfully.

"You are thinking about the Litsa problem," he said.

"That, and I have a job. Did I tell you I have a job?"

"Sounds to me like you are planning to stay in Greece."

"Greece doesn't want to let me go."

"She does that. Greece has the world's longest umbilical cord. Even when Greeks leave, Greece haunts them."

"Dad never could quit talking about the place," I said.

"Your father has always been a talker. Your father, Rita, and that *kolopethos*, Kostas. That boy … everything that came out of his mouth was *skata*. As an adult he is the same shit."

Kolopethos. Butt-child. Greeks have a way with insults.

"I wonder where Grandma put him?"

"Only God and Katerina know. They have secrets, those two." He chuckled and took a long pull from the retsina bottle's narrow neck.

I glanced at my phone, just in case Donk had called me back and I'd missed it. But I'd missed nothing. Maybe my new phone wasn't working. No—the family gadget whizz never messed up so I knew my phone was working at peak efficiency. All the same, I rang Baby Dimitri's nephew again, just in case.

The languid chorus of Snoop Dog's *Drop it Like it's Hot* wafted through the wall.

"Heh," Monobrow said. "What a coincidence."

I raised my eyebrow at him. "Is there someone in the next cell?"

He shrugged. "Who can say?"

I let myself out of his cell and knocked on the neighboring door.

No answer.

"Donk?"

Nothing.

"Grandma will give me the keys if I ask, so you may as well open the door and let me in."

There was a pause, then: "Are you alone?"

"Yes, unless you count Makria's only homeless person, who doesn't seem to have a name."

"Are you sure?"

"Positive."

The small flap in the door flipped up and Donk's face appeared. Well, a rectangle of it. His eyes darted left then right, then they stuck to my chest.

I crouched down until we were eye to eye. "If you say anything about my breasts, I'll tell the world you're hiding here."

"Hey baybeeeee. Nice ass," he said, massacring the English language.

I raised my phone. "With the press of one button, the whole world can know you're here."

"Whazzup, homes? You so cruel, boo."

"You need to slow down on the rap. It's no way to learn English."

"Will you teach me?"

"That's what school is for. Let me in."

The door swung open. Donk peered out, then he hauled me in and slammed the door. Donk talks big but he makes a toothpick look like it's battling a weight problem. If he were a bird he'd be a cocky little bantam rooster. But his heart is in the right place, even if the only brain he has lives in the crotch of his sagging pants.

His cell was a less cluttered version of the one next door. The bed was a tangle of sheets and covers, and there was a pile of candy wrappers and chip bags on the floor. And there was a smell …

"What is that?"

"What is what?"

"It's coming from …" I turned in a tight circle until I spotted a sock draped over the desk. "… there."

Donk's tan faded fast. He lunged across the room, grabbed the sock, dropped it on the floor and kicked it under the bed.

"Wow, did you use that sock in a crime or something?"

Monobrow laughed in the next cell. "A crime against nature, if you believe the Bible."

It was late. I was reaching the point of mental saturation. And apparently I had to be at work by nine the next morning. So it took a moment for his meaning to sink in. When it did, I leaped back.

"Jesus H. Christ!"

Donk turned red.

I avoided eye contact with the sock under the bed and threw the kid a lifeline.

"So what's going on?"

"I am hiding."

"Why? And why here?"

"Can you think of anywhere safer?"

"That depends on what or who you're hiding from."

He looked at the floor and scuffed it with his shoe. "I did something stupid."

"You were sleeping with Litsa."

His head shot up. "How did you know?"

"I'll never tell."

Monobrow chuckled. "Baboulas has the whole compound rigged up with cameras. If you can fart without her seeing your cheeks flex then you are a hero."

"Okay," I conceded, "so maybe I saw you on camera, going to her apartment."

Donk flopped down onto the bed, head in hands. "We were in love."

Jeez, poor kid. My knees folded and sat my bottom on the bed alongside him. I patted his back.

Loud, obtrusive snorts blasted out of Monobrow's nose. "Maybe your *poutsa* was in love, but your heart? The heart cannot love a scorpion, and that one was a scorpion. A big, *poutsa*-eating scorpion." He mimed PacMan with one hand. "Chomp, chomp, chomp, man to man, *poutsa* to *poutsa*. That one had more *poutsas* than I have had hot dinners, and I am a man who has had a lot of hot dinners." He patted his belly.

"It was love," Donk wailed.

"How did you two end up ... together?"

Donk sniffed. "You mean in love? We met at a party."

"What party?"

"A party here."

My eyes narrowed. "Which party?"

Monobrow snorted. "He means your funeral. They met after your funeral."

"I knew her before that," Donk said. "Sometimes she used to come to the school."

"When her boys were in trouble," I told Monobrow before he mentioned the possibility of Litsa cruising the high school for jailbait. Casting unfounded shade on a dead woman seemed like bad juju. "Who started it?" I asked Donk.

He lifted his head long enough to waggle his eyebrows at me. "No woman can resist the Donk. Donk is outta sight."

Someone really needed to stage a rap intervention on this kid.

"So ... you?"

"Did you see her ..." He juggled invisible melons. "I told her I liked them. I couldn't help myself, they were just there."

Good thing Marika wasn't down here or she'd be slapping his head, left and right.

"Do you think she is dead because of me?" he asked, face pinched. "She went to see my mama the other day. What if she told Mama about us?"

I gave him the only answer I could. "Nobody knows anything yet." I eyed him. "Do you know anything?"

"Like what?"

"You were sleeping with her, and you're hiding out here. Maybe you know more than you think you do."

"I don't know anything," he said in a whoosh, "except I don't want to die."

"If you're lucky nobody knows you're here, so you're probably safe."

"He is safe, he is safe," Monobrow said. "If someone comes here to hurt the boy I will shoot them."

"With what? A dirty look?"

He belly laughed. "No, with a gun."

"Grandma gave you a gun?"

"No. I bought my own." He winked. "It is a big one."

Around here that wasn't a euphemism. When someone connected to my family said they had a big gun, chances were better than even they had a really big gun.

Donk wasn't buying it. "What if there are spies? My uncle says someone is always watching, waiting to snatch it all away and stuff him into a prison cell, where he'll be forced to eat *poutsa* for the rest of his life."

Something told me that wasn't how things would go if Baby Dimitri wound up behind bars. Not that he would. Guys that canny and old had contingency plans on their contingency plans. Mind you, I would have said that about Winkler, too, before Grandma took her down.

"There aren't any spies."

"Promise?"

I opened my mouth to pinkie swear, then I remembered something. I texted Melas.

What did Hera say?

His reply was immediate. *Nothing yet.*

That witch. She'd locked up shop and gone into denial mode. What was she up to, and was she doing it with a Melas clone?

Stuff clanged around in my head. Plumbing happened. Connections were made.

"I have to go. You," I told Donk, "stay here. And wash that sock."

Monobrow laughed. "Only fire can help that sock now."

Chapter 12

Grandma's dungeon has a super-secret exit, forged by—
legend goes—Dad and his buddies. It's hidden behind the
stony facade in the window dressing dungeon beyond the
real dungeon.

I shut myself in the second cell, popped the hatch, and
entered the narrow tunnel that lead to the free side of the
compound's wall. Last time Xander had been behind me,
up close and borderline intimate with my butt. This time I
was alone and considerably less self-conscious about
my rear.

A few moments later I popped out into the night air …
after a brief tussle with a wall of vine and foliage. Night
was here, and it had hauled along more cool air than the
previous evening. Another season was on its way and I was
still showing no signs of leaving Greece. Now I had a job I
didn't want, ties, commitments. I really hoped the government didn't run out of all of Germany's money before I
retired. Mind you, if Grandma had her way—

Wow. Come to think of it, now that I knew Grandma

was straddling both sides, light and dark, I wasn't sure what her plans for me were. Obviously she didn't want me to propel the family toward greater debauchery.

There was another factor now, too. Dad. He was alive, well, and completely alive enough to take over the family business when Grandma eventually kicked the bucket, which hopefully wouldn't be anytime soon.

My whole life was up in the air. Maybe that's why I'd let myself be talked into take the morgue job. A job was stability. A job was ... okay, it wasn't exactly granite under my feet, but it was hard-packed sand, something I hadn't felt in weeks.

I covered up the evidence of my escape, dusted my jeans off, and looked around for shadowy figures. Well, one shadowy figure. Xander had a way of peeling himself out of the night's dark pockets and appearing at my side. Mind you, this wasn't really an escape. I was hunting. Last time I saw Hera she was lurking around Grandma's property, hiding out in my car. I was taking my chances that she was still hanging around out here somewhere. All I had to do was walk around until I caught a whiff of Eau De Ho and followed it back to the bottle.

I trotted toward the front of the property, to where I'd spotted Hera last. She'd be sticking close to the road for a quick getaway if Grandma decided she wanted to put her slipper-clad foot up Hera's perky ass.

Oh boy, that was another one of those relationships that had taken a more complicated turn, now that Dad was NIS for sure and Grandma was Interpol.

Somebody really needed to flowchart things for me, preferably on a phone app that would update with any changes.

The dark was thin, chilly, and tinted with wood smoke. One of Melas's fires? Every so often I heard a scuffling from an animal that probably wanted to eat me. To mini-mize my chances of survival I tried to make myself seemed bigger than I was and invisible at the same time. Given that nothing ate me, I guess you could say I was successful. Go, me.

I stopped. I listened. Like a dog, I sniffed the air. An absence of Eau de Skank. There was something else though, beyond the smoke: food. And I didn't think it was coming from the compound or the farm. It smelled like sadness.

Someone was eating ramen noodles.

I followed the fragrant chemical trail. Low and quiet, tree to tree. I was almost good at this. Okay, maybe not good, but I definitely didn't suck at it. Not surprising, given that a fifty perfect chunk of my DNA was super-secret agent.

And there it was, in between the trees: an NIS van, doors open, bouzouki music low (a bouzouki is the twangy missing link between a guitar and a banjo), two of Hera's buddies eating bowls of sadness on milk crates.

Suckers. I'd caught them. Little ol' me. Bill collector. Morgue receptionist. Okay, so neither of them was a Melas lookalike, but that would have been too convenient anyway.

"Stop," a voice said behind me.

Rats! There was a third one. How very Jurassic Park of them, setting themselves up like velociraptors.

"I live here—well, live-ish here—I don't have to stop."

"She has a point," one of the sad ramen eaters said, setting down his bowl.

The guy behind me poked me with something hard and probably deadly. I looked over my shoulder at his poking thingy. Gun. Yup. Definitely deadly.

Jesus on a jet ski, what was with these goobers and their

guns? I was so over being on the wrong end of gun. I selected a trick from Marika's bag and smacked it out of his hand.

He reached out to slap me but a hand came out of nowhere and stayed his wrist before it made contact. A bigger hand, attached to a stronger body.

Xander.

And if I had to guess from the twist of his mouth and the Arctic freeze in his eyes, he wasn't happy.

"You're late," I told him.

His eyes thawed for a moment. He was mad, but not at me. Someone didn't like me being manhandled.

Back on silent mode, Xander didn't say a word. He nodded once, released the guy's hand. The NIS guy stooped to grab his gun. Into its holster it went.

"Why are you here?" That was the goon with the noodles. He was talking through a thin, starchy mouthful.

"Are those ramen noodles? Because that's the one thing I never expected to see in Greece."

"Ramen noodles are everywhere," he said, "like those guys with kitchen towels on their heads."

"Could you be more of a bigot?" I asked him.

He shrugged. "This is me after sensitivity training."

No wonder he worked with Hera. They were cut from the same poop-stained cloth.

"I'm looking for Hera. Is she here?"

Looks were exchanged. Noodles were set down. In my head I assigned them all names. Noodles One, Noodles Two, and the guy with the gun was No Noodles.

"What do you want with Hera?" Noodles Two asked.

"We were supposed to have a pajama party, do each others nails, and call boys and hang up on them."

They didn't look convinced. "Hera? Pajama party?"

"I do not think Hera does pajama parties," Noodles One said.

"Hera does not wear pajamas," Noodles Two said.

They all snickered.

I looked around. "So … is she here?"

Noodles did the up-down chin chuck. "No."

"Where can I find her?"

They exchanged more looks. Heavy things. Loaded. Three bags full.

"Bueller?"

The looks shifted to me and turned hazy. Probably they hadn't seen that movie.

"Who knows?" No Noodles said.

"I was hoping you'd know. You're always with her. You work together. You've got this whole creepy NIS—"

"Allegedly," Noodles One said.

"—van skulking around my family's property going on, and I'm pretty sure that was Hera's idea, not yours. So I figured you'd know where she is."

"We have not seen her today," he said.

"Day off?"

"Hera does not take days off. The NIS—"

"Allegedly," Noodles Two said.

"—is her life."

"What's her phone number?" I asked.

There they went again with the fully loaded looks. I rolled my eyes.

"I just want to call her," I said.

"She will kill us," Noodles One said.

"I'll kill you. Okay, maybe not kill, but I'll do bad things to you."

"Like what?"

I grabbed his noodle bowl and upended the ramen on the ground.

He let out a pained cry. "I was going to eat those!"

"You can still eat them. They have extra seasoning now."

"Okay, okay, I will give you her number." Noodles One reeled off a short string of digits, which I tapped into my new-new phone. There was a stretch of silence so long I could probably pack an elephant into the space, then Hera's phone began to ring.

Chirp.

Chirp.

I lowered the mouthpiece. "I thought you guys said she wasn't here."

No Noodles puffed up like a blowfish. "That is what we said. Are you calling us liars?"

"No—just hearing impaired."

I was totally going to follow the sound when Xander held up his hand. He wanted me to sit and stay. I wanted to sit and stay, too, but since he was giving orders, my DNA kicked in and threw a handful of gravel at the bits of my brain that took care of things like obedience.

"Stand aside, my good man," I said.

Xander stared at me with the patience of a long-suffering saint.

Common sense slapped my DNA aside and reminded me that Xander was a henchman-slash-NIS agent, and a pretty good one because he was still alive, despite playing for both teams. So I should probably follow him instead of leading the way. Greece had snakes, and I wasn't sure when they'd head underground for the winter. They could be out there right now, hunting Americans.

"Okay, you can go first, but only because of the snakes."

Everyone looked at me like I was several souvlaki short of a feast.

Xander shook his head and headed for the tree line, following the sound of Hera's phone. I followed but not too closely (snakes, remember?), stopping when he crouched down about fifty feet into the orchard and snatched something up off the ground.

Hera's phone.

Without Hera.

This was one of those mixed blessings. No Hera was definitely good Hera, but it didn't seem to me like she was the kind of woman who left anything behind, particularly her phone.

Xander swiped through her phone, probably looking for clues.

"Is that a good idea?"

He looked at me.

"Forget I asked." I eyed the phone. "Anything good?"

He looked at me again.

"I meant useful—anything useful."

He pocketed the phone.

My voice dropped to a whisper. "Are you taking that as an NIS guy or as one of Grandma's henchmen?"

He turned me around, put his hand in the middle of my back, and pushed me away gently, leaving a puddle of heat where his hand had been.

The NIS guys were still sitting around, not doing much of anything. Probably these guys weren't being paid enough to leap into action, not even for Hera's sake. I'd eavesdropped on them once or twice in the past and over-heard Hera berating them. Someone had forgotten to show up to school on the day the teacher talked about catching more flies with honey than vinegar. The way she talked to these guys it was a wonder they didn't bounce her out of the van during a high-speed chase.

Or maybe they did.

"Good news, gentlemen. Or maybe bad news, depending on whether you hate your boss as much as I do—"

"She is not our boss."

"Definitely not our boss," Noodles One said.

"Definitely not," Noodles Two said.

No Noodles had other ideas. "She is maybe our boss."

The other two goobers looked askance. No Noodles explained his logic.

"We take orders from her, no? That makes her our boss."

Huh. His logic actually had logic in it.

Noodles One spat on the ground. Greek men, especially of a certain age, seemed to suffer from an excess of saliva and mucus. None of these guys had seen their thirty-fifth birthdays yet but they were practicing their spitting skills in preparation for old age. At least they weren't blow nose oysters, so that was something. Not much, but something.

"I take orders from her," Noodles One explained, "because I like to look at her *vizia*."

Boobs. He meant boobs.

"She does put them out there," Noodles Two agreed.

No Noodles wasn't impressed. "Plastic."

Noodles One rolled his eyes at his coworker. "Plastic? What plastic? I touched one once and it felt real to me."

No Noodles laughed. "How would you know, *pousti*?"

"*Parta!*" Noodles One gave him a *moutsa* and told him to "take it."

Noodles Two cackled.

"They are real," Noodles One told me solemnly.

"I couldn't care less if I tried. When did you last see her?"

Shrugging happened. "Earlier," No Noodles said.

Greek time: it's like fog. "Can you be more specific?"

He gnawed on that a moment. "This afternoon."

"Hey, wait, why is this girl asking us questions? We are the government agents!" Noodles One said.

"Allegedly," Noodles Two added.

"We are the ones who ask questions," Noodles One went on. "If Hera is missing she went missing on your family's property, so where is she?"

They all looked at me.

"Wait, what? I'm the one looking for her. Why would I be looking for her if I engineered her disappearance?"

"You would be amazed what guilty people do," No Noodles said. "The things we have seen … Terrible things. One time, we caught a man making love to a donkey. He denied it! We had pictures, tape, everything, and still he denied it."

"Wouldn't you?" I said.

"So we are saying maybe you made Hera disappear." Noodles One sounded happy about that.

My eyes rolled skyward. "Any idea where she might be?"

They laughed. "Why would we tell you? We are the NIS," Noodles One said.

"Allegedly," Noodles Two said.

"Allegedly," No Noodles agreed.

After some more eye-rolling, some serious sighing, and one of my best dirty looks, I sent a message to Grandma, asking her if she could send some food out to the unwashed and hungry trio. No one deserved to eat packets of ramen, not when there was a whole country of Greek cuisine out there.

I'm a lot of things, but I'm not a monster.

XANDER and I were leaning on a wall. One of us was doing all the talking and it wasn't him.

"I should call Melas," I said. "He needs to know that Hera is missing."

So that's what I did.

"Did you talk to her?"

"Who?"

"Hera."

"No."

"Well, I wouldn't call her phone if I were you."

"Why not?"

I sketched out the last few minutes for him, right down to the imminent food delivery.

"You fed them?" He sounded astonished.

"They were eating ramen. Ramen is sadness. It's for desperate college kids, not adults with jobs."

"This is Greece. Sometimes we do not get paychecks. We know sadness."

"All the more reason to feed them."

"Some might think you're buying them."

I was this close to leaping into verbal action, attempting to defend my honor, when I realized his voice had a laugh in it.

"Are you mocking me?"

"No, I like that you sent them food." His tone changed again, darker, lower. "Look, do not worry about Hera. She can take care of herself."

"Do you think she would leave her phone behind?"

"As long as it was not her handbag, I am not worried. Was her handbag there?"

"Just her phone."

"Then she is fine. Hera is a professional."

A professional headache, more like. But he was maybe, probably, right about her bag. She kept all kinds of fancy gizmos in her handbag, things that went *zap*, *pew-pew*, and *bang-bang*.

"You don't think maybe she stole Litsa's body and went into hiding for some weird reason?"

"What weird reason?"

"Human sacrifice? I don't know. What does anyone do with body parts? Maybe she's a cannibal." Maybe she bathed in blood. It would explain why her skin was so smooth.

"Forget it, okay? The two are not connected. Hera is fine, I am sure of it."

Something in his voice didn't sound right. Was he trying to convince me or himself that the two things weren't connected?

Melas's tone changed again. "What are you doing tomorrow night?"

"Nothing. We're all still in mourning."

"Then how about we try a date at my place again?" His voice came out dipped in chocolate and rolled in velvet, but less linty.

"Okay …"

"Katerina?"

I nibbled on the edge of a nail. "Huh?"

"Are you okay?"

"Just thinking."

"About?"

"Our date," I lied. I wasn't think about our upcoming date night do-over at all. My mind was fixated on Hera and her abandoned phone. Handbag or not, the phone didn't sit right with me. But why did I care anyway? It wasn't like Hera and I were friends. Or acquaintances. We didn't even have enough respect for each other to be mortal enemies. Mostly we wallowed around in mutual contempt and disgust. Unless those were synonyms, in which case it was just one of those things.

————

GRANDMA WAS IN THE KITCHEN, doing what looked like prep work for more baking. She looked up when I came in, sans Xander, who had mimed a vaguely pornographic freestyle stroke before we parted ways. Maybe it wasn't pornographic at all; maybe it was just me. Hormones are stupid. Lately mine seemed to be dumber than most.

"Did you find what you were looking for?"

"Yes, but I lost something else."

"What kind of something else?"

"Nobody. Just Hera."

Grandma snorted. "Of all the things you could lose, I think that would be a good thing. I do not like that one." She tapped her temple with the fingers that weren't curled around a wooden spoon. "*Trela*."

Crazy.

I couldn't disagree. Hera had issues and a gun. Never a good combination.

"Do we have any spare sheets?"

"What for do you need sheets?"

"It's a job thing."

"If you needed a job I could have given you a job."

"This was more of an accidental job thing. Wrong place, wrong time, wrong facial expression, and not enough protesting."

She waved the spoon. "Work on that. That kind of thing can get you killed in my business."

"Which one?"

"Both. I will have sheets for you before you leave in the morning. Someone will take them to your car."

I kissed her leathery cheek and said goodnight, then headed back out into the night for my new digs. Not far away, I could hear the rhythmic splash of Xander cutting through the pool's crystal surface. My feet wanted to turn but my head was steering my body. It had control of my hormones, more or less.

Wouldn't hurt to take a peek, would it?

"Thea Katerina?"

Tomas had found me, and he was carrying a stuffed … Einstein?

"Is that Albert Einstein?"

"Alan Turing."

I inspected the head. No mustache. Hair styled by fork in a live socket. I knew about sockets. When I was eight I pulled one apart and touched the pretty copper part. Regrets, I had them.

"What happened to his hair?"

"I used to chew on it when I was little."

Said the boy who was still classified as teeny tiny.

Stavros and Elias were right behind him, carrying more of his clothes.

"Moving in with me?" I asked the little guy.

"Can I?"

"You can stay for tonight, but I need to talk to your father before we make bigger plans, okay?"

"He's too busy for me," Tomas said. Sad words. Matter-of-fact tone.

"Busy trying to find the you-know-what," Stavros said.

"Katerina, we will be outside the door until Xander is finished in the pool, okay? Scream if you need us." He kissed me on both cheeks and closed the door behind us.

"Were you having fun with Stavros and Elias?"

Tomas plopped down on the couch. "I saw them kissing."

"Huh." I carried Tomas's things into the bedroom and placed them on the second bed. Then the words sank in. I walked backwards until I could see Tomas, swinging his lefts on the couch. "Wait—what? You saw Elias and Stavros kissing?"

Tomas's head bobbed.

"You mean like Greeks do, on the cheek?" Greeks are kissy-kissy people. Even the men are affectionate in a way that would make most American guys twitch. A child or an adult in need of LASIK could easily mistake it for more.

"On the mouth."

"Maybe it was resuscitation."

"Maybe," Tomas said. "Theo Stavros did look look distressed when he turned around."

La-la-la-la. I couldn't hear him. This was way too much information territory. Not that I was bothered or offended, but this was one of those out of left field things, like Dad's old pals in the back of the mattress shop, or my former fiancé and his unexpected (to me) penchant for penis.

"Huh," I said as nonchalantly as I could. "Who knew?"

"Nobody, I think. And I know pretty much everything because nobody is careful what they say in front of a little boy, unless it's bad words. Which is silly because I know all the bad words anyway. I even know how to spell them."

I tucked Tomas into bed with Alan Turning, code-breaking genius, and settled down on the comfortable couch in living room. My new place was nice. Small but cozy. The kind of place I wished I could afford back home. In Portland you can rent a lovely potential meth lab for an arm and a leg. Want to buy a home? You'd better have several firstborn children to pitch in at closing. Migrating Californians and wannabe hipsters had dragged real estate prices north with them.

I got two tall glasses out of the cupboard, filled them with cold water. A moment later there was low whispering outside—Elias and Stavros were switching shifts—then there was a quiet tap on the door.

Xander.

His hair was slicked back and wet from the pool and the subsequent shower. He did tasty things to basketball shorts and a white t-shirt. He helped himself to the other end of the couch and leaned his head back on the backrest, eyes closed.

"I poured water," I said. "Want some?"

Nothing.

"Xander?"

More nothing.

I waved my hand in front of his face. No reaction. He was out cold, chest rising and falling slowly. Boy, swimming really wore him out. I grabbed a blanket from the bedroom, covered him from chin to foot. Pillow on the couch where he could find it during the night if he shifted positions (I suspected he slept sitting up or hanging upside down in a closet). Lights out. Then I eased into bed, taking care not to disturb Tomas, who was curled like a comma around his stuffed toy. On the nightstand my phone sat silent and still, mostly because I had turned the ringer off. I checked messages one more time—nothing—and then rolled over.

Sleep came.

———

SO DID MORNING. And it came on like a headfirst collision with a train, all bright light and tunnels.

I jerked up into the sitting position.

That lying liar, Nikos Melas. That's why he had sounded funny last night: because he was lying his perfect running-sculpted buns off.

Rat bastard.

Grumbling, I showered, crammed my hair into a sock bun, and pulled on clean jeans and my black shirt. Shopping was in my future; I couldn't wear this shirt until the family's mourning period was over, not unless I wanted to kill people with my body odor. Before bolting out the door I grabbed the big coat Elias had given me yesterday. False winter was coming.

Outside the garage, Elias was waiting with a white cake box and two tall paper cups of coffee.

"Baboulas made coffee," he said.

My nose twitched. "I smell sugar."

"*Koulourakia,*" he said, holding up the cake box.

I eyed the box suspiciously. "Are they green?"

"No."

I flipped the lid up, grabbed two cookies, stuck one in my mouth and stuck the other between Elias's teeth.

He grinned as best he could with a twisty Greek cookie in his mouth.

"Let's roll," I told him. "It's time to head to the coal mine."

"A coal mine would be warmer."

He wasn't wrong.

On the Beetle's passenger seat someone had left a stack of sheets, just like Grandma had promised. Some were threadbare but they were clean and they were sheets, which meant Gus would be happy.

And he was.

"Sheets!" he cried, dabbing his eyes. "You brought me sheets." His gaze slid to the box in Elias's hands. "What is in the box?"

"*Koulourakia*," I told him.

"Homemade?"

"With my grandmother's two hands."

He flinched. "Are they poisoned?"

"Would my grandmother poison you?"

"Maybe. I don't know. What have you heard?"

I dumped the sheets in his arms, then took the box from Elias and marched around to the reception desk with my coffee and cookies.

"More *koulourakia* for me if you're too paranoid to eat them."

"Look at me: I am surrounded by death," he said. "That would make anyone paranoid."

"By choice."

"What choice? There was no choice. One day I came down here to get a signature and they never let me leave."

On that mysterious note Gus vanished down the hallway with the sheets, leaving me with Elias and one extra body.

"Who left that here?" I barked.

Elias swung around to look. "Which one?"

"The one by the elevator."

I recognized it from yesterday. That darn orderly had snuck back down here sometime between when I'd chased him away and this morning. Not cool.

This was war. And like in any war, there were already too many bodies.

I grabbed my coffee and a *koulouraki*, and jogged

upstairs. Foot traffic was heavier now, with visitors coming and going. How was I going to find that orderly?

Clever me, I hadn't even bothered to get his name yesterday. It was right there on the badge and I'd been too busy trying to win the battle, armed with inherited bossiness and my one good stink eye. People swarmed past me. Too many faces and body odors.

This was futile. Big hospital. Lots of employees. Even more visitors.

I nibbled the cookie and thought about it. Actually, mostly I was thinking about *Field of Dreams* and how "if you build it he will come." Somehow I knew that had a practical real-life application.

Then it came to me.

I hoofed it back downstairs, where the deceased was waiting, under the sheet.

"You're with me," I told him or her. Her. She had breasts. Or he did. Safer not to assume.

We rolled into the elevator.

Elias looked amused. "What are you doing?"

"Human sacrifice."

"I am not an expert, but I think they are supposed to be alive before you start."

"Elias?"

"What?"

"Your logic has no place here."

He grinned. "Yes, boss."

I stabbed the lobby button with my finger. The doors closed. When they opened, I rolled the stretcher into the lobby and laid it to rest—temporarily, I hoped—against a coffee and *koulouri* cart.

The vendor, a rusted twist of wire in a blue and white striped apron, twitched his mustache in my direction. "You cannot leave that there."

I held up both hands. "Oops. I just did. Better call an orderly."

"At least buy a *koulouri*," he called after me.

As far as ideas went, that was a good one, so I doubled back and bought three *koulouria*. Despite the similar name, *koulouria* and *koulourakia* were only distantly related. The *koulouri* is like a soft pretzel, dipped in sesame seeds and served warm. By the time the elevator opened in the morgue I was in need of a toothbrush, floss, and a nap. I gave the second *koulouri* to Elias.

Gus brightened up when he spotted the third *koulouri* in my hand.

"Is that for me?"

I handed it to him.

He chewed while he counted bodies. "Nobody ever buys me *koulouri*, and I can never go up to get one because if I do then more bodies appear down here. There was one more in the lobby when I got here this morning."

I told him what I'd done and he lowered the *koulouri*, staring at me like I walked on water.

"Never leave me," he said reverently. "We had three other new arrivals overnight. I do not suppose you could get rid of those, too?"

"I could try."

He led me out back, to the cold lockers.

"Why are they in here?" I asked him.

"You will see."

He yanked on the first locker's latch. My hand snapped out.

"Wait!"

"What?"

"I don't want to see them. Can't you just tell me who they are, and I'll contact their families?"

He tipped back his head and laughed. "You," he said,

"you are very funny. I already told you, almost nobody comes to pick up their dead relatives these days. They are too busy spending what little money they have on luxuries like food and the ProPo."

ProPo is the Greek lottery, except instead of numbers they pick the winning soccer teams. Never call it soccer though; it's football.

"Is it too much to ask that these people have contact information?"

"Today is your lucky day. Two were patients here, and the third came in with her handbag tied around her neck.

Gulp.

"And her handbag is …?"

"Still tied around her neck." He shrugged. "What? The police would make me eat wood if I tampered with evidence."

"Do the police know you've got a murder victim?"

"Sure. I left a message." He gave me a funny look. "Wait—how did you know she was murdered?"

"Handbag. Neck. That kind of thing doesn't happen by accident. I've seen all the CSI shows. Even the one with LL Cool J."

"Oh—I thought maybe you had inside information."

"Inside information?"

"You know. Your family."

"You think someone in my family murdered your murder victim?"

"No!" He waved his hands, Muppet-style. "Forget it. Just get rid of these people. Handbag Woman gets a pass for now, at least until the police look at her. But call her family anyway." He thrust three charts into my hands, then he reached for the locker door again. This time I stayed quiet as he rolled out a body covered from head to toe in a sheet splattered with toy trucks. Sheet down, far enough to reveal a large orange shoulder bag with lots of shiny buckles.

My zeroed in on the leather handbag. Big. Roomy. Familiar. Very familiar.

I knew that bag.

It belonged to Hera.

Chapter 13

"*Ung*," I said, trying not to barf. "I know that bag."

He brightened up. "Do you know her?"

My gaze slid upward to the dead woman's face and hair. Whoever she was, she wasn't Hera. Blonde, but a cheaper shade. A wide strip of dark roots. The face wasn't Hera's either.

Poor woman.

"No."

"Then how do you recognize her bag?"

"I must have been mistaken. Someone I know has one just like it."

"Expensive," he said, checking the designer's label.

"You know bags?"

"My mother collects pictures of bags. She does not have one like this but she would like one. These bags have to be ordered from the designer. You cannot buy them off the shelf."

"And looking at this woman's hair, I'm guessing if she didn't have money to burn on coloring her hair, she definitely couldn't afford this bag."

We were on a roll. Probably on a roll to the Land of Shoddy Conclusions, where someone is always making an ass of u and me. But we were rolling. Which was more than I could say for the police, who were distinctly not here.

"Therefore," I went on, "she stole the bag."

"Or swapped it for sexual favors."

I hated to do this, I really did, but like it or not I was a morgue employee now, which meant sometimes I would have to do weird, gruesome things. That knowledge didn't quell the grease trap taste that was forming at the back of my throat. What I hated to do was ask to see what she'd worn to her own murder.

"Can you …" I waved my hand at the sheet.

Gus twitched the cotton down further. The dead woman was all dressed up with no place to go except the grave. If her family came to collect her, that is. Somewhere a pole was missing its stripper; a corner was missing its third best working girl; a porn shoot was missing the woman who'd ordered the pizza with extra sausage. The early 2000s had come calling and slapped her chest with glitter powder. Mini skirt in a violent shade of pink. Buttons and buttonholes at the end of their rope said her pink shirt was too tight and had been since the beginning. Red platform heels. She and this bag weren't from the same strip mall.

A goopy sensation was gathering in the pit of my stomach. Here was—not to judge her—a dead sex worker of some kind, in possession of what looked like Hera's expensive handbag.

But where was Hera?

"We should check the bag for identification. And by we I mean you," I said.

"You already know who the bag belongs to, yes?"

"Maybe." I was hoping I was wrong. "But I want to be sure."

"Who?"

"Its owner, if it's hers, is NIS."

Gus crossed himself then went diving, hand first, into the bag. He yelped once, and then fell on the ground, out cold. Yikes! I knelt down beside him and felt around for a pulse. Heartbeat present and accounted for. After grabbing a cup from the kitchenette and filling it with cold water, I flicked icy droplets at his face. Dumping the whole thing on him would be cruel in this false winter weather.

Gus sat up. "I am okay," he said through chattering teeth. "Am I okay? Did I *ouro* in my pants?"

No wet stain. "You're dry, except for your face."

"Thank the Virgin Mary."

I helped him up.

"There is something in that bag," he said. "Something evil."

"Probably a Taser or a stun gun."

Definitely Hera's bag. Which meant Hera was now separated from her bag and her phone. The question now was: whom should I call first? Melas the cop or Xander the undercover NIS agent?

Decisions, decisions.

For a moment I'd forgotten there was a third option now: Dad.

Although I hadn't asked, I assumed Dad outranked Hera. Even if he didn't, he'd know what to do about the missing NIS agent. But wait, was he still hiding or was he semi-undercover now that Winkler was behind bars or Plexiglas or wherever they put Greek-German criminal masterminds?

I sent Dad a text and waited for his reply. Ten seconds later I got one.

We will be right there.
I felt better already.
Just kidding.

———

THREE GREEK MEN swaggered into the morgue. Their swaggers lasted as long as it took for the refrigerated air to body slam them. One of them should have known better; he'd been here before.

I laughed inside my winter coat—my warm winter coat. I held up my hot coffee cup with both hands.

"Welcome to the morgue," I said. "You don't get to leave unless you take a body with you."

"You are good at this," Melas said.

"You think I'm joking?"

Elias raised his eyebrows at Melas, Dad, and Xander. "She is not joking."

Dad laughed anyway. "How does it work? Do we just pick one we like?"

"That works," I said. "As long as you get them out of here."

Like our clientele, his smile died. "Is this the job you really want?"

Gus popped around the corner. Popping around corners was a habit of his, I'd noticed. "No, no, no. Do not think you can talk Katerina into taking a different job. I need her."

"He needs me," I said, hugging my coffee.

"If you are happy, I am happy," Dad said, looking distinctly not happy.

"I wouldn't go that far," I told him. I hooked a thumb down the hall. "She's down there. Cool entourage." I eyed Xander and Melas, who were doing their best to fake being warm. To Xander's credit he was pulling it off, but then I wasn't sure he was made of the stuff regular people are made of. But even he couldn't hide the goose bumps bursting out all over his neck.

I traipsed after them, not because I wanted another look at the poor dead woman with Hera's bag wrapped around her neck but because I didn't want to be forced to eavesdrop. What if I missed something important?

Greek genes; they're assertive and also nosy.

Hands buried in their pants pockets, Dad and Melas jiggled in place while Gus rolled out the dead woman. Xander planted himself on the floor, arms folded, refusing to give in to the cold. Meanwhile, Elias and I were snuggly and warm in our winter wear.

"Nice sheet," Dad said. "Let us take a look at her."

Gus peeled back the sheet to her shoulders. For a moment nobody said anything. The bag around her neck did all the talking.

Dad crouched and squinted at the bag's handle. "Are you sure this is Hera's handbag?" He was talking to me.

"It bites."

He chuckled. "Field agents always get the best toys. One time I had a pack of cigarettes that could put a grown man to sleep with one puff. Very useful in Europe. In America, not so much."

"You do spy work at home, too?"

For decades Dad had faked a career as a truck driver.

He looked uncomfortable. "Once or twice." He nodded to the woman. "That is definitely not Hera. Do either of you two *malakes* know her?"

Melas and Xander both did the chin lift thing, indicating that they had no idea who the dead woman was.

"We should have brought Takis," Dad said. "He knows all the working girls."

Using his phone, Melas snapped dozens of pictures of the woman and her fatal boo-boo. The forensics team, such as it was—a shivering constable carrying a train case —took what it needed from the woman, then Dad conjured up a set of small clippers and sliced right through the handbag's durable straps. Bag aficionados all over the world felt a disturbance.

Gus winced. "That was a very nice bag."

"Now it's a nice clutch," I said.

"You are an optimist," Gus said. "We need an optimist around here."

Rather than go digging blind in Hera's bag of nasty tricks, Dad laid it on a steel tray and hacked through the leather. He splayed open the leather flaps he'd made. The contents spilled out onto the tray. Dad poked at them with his clippers. He separated the purse from the other contents and handed it to Melas.

"It's Hera's," Melas said.

"Are you sure?" Dad said.

Melas made the purse vanish into his pocket. "Positive."

"What is it?" I asked him.

"Nothing."

Nothing, my lily white butt. Men didn't clam up over nothing. "Did you buy it for her?"

"Years ago."

My heart rolled over and pouted. It didn't bother me that Melas had a history—everyone had a history. No, what bothered me was that Hera was a skanky beast. Not that I could talk; my ex fiancé had been a closet dweller.

They inspected Hera's other belongings.

"Stun gun," Dad said, pointing to a small device that looked like a lipstick. "That's what bit your friend," he told me.

"Technically I am her boss," Gus said.

Dad snorted. "Give her time and she will be the boss of you.

Everyone laughed except me. Was it my imagination or were Melas and Xander laughing harder than the others? Nope. Not my imagination.

"It's a good thing we're trying to get rid of bodies here," I said, "otherwise you two would be toast."

The laughing stopped. Everyone except Dad tilted their heads as they tried to figure out what crunchy bread had to do with anything.

I didn't explain. Unfulfilled curiosity, for Greeks, is hell. Let them suffer.

Hands on hips, I turned to face Melas. "Still think she's not missing?"

"Hera is tough. You would need an army to take her out." But his face said he was worried.

"She's out there somewhere without her phone, her handbag, or her lipstick. Hera would never go anywhere without those things. She probably sleeps in makeup."

Sometimes I sleep in makeup, but only because I'm too lazy to spend all that time washing it off. According to fashion magazines I'd be sorry about that someday, but not today. Yesterday's eyeliner and mascara is today's no-makeup makeup look, with a bit of careful wiping along the lower lash line.

"She's fine," Melas said.

"Do you really believe that?"

"Yes."

"Liar."

"Forget it," Melas said. He strode out of the room, shoulders square, trying to pretend he wasn't freezing his balls off.

Everyone else followed except me.

I helped myself to Hera's lipstick-shaped stun gun and hid it in my pocket.

One of these days it might come in handy.

———

NO CLOSER TO identifying the dead woman, we straggled back into the lobby, where there was a new body waiting. A new-old body.

"I don't believe it," I groaned. "I'm going to strangle that orderly."

"There are better ways to kill someone," Dad said. "Especially if you are a woman. You do not have the same strength in your hands that a man has." He glanced sideways at Melas, who was conveniently ignoring him. "Or so I have heard."

Gus shivered. "Your family scares me."

"They scare me, too," I told him, while I considered my next move. Someone—the orderly—was playing a game of checkers, and I wasn't about to let him win. I grabbed the stretcher again and, in a huff, began to roll it towards the elevator—again.

"Wait," Melas called out.

I stopped. "What?"

"It moved."

"Moved?"

"The body."

Yikes! I jumped up and back. My heart went all wonky until dark spots danced in front of my eyes. Was Marika right? Was this the zombie apocalypse?

"Save yourselves," I said, grabbing Dad and Elias. I shoved them toward the stairwell. Melas and Xander were next. Well, Melas. Xander was advancing on the stretcher. Oh God, he was going to get bitten and turn zombie.

Zombie Xander? He'd be unstoppable.

"Gun," I shouted. "Somebody shoot Xander in the head if he turns."

Xander reached forward and yanked away the sheet. The body underneath sat up and yelped. When she spotted Xander holding the sheet, she slapped his hands and snatched it back.

"What is wrong with you? I am trying to be dead here and you are blowing my cover."

The woman was short, dark haired (part wig, part dye), with curves like a collision between a mountain range and a garden gnome. Her name was Dina and she was Dad's ex-girlfriend; the one he'd jilted before skipping off to the Americas to hook up with my mom and live happily-ever-after-ish … until Mom got cancer and ruined their American dream.

Dina laid back down, draped the sheet over herself.

Melas looked around at us, confused. "What just happened?"

"That happens sometimes," Gus said. "The dead are not always dead. One time I went to make the first cut and the corpse ran away, screaming."

"Cut me and I will cut you harder and deeper," Dina said from under the sheet.

"Kyria Dina?" I said. "What are you doing?"

"Who is that?"

"Katerina."

"Which one?"

"Katerina Makris."

She signed like I was killing her. "You again. What do you want?"

"I work here." I jerked the sheet down so I could see her face. "What are you doing?" The last time I saw Dina she was trussed up in the back of one of the family SUVs in Germany, tied up my by Uncle Kostas. He'd shot at her and left her for maybe-dead. After that, she had vanished. I hadn't seen her since. Until now.

"Working."

My eye twitched. I had an inkling what Dina did for work and it wasn't legal in most American states.

"Working," I said faintly.

"I have a client who misses his mother and likes to—"

Before she could finish that sentence, I covered her back up. My psyche had enough scars.

"Dina?" Dad said.

Dina sat up. She looked at Dad. A wild scream burst out of her throat, then she dragged the sheet over her head.

"Tell me that is not your father." Her voice was muffled by the cotton blend.

Melas elbowed me. "This is getting interesting."

Gus glanced from me to Dina and back again. "I do not know what is going on. The living are strange. The dead are less dramatic." He shook his head and disappeared back down the hallway.

"Dina," Dad said again.

Dina sat up again. The sheet fell away. She sniffed and flicked back her combination real-fake hair. "Michail? You got old."

"You got fat."

"You abandoned me, so I ate to fill the void. What is your excuse?"

"For leaving or for getting older?"

Dina swung her legs around, using the sheet to preserve what modesty she had left. I'd already seen more of Dina than I ever wanted to. Dina was a bona fide whacko who was still madly—heavy on the *mad*—in love with Dad.

"What is wrong with you that you could not say good-bye? You said you loved me—"

"I never said that," Dad answered.

"You said we would always be together, no matter what. Even though your family hated me." Her voice was gaining pitch.

"I never said that either."

"Maybe you did, maybe you did not. But that is what I heard."

"But I never said it!"

"Dad, your logic has no logic here," I said in English.

"So I am learning," he muttered. "What is wrong with this woman?"

Loose screws and abandonment issues. "She's *your* ex. You tell me."

"Virgin Mary," he muttered.

"I don't think religion can help you with this one."

He glanced at his phone. "I have to go. I have a thing."

"You do not have a thing." Dina didn't look happy. "You are trying to abandon me again."

"You want me to defy Baboulas? Nobody defies Baboulas."

I snorted. "Please. I defy her all the time. I'm still here, aren't I?"

Neither of us mentioned her secret in any language, that Grandma was more good guy than bad. Xander spoke English, and God only knew how passable Melas's English was. As for Dina, she was a new, unknown quantity. At first I'd assumed she was the Greek version of a crazy cat lady, with Dad instead of cats. But somehow she'd escaped unscathed from being shot, and she'd performed a semi-decent stakeout on Johnny Deadly's place. And now she was here in the morgue. There were dots—dots that weren't adding up to a picture yet, but in time—if I was lucky—there would be more dots, and I'd be there with a pencil when they appeared.

"You are her only granddaughter," Dad went on. "She has another son."

He winked at me, shot Dina a worried look, then headed for the stairwell.

Dina wasn't having that. "No! You do not get to run away from me again. If you leave now, what will happen this time? More wives? More children? Pets? Beach houses in places people buy beach houses."

"People buy beach houses here," I said helpfully. Maybe her geography was bad, I don't know.

"*Skasmos*," she snapped. "You will not stand between us anymore."

"I wasn't standing between you before."

Dad leaped to my defense. "You cannot talk to my daughter that way."

"How do you know she is even yours, eh? Look at her."

All eyes turned to me.

"Can we not stare?" I said. Something popped into my head. "Kyria Dina, were you here when some guys stole a body the other day?"

"Maybe."

"Yes or no?"

"What is it worth to you?"

I looked at Dad.

"No," he said. "Do not even think about it."

"One date," I said. "Or just go to her house and admire her handicrafts. A woman was murdered and dismembered. A woman who was family." I pressed down hard on that last word to tug on his guilt strings.

"Fine. But after this I am adopting you out."

"Deal," I said.

Dina beamed. "I like the part where you give her away.

Now there will be nothing between us. I heard them but I did not see them because I was waiting under the sheet. Two men. Very talkative. One was complaining because the other man got the bag with her *vizia*."

"Men are weird," I muttered.

Melas's phone beeped. "I have to go," he announced. "Fire. This time it is an old olive factory up on Pelion."

The men skedaddled, leaving me with Dina. This didn't thrill me. It didn't thrill Elias either because he went to hide behind the reception counter.

Dina jumped up and gathered the sheet around her.

"You can't keep that," I said, indicating the sheet.

"This? Okay." She dropped it on the floor, putting all of herself on display.

Behind the counter, Elias made a horrified sound.

I threw the sheet at her. "On second thought, keep the sheet."

"There is something very wrong with you," Dina said, tying it like a dress sarong. "You cannot make up your mind."

"Where are your clothes?"

"At home."

"You came here naked?"

"It is a long story."

A story I didn't want to hear.

Sarong fastened, Dina shot me a look I didn't like. It was full of expectation and unasked favors. I didn't want to do Dina any favors.

"How am I supposed to get home?" she asked me.

"Bus?"

"My skin does not come with pockets."

Gus appeared. "That is not completely true. You would not believe the things I find in the human *kolos*. And that is just the men. The women have an extra hiding place. One time I found a whole souvlaki stashed up there, still in the wrapper."

Twitch. "How did you get here?" I asked Dina. "You should do that but in reverse."

"Ambulance."

Despite the abundance of ambulances coming and going, she couldn't catch a ride home. Ambulances are kind of a one-way thing. I went digging in my bag and pulled out some cash. I gave her the twenty euro and told her to stay away from my father after their one date. Dina was the kind of crazy he didn't need in his life.

"Are you joking? This time I am going to play hard-to-get. He will fall in love with me again, you will see."

Yikes.

Chapter 14

At lunchtime I snapped a photograph of the dead woman and drove to Penka's stoop. On the way I stopped to grab lunch for three. Giant chunks of *spanakopita*—spinach pie —with crispy phyllo pastry.

Out on the sidewalk, Penka was staring up at the sky, using her hand as a visor.

"Oh," she said when she saw us. "It is you. And him."

Elias didn't take it personally. He was just glad he wasn't expected to kill people for a living on a daily basis anymore. As far as assassins went, he'd never moved out of the wannabe category, which was good for me because I was supposed to be his first hit.

I held out my phone and the bag of food. "Pick a hand."

She took the bag. "Autumn and winter are terrible for my waistline. All I do is eat, eat, eat because I am bored."

"What about church?"

"That is one day of work. There are six others."

"Have you considered seasonal work?"

"Funny you should mention that. Baby Dimitri's sister offered me a job."

I could only imagine what kind of job she'd offered Penka.

"Doing what?"

"Makeup and wardrobe. She likes my style."

That made sense. Penka's style was prostitute-on-a-shoestring, which dovetailed nicely with porn. "Are you going to take it?"

"Maybe. The economy is not so good. I could do house calls to sell my classy drugs but I do not exactly blend in."

Nobody in Greece really blended in. Even widows stood out. Turns out black is really noticeable on bright summer days.

"She offered me a job performing," I told her.

Penka nodded. "With your background you could make a lot of money. Everyone wants to see Baboulas's granddaughter do kissy-kissy with a German shepherd."

Eww. No thanks. "Can't. I already have a job, remember?" A low-paying job schmoozing with the dead. But at least I got to keep my clothes on. In fact, I got to wear extra clothing. Lucky me.

"She has been trying for a long time to get someone from your family to join her business. When you turned her down, apparently she tried to convince that one woman."

"Which woman?"

"The one from Baby Dimitri's shop."

"Litsa?"

Penka nodded. She forked a healthy bite of *spanakopita* into her mouth and chewed.

I pulled up the picture of the dead woman. "Have you ever seen this woman before?"

Penka peered at the screen. She pulled away and thought for a moment.

"Yes, but only because you bought lunch. I like people who bring lunch."

"You like me, admit it."

"Maybe, but only because we are both foreigners."

"So, who is she?"

"I don't know. I said I have seen her before, not that I know her. I have seen this one before ..." she nodded at Elias "but what is his name? Who knows? Who cares? Skinny man in a ninja costume."

"I have been working out," Elias said in his own defense.

"You look fine," I told him. "So you've seen her but you don't know her?"

"This is good *spanakopita*." She gave the bag in my hand a meaningful look. I sighed and handed over my lunch. "Okay. She works for a lawyer. I know because I have seen her at the police station. I am surprised you did not recognize her. She is dating a Makris."

Now that I didn't see coming. "Which one?"

"Who knows? They are all the same to me except you, and only because you have a funny accent and a yellow car."

"Hey—you have a funny accent, too."

"I have a Bulgarian accent. There is nothing funny about it."

On the way back to the morgue I called Dad and passed on Penka's revelation.

"Have you ever thought about joining the NIS?" Dad said, sounding impressed.

"No."

"Good. It is a dangerous business."

"Says the mobster's son."

"Baboulas is not just a mobster. She is much worse than that." In the background, something hard struck something less hard. Dad yelped. "*Re*, Mama, I was joking."

"You are not too old to get the *koutala*," Grandma said in the background. I winced. She'd just launched the wooden spoon at him. She took the phone from him.

"What are you two saying?"

I repeated what I'd told Dad.

"Send me a photograph," she said.

———

AFTER WORK, I drove back to the compound. I was eager to see if Grandma had discovered whom the mystery dead woman was dating. On the way across the courtyard, someone hollered my name.

Marika was on her balcony, waving.

I jogged upstairs. Her door flew open before I had a chance to know.

"Why are my children not as well behaved as little Tomas?"

"Tomas is different. For what it's worth his brothers are zoo animals."

"You always know how to make me feel better." She hugged me, then pulled away and made a face. "You smell like dead people."

I sniffed my hair. She was right, I smelled like fake pine and real decay. Ugh.

Little Tomas was sitting on Marika's bedroom floor, fiddling with a safe. Square. Black. About two by two by two. Feet, not meters. On the front was a keypad. The numbers were an angry shade of red.

"Is that Takis' safe?" I asked her.

"If he thinks he can keep secrets from me, I will make him eat wood."

Tomas's face lit up when he saw me. "Thea Katerina! Guess what I am doing!"

"Baking a cake?"

He giggled. "Cracking this safe."

"How's it going?"

"This one is harder than the others."

I raised an eyebrow. "Others?"

"Sometimes people in the family ask me to open a safe. It's fun."

I left him to the safe and followed Marika into the kitchen, where she was slicing potatoes into thin strips. Takis had a thing for *tiganites*—fries—and Marika was only too happy to feed his habit.

She shoved the bowl of potatoes in front of me. "Here, spit on these."

"You want me to spit on your food?"

"Not my food—Takis' food."

Takis was a henchman. Spitting in his food didn't seem smart, even though some would say I outranked him in the family hierarchy.

"I have to go," I said. "Grandma is waiting for me."

Not waiting, exactly. But close enough.

Marika's eyes lit up. "Is she going to send you on an adventure? I could use a good adventure."

"Even after Naples?"

"I got to see Italy."

She got to see the inside of a Ferrari, sleep on a stoop, and almost drown in a sea cave. "What about Germany?"

"German men love me. They like their women big and comfortable, like furniture."

"No adventures on the horizon, sorry. But you can come to work with me tomorrow if you like."

"At the morgue? What if they turn into zombies?"

"There's no such thing as zombies." Never mind that earlier I'd experienced my own paranoid zombie apocalypse moment.

"You say that now," she said darkly, "but waiting until you are shambling around, trying to eat brains. Tomas, come spit on these potatoes."

I kissed her on both cheeks, waved goodbye to Tomas, and trotted back to Grandma's hovel. Grandma was hosing down the concrete with a look of fierce determination on her face. She was talking to herself.

"Here she is now," Grandma said as I pushed through the gate.

"Here I am. Talking to yourself?"

She plucked an ear bud out of her ear. "I am not crazy —yet. But I think you will make me that way." The ear bud resumed its position. "I will send her to see you. Go to the waterfront and see your cousin Yiannis."

"Are you talking to me now?"

"Yes, I am talking to you? Who else would I be talking to?"

I shook my head. "Nobody." The Makris family tree had a dozen branches and twigs named Yiannis. I couldn't pin a face to this one yet. "What's at the waterfront?"

"The souvlaki shop."

My head tilted. Words were coming out of Grandma's mouth but their meaning was lost on me.

Grandma's lips tightened into a colorless line and she shook her head. "Not all my business is criminal, Katerina. The Makris family has legitimate business, too. The souvlaki shop is one of them."

"What am I doing there?"

"Take Yiannis to the morgue and have him identify the woman."

"The morgue is closed."

"Then find a way to open it. A little squirrel told me you know how to open a lock."

"Was this squirrel Aunt Rita?"

"No."

"Did it have a monobrow and a good grasp of classic literature?"

She zipped her lips and dropped the invisible key in her cleavage. Given that Grandma's bosom was almost on talking terms with gravity, the key had a long way to fall. Not for the first time I made a mental note to go for a bra fitting. It was never to soon to fight physics.

"Go," she told me. "Elias is waiting."

———

ELIAS WASN'T the only one. Marika was waiting in the Beetle's passenger seat, huge shoulder bag sitting on her lap. Her hair was damp and she'd dunked her face in a makeup palette and emerged in conflicting colors.

"I heard you were going for souvlaki," she told me.

"Souvlaki then the morgue."

"I can handle anything after souvlaki, even zombies. Anyway, we have a bodyguard to protect us if the zombies attack." She swiveled around and gave Elias a meaningful look.

"Zombies are not in my job description," he said. "Baboulas does not give us weapons to deal with the undead."

Marika rolled her eyes. "This one," she said. "So many excuses. Lucky for you I brought supplies in case the zombies rise. I have been prepared since the last time we had to go to the morgue. Good thing I kept my bag packed." She patted the smooth leather and fluffed her hair.

"Supplies?"

"This I have to see, otherwise I will die from curiosity," Elias said.

We peered into the Beetle, waited for Marika to unzip her bag.

Stakes. An axe. Holy water. A compact machine gun.

"Stakes are for vampires," she said. "Axe for zombies. Silver bullets for werewolves, and holy water for evil. Everything works for regular people, too, except the holy water."

"I guess someone could drink that if they were thirsty."

Her nose wrinkled up. "I do not recommend Father Harry's holy water. He does not always change the water after a baptism."

Greek baptisms happened when an infant reached their third month of life. On that day they scored a name and a free bath in a tub of holy water.

Elias shook his head. "What if your children found those things?"

"Who do you think helped me pack my bag?" Marika said.

My head hurt. Two women were dead and Hera was missing—unless she wasn't, if Melas was to be believed. Right now I wasn't sure I couldn't believe him. But why would he lie to me?

Oh God. They were back together, weren't they? He had her stashed away in his renovated firehouse, cooking naked except for an apron and scrubbing his floors on her hands and knees.

Pain—the psychological kind—whacked me in the stomach. My butterflies dropped dead en masse.

"Do you have any food in there?" I asked Marika.

ALEX A. KING

She riffled around. "Do I have food? I am Greek and I am a mother, of course I have food. Wait—no, I ate it."

Elias reached into his jacket pocket and presented me with one of Stavros's muffins. Barely pausing to peel away the plastic wrap, I bit into the tender crumbs.

"I love you," I said, mouth full.

Elias grinned.

"Are you eating your feelings?" Marika said. "Because it looks to me like you are eating them."

"Marika?"

"Yes?"

"Are you ready for an adventure?"

"No, but I am ready for a souvlaki and that is kind of the same thing when you are pregnant."

I crammed the rest of the muffin into my mouth and hit the gas.

———

I HIT the waterfront and kept on going. That's what Marika told me to do.

"Where is this place and why didn't I know about it until tonight?" I asked her as I crawled along behind a string of traffic heading east.

"Baboulas has so many businesses it is hard to keep track."

Fair enough. Still, it would have been nice to know there was a souvlaki joint in the family. I really liked souvlaki.

The eatery was located not far from Volos in one of the villages that was now officially considered part of the city. Ask the locals and you'd get a different story, Marika told me. They would never, ever be city people, no matter how many vending machines and yoga studios opened in their

194

village.

The village was typical for the area: ready for its post-card close-up on the main streets, and grubbier along and the seams and interior, where the villagers did their living. I was growing fond of the real Greece, the bits that didn't make it onto the postcards and calendars. It smelled like chickens and brined olives. I parked next to a tree filled with roosting turkeys, then decided birds and convertibles weren't a good combination, so I scooted forward until the tree was in my rearview mirror. If they pooped in my car I'd tell them all a bedtime story about a little holiday Americans like to call Thanksgiving. The souvlaki joint was down the road and around the corner, on one of the promenade's busiest corners. It wasn't all that busy now, what with the tourists flitting back home for the winter, but it was still doing brisk business with locals.

My cousin Yannis was behind the counter, slapping meat into pita bread and slopping *tzatziki* on top. Like many of the family's men he had a potato for a nose and a slicked back mop of black hair. He looked like he'd cut you if you complained about his cooking, but no one seemed to be complaining. His face broke into a welcoming grin when he spotted us.

"Come, come. Eat," he said. He quickly wrapped three souvlakia and threw them to us.

"Those were mine," a waiting customer said.

Eyes of steel landed on the customer. "Was your name on them? I do not think so."

"But …"

"*Malaka, skasmos* before I throw you out the door, eh?"

The man shuffled aside, not wanting to get tossed out before he got his food.

Sizzling meat and warm pita bread aromas wafted up

my nostrils. My stomach growled. I was starving but I couldn't eat. Not yet.

"We need to talk," I told my cousin.

"So talk."

"I was thinking somewhere private."

He laughed. "Privacy in Greece." His voice climbed a few decibels. "She thinks we have privacy in Greece." The other customers laughed along with him.

"It's about your girlfriend."

"I do not have a girlfriend. I have a wife. She will not let me have a girlfriend."

The customers laughed again, especially the ones with wieners.

This wasn't going how I expected it to go. I leaned across the counter. "Does your wife work for a law firm?"

The tips of his ears pinked. "Opa! Would you look at the time? I need a cigarette." He grabbed one of his workers by the shirtsleeve and shoved him into place, then he wiped his hands on his apron and nodded to the door.

"Outside."

Once he was out there he didn't light up.

"What do you know about Voula?" he demanded. "Are you going to tell my wife?"

I scanned my memory banks, trying to figure out which wife went with this particular cousin. For the most part they were variations on a theme: the good mother in stretchy capris pants and scoop-necked shirts. "Which one is your wife?"

His eyes went shifty. "Never mind. How do you know about Voula?"

"I ran into her at work. Have you been together long?"

"A few weeks. Why?"

Grandma wants you to take a ride with us."

He squeaked and took a step backwards. "You are going to kill me, your own cousin?"

"What? No. We're just going for a ride. I'll even bring you back in one piece."

He didn't look convinced. "One piece with holes?"

"You won't have a single hole more than you have now, I promise."

"*Gamo tin Panayia mou,*" he said when I eased into the hospital parking lot. "You are going to break my legs and dump my broken body in the emergency room."

Marika reached back and slapped him. "Watch your mouth, there are children around."

He held both hands up. "What children? There are no children."

"I am pregnant."

They spent the next five minutes bickering about whether fetuses can hear and understand Greek. Meanwhile, I trotted down the stairs to the morgue and found it locked up tight.

"You work here," Marika said. "Why not call your boss?"

"I guess I could do that," I said.

I dialed his number. Somewhere beyond the door, Gus's ringtone sang out.

No answer.

My gut started getting bossy, telling me that nothing about any of this was okay. Gus wouldn't not answer his phone, it said, and what was Gus doing here anyway?

My gut obviously didn't understand that Gus was a workaholic who lived, breathed, and possibly did other unsavory things with the dead. But my gut wasn't an idiot like my hormones; it knew when trouble was brewing.

"We have to go in," I told Elias.

"You want me to shoot the lock?"

197

Marika rolled her eyes. "Listen to him. Shoot the lock. Ha! I have an axe." She rifled around in her bag and thrust the axe at my bodyguard. "Chop down the door."

"It's metal," I told her. "I'll pick the lock."

Yiannis didn't look happy. In fact he looked like he expected fifty armed cops to descend on us at any moment. "What are we doing at the morgue, and what does this have to do with Voula?"

My phone rang. Melas was on the other end.

"Where are you?"

"Why?" I said. "What did I do?"

He chuckled. "I am standing at your door but you are not here."

I slapped my forehead. "We're supposed to be on a date, aren't we?"

Yiannis made kissy sounds.

"Who's that?" Melas wanted to know.

"One of my cousins. He thinks I'm going to kill him and he might be right."

That shut Yiannis up.

"Can you wait?" I asked Melas. "I'll be back soon."

"You mean wait here with your family?"

"Or we could do this another night."

"What exactly are you doing?"

I turned around and spoke quietly into the phone. "I'm at the morgue."

"Isn't it closed?"

"I'm working late. It's important."

"Is this something I should know about?"

"Would you look at the time," I said. "I have to go. I'll see you in an hour."

"Katerina …"

I ended the call, pulled up a schematic of the lock, got my lock-picks out.

Yiannis took them from me. "Give it to me."

Before I could protest he'd popped the lock. I looked at him in awe.

He shrugged. "Everybody in the family can pick a lock. Baboulas makes sure we are all versed in the basics."

"It is true," Marika said, bobbing her head. "Takis could pick a lock before he spell his own name."

I wasn't sure Takis could spell his own name now, so that might not be something to brag about.

"What about you?" I asked Elias.

"I am still learning. Stavros is teaching me many things."

A lot of things, apparently. Not that there was anything wrong with that. "Let's find Gus."

"I will wait here." Marika hefted her axe. "Somebody has to keep a lookout for zombies." She glanced at the dozens of sheet-draped bodies crowded into the lobby. "Maybe I will wait upstairs." She bounded up the steps.

The morgue was dark, except for a light in the room where we had all been inspecting the dead woman earlier. An eerie glow radiated down the corridor.

"Stay here," Elias said. "I will make sure it is safe."

"Forget it. We stick together."

"You let Marika go."

"The most trouble she'll get into is the culinary kind."

Elias gave me a wan smile. "I was hoping you would not let me go alone."

Heart hammering in my chest, I volunteered as tribute and set off down the corridor. The men followed.

We found Gus on the floor, hogtied and gagged with the same sheet. Elias cut the makeshift gag away first. When he did, Gus was like a toddler on high fructose corn syrup. His mouth had one speed.

"It is so exciting," he said. "I was working late, then I

heard somebody come downstairs. You were not here, so I went to make sure nobody wanted to leave another body." He shot me a wounded look.

"I don't get paid overtime. Come to think of it, I'm not sure I get paid."

"There was nobody here, so I went back to work. Next thing I know some men came up behind me and tied me up. I have never been tied up at work before."

He was practically humming with excitement. Probably after dealing with so much death this was a refreshing change.

"Men? Did you get a look at them? Did they look like Detective Melas?"

"I did not see them. I only heard their voices."

"What did they say?"

"Take the body, leave the *malakas*. Normally I would be offended that they called me a *malakas*, but they did take a body so I cannot complain."

"Which body?"

He shrugged while Elias cut the rest of him loose. "One of the men hit me and everything went dark until just now."

My gut started jabbering again, this time about how I should open Voula's locker. The locker opened with a loud click.

It was empty.

Chapter 15

"Two murdered women connected to the family, two stolen bodies," I said.

Yiannis threw his hands in the air. Both of them. Big. Greek. Dramatic. We were back upstairs, and only the dying and battered waiting in the ER were around to witness his performance. "What does this have to do with Voula?"

I sighed and showed him the pictures I'd snapped earlier.

He took the phone from my hands, crossed himself, and let out a string of brightly colored curse words. Then he burst into fat, wet tears.

I patted him on the back. "So that's definitely Voula?"

He nodded. "That is my Voula."

Marika glared down her nose at him. Not easy for someone a good six inches shorter. "I know your wife."

"If you tell her she will cut off my *poutsa*."

"She should cut off your *poutsa*."

"You do not understand."

"Help us understand," I said.

"Voula believed in me. My wife, all she did was complain and complain when I went to work for the souvlaki shop. She wanted me to keep doing crime for Baboulas. There is much less money in souvlaki, even very good souvlaki. Voula understood that I wanted to get away from crime. She got away from it and went straight, too."

"She was working for a law firm, right?"

"Yes, but doing honest work."

"What was she doing before that?"

"Dancing."

"How did you meet her?"

"There was an advertisement on the internet for souvlaki delivery men for the entertainment industry, and there I was with a souvlaki business and a delivery motorcycle. So I called the number, went to the address, and Voula was there. I was supposed to give her my souvlaki."

A little light was flashing in my head. "What kind of entertainment?"

He looked uncomfortable. "Movies."

"Were these movies porn?"

"They do not call it that. It is adult entertainment. But I did not give her my souvlaki—not then, anyway. Baboulas would skin me alive if anyone in the family got involved in the pornography business. She is against the exploitation of women, you know? And the company hiring belonged to Baby Dimitri's sister, so Baboulas would have skinned me alive and fed me to the cats. Can you imagine being eaten by cats, with those rough little tongues?" He shuddered.

"So you met Voula on a porn shoot run by Baby Dimitri's half sister?"

He looked surprised. "You know her?"

"She offered me a job."

He nodded like he knew. "She likes people with

connections, that's what Voula told me. People with interesting backgrounds and connections sell more."

"So did Voula take the job?"

He made the little tst sound and puffed out his chest. "I convinced her not to. One taste of Yiannis' *loukaniko* and she was cured."

Marika and I rolled our eyes. Every guy on the planet believed his sausage was magic.

"I cannot believe she is dead. She is dead, yes?"

"I'm sorry," I told him.

He took the time to light up a cigarette and smoked it halfway to the butt before responding. "That is too bad. If I was not already married I would have married her."

"Why not get a divorce?"

"The Makris do not get divorced."

"Aunt Rita did."

"Aunt Rita is Baboulas's daughter. Baboulas would not kill her own daughter. I am just a cousin. One of many cousins. We are like wrenches: if one breaks she buys another."

"Has she ever actually killed anyone in the family?"

He thought about it a moment while he puffed thin clouds of stinky smoke into the air. "There are stories …"

There were stories but were there bodies? I was starting to think not.

"Can you think of anyone who might have wanted Voula dead?"

"Only my wife if she found out, and she did not find out or she would be wearing my *archidia* as earrings."

"Do you know anyone who would take Voula's body?"

"No. Her family is poor; they do not have money for a funeral. When you find her body, I will pay for her burial."

"*When* I find her body?" Wow, he really had faith in me.

He shrugged. "That is what you do, yes? Lately you are the one who solves these kinds of problems. You have a reputation in the family now, and a nickname."

"I have a nickname?"

Marika jumped in. "Do I have a nickname?"

"You are Katerina's sidekick."

"Bodyguard. You mispronounced 'bodyguard'."

Yiannis laughed until Marika glared the mirth out of him.

I sent Grandma a text letting her know that the dead woman had been identified as Voula and that her body had been stolen. Gus promised to go upstairs to the emergency room to get his head checked out. While he was doing that I sent Marika and Yiannis back to the Beetle. Elias and I canvassed the area, looking for someone who might have seen a couple of thiefs making a hasty exit with a corpse.

The other night Melas and I had gotten lucky. Tonight there was nobody. Everyone was either coming or going. Nobody was hanging around, waiting for drama. I dropped Yiannis off at his souvlaki store and waited while Marika grabbed another lamb souvlaki to go.

When we got back to the compound, Melas's cop car was nowhere in sight. Disappointment washed over me. I wondered if there had been another mysterious fire.

Something niggled at the back of my brain where the under-the-bed and closet monsters lived. I couldn't grab its tail, so chewing on my cold souvlaki, I wandered toward Grandma's place. Dogs materialized at my side, mouths open, tongues lolling. They didn't care that the lamb was cold, only that it was food and they wanted some.

"Doesn't anybody feed you?" I crumbled pita bread between my fingers and made it snow crumbs. My goat ambled over for a share of the late-night snack. I scratched his head and wondered how my cow was doing on the farm. The cow was a gift from my bank, whose India-based call center accused me of stealing my own identity. I wondered if the farm had a surveillance camera hooked up to Grandma's bunker. Suddenly I wanted to see my cow, to know she was okay and not burgers.

I didn't feel like going back to Grandma's yard. She had company still—Dad, Papou, Aunt Rita—none of whom were Melas. I cared about them all but I wasn't in the mood to socialize. So I knocked on Xander's door and hoped he was home.

The door opened and Xander was there, fully dressed, hair dry. He was wearing jeans and a white t-shirt that made his bronze skin glow. He reminded me of Talos, the bronze automaton that protected the king of Crete's mother, circling the island three times each day. Hopefully he had more than one vein, because things didn't go well for Talos.

When he saw it was me he opened the door wide enough for me to slip in and under his arm.

"No swim tonight?"

He shut the door and did the up-down chin thing. He folded his arms and waited for me to get to the point, which I did. I liked Xander—more than I wanted to—but I needed some alone time.

"Can I use the hatch to the bunker?"

He gave me a questioning look, his dark eyes serious, curious, with a flicker of worry.

"I want to check on my cow," I said.

The worry gave way to the kind of amusement that suggests the person on the receiving end is missing several marbles and a bunch of nuts. He pulled back the rug, revealing the hatch that led to the bunker. He entered the PIN. The steel hatch opened.

"Thanks," I said.

He grabbed my hand and helped me down the ladder. It wasn't necessary but it was nice. That type of nice gives a woman ideas. Like right now I was planning a wedding in my head. Big fluffy dress. Skyscraper cake. Lots of guests, most of them with the family nose. The trouble was the groom.

What was the problem?

There were two of them, for starters.

And they were both mostly naked.

A hot flash stained my face pink. I scooted down the ladder and dropped down to the floor below before Xander could get inside my head and rifle around. Mumbling to myself, I flopped into the captain's chair and tried to focus on the screens. The farm's main building—the barn, I guess—was brightly lit. The gaggle of cousins who worked the land and reared the animals (not literally, I hoped), were crowded around a backgammon board. Things looked like they were about to get violent. Greeks take their games seriously.

A click of the mouse later and I was in the barn, looking at my cow. She looked happy enough—as happy as animal can look while it's asleep. Unlike her brethren she was wearing a coat. Something was printed on the side. I couldn't quite make it out.

Squint.

Do Not Eat.

Ha-ha-ha. Very funny, my cousins. But whatever worked. My goat was fine. My cow was fine. Dad was alive and, for the moment at least, safe.

I checked out the other feeds. Greece was winding down for the night. My mind skipped back to Melas and our date that wasn't happening. I glanced at the police station's feed—the one he didn't know about—and saw

Melas at his desk, tapping a pen on paper. Every so often he'd reach for his coffee cup and take a long swig. His smooth forehead was crumpled. Something was bothering him. The fires maybe?

I sent him a text message.

Working hard?

His phone lit up. He glanced at the screen and smile flashed across his face. It didn't last. He closed his eyes, tilted his head back, hands supporting the back of his neck. Greek police budgets didn't extend to good chairs.

Then he reached for his phone.

I could not wait, sorry. Tomorrow night?

Sure.

If it were up to me I would let the world burn so I could keep a date with you.

My cheeks burned. Sure, it sounded like a pickup line —and I'd heard my share of them—but I wanted it to be true.

The police station door opened. Normally the squat building's air conditioning was a stack of bricks that held the door open so a stray breeze could pass through on its way inland, but on these cooler nights the cops were using the bricks as paper weights. A woman sashayed in.

It took me a moment to place her, then it clicked. Baby Dimitri's half-sister (and Donk's mother) sauntered between the desks on spiked heels that could cook gyro meat. She was wearing a bright pink trench coat that I hoped wasn't about to end up on the floor.

What was she doing there?

Melas set aside the pen and paper. His face had shifted into the neutral position. Whatever the adult entertainer was saying it had triggered his cop mode.

Why didn't this thing come with sound?

Donk's parental unit waved her hands as her mouth

sprayed words. Melas listened and pocketed his phone. When she was done, he stood and came around to the other side of the desk. He touched her shoulder and walked her to the door. As soon as they stepped through they vanished from view. Stupid camera and its stupid limits.

I called Aunt Rita.

"Do these cameras move?"

"Use the mouse," she said.

Duh. I seized the mouse, selected the feed's link and brought it up on the computer screen. The camera didn't move fast but it did move until I caught sight of the police building's exterior through the open door and windows. Melas was standing in the doorway, talking to Baby Dimitri's half-sister. All I was getting was the back of his head and his butt, which was brought to this world by lots of running. I paused to admire the view for a moment, until he moved out of range again. I wiggled the mouse but the camera had reached its limits.

Damn it.

Time passed. My lids got heavy. At some point I drifted off. When my head jerked up, I was wearing a puddle of drool as a brooch. Fancy.

Melas still wasn't back. Maybe he'd been and gone again, but his papers were arranged exactly how he'd left them.

I messaged Melas again.

Let me know if you need a rescue party.

I added a winking face.

Nothing.

There was a noise beside me and then a large, male hand came out of nowhere and snatched the phone out of my hand. I leaped sideways, arms windmilling.

"Are you crazy?" Xander barked.

Xander had spoken. Again.

"You scared the heck out of me! You made me wind-mill! Why can't you make noise like a regular person?"

He stood over me, face grim, my phone in his hand. "You want Melas to know he is being watched at work?"

Embarrassment lit my cheeks. He was right, damn him.

"Well?" he said.

"No."

He thrust the phone back at me. "Don't do it again."

"Text Melas?"

"As much as I'd like that, that's not what I meant."

"You don't like me texting Melas?"

He changed the subject. "How is your cow?"

"Alive and wearing a coat." If he could change the subject, so could I. "What are you doing down here?"

"Tomas was looking for you. He can't sleep."

My eyes scanned the bunked. "You didn't bring him down here, did you?"

"He's with Kyria Katerina and your father."

"Oh good, that should warp his mind nicely for life."

"Your Grandmother raised me. I turned out okay."

"I didn't realize you had a sense of humor."

"There's a lot you don't know about me."

He was right about that. "Like what?"

His mouth did this sexy half-smile thing that some people might call a smirk. But on him it was less arrogant, more tasty. I picked a spot on the wall behind his head and stared at that. Safer that way.

"Like I know you're planning to sneak out of here and march to the police station."

"Am not. And that's something about me, not something about you."

He dumped my phone on the desk and folded his arms.

"Okay. You want to know something? I like you, and I think Melas is all wrong for you."

My face went up in flames again. That spot behind his head was looking mighty interesting. "I suppose you think you're right for me?"

"No. I'm no good for anyone, least of all you. I already told you that."

"Why not?"

The conversation pivoted again. "Whatever you think is going on, whatever you saw in the camera, Nikos Melas is okay. He can look after himself."

"That's what he said about Hera, and she's missing, too.

"Okay. Tell me what you saw."

I told him about Melas's exodus with the area's queen of porn.

"Baby Dimitri's sister doesn't have any reason to hurt him," Xander said.

"I don't understand all the dynamics, but she is a mobster's sister."

"Half-sister," Xander said. "And from what I know Vikki's business is completely independent of her brother's. I'm not sure he even knows how she makes a living. She's discreet. The only rumor I have heard is that she has a thing for performers with interesting backgrounds. It's her company's hook. But the Greek market is limited, so she has been trying to branch out to bring in notable and connected women from other regions in Europe. But that's not a crime. We're not talking human trafficking here."

"So what does Melas have to do with her business?"

"Nothing that I know of. He is busy investigating the fires."

Yeah, right. My eyes hadn't lied to me. Melas had left the police station with Baby Dimitri's sister. Just because Xander didn't hear the tree fall in the forest, didn't mean it didn't fall. But it was obvious Xander wasn't on board with my hypotheses.

"You like me?"

"You're cute. You're sexy. You're funny. Want me to keep going?"

"Yes and no."

I glanced at the screens but nothing registered. Slowly, I stood up. My plan was to scoot around Xander and take off into the night to see what was going on at the police station.

You know what they say about plans. Once I was standing in front of Xander, the space between us shrunk, the air thickened, and things turned biological.

Lump in throat, I tried to swallow. I didn't know what to do. Melas was out there somewhere, doing God only knew what with Vikki. Then there was Xander. Hot, sexy, oh-God-I-can't-believe-how-good-he-smells Xander.

Maybe Xander was right. Maybe Melas was fine. He was a grown man and a cop. He even had a gun.

My hand touched his chest, flat against the hard muscle. For a man who looked like he was made of marble he was warm. His shoulders were tense, his body poised. He was waiting on me to make a move.

"Katerina?"

"What?"

"Are you asleep?"

My hand moved lower. He was muscle all the way down to his belt.

"I hate to do this," I said, looking up into his eyes.

He jerked back slightly. His eyes clouded over. "You

don't have to do anything you don't want to do. I like my partners willing."

"Not that. I want to do that." At least I thought I did. My hormones definitely did. My head was having a hard time reconciling my body's wants and my head's needs. "I mean this." I thrust my hand into my pocket and pulled out a little something I'd found in Hera's bag.

Zap.

Xander collapsed like sack of flour.

Huh. It really worked.

I felt bad—I really did—and I wanted to put him somewhere comfortable so he wouldn't wake up with a stiff neck. But he was build like a fire truck and I barely have enough strength to squeeze a garlic press. As a compromise, I grabbed a pillow and blanket from one of the cot beds in the bunker's living quarters. Xander taken care of, I scrambled up the ladder and exited via his apartment. But first I dragged the couch over to the hatch.

Night was gone. Dawn was minutes away. I wasn't sure how long I had before Xander came to, but I knew once he woke up he'd launch a manhunt to find me. Maybe a one-man manhunt, but definitely a manhunt.

What I needed what a hiding place.

I jogged around to the garage. My Beetle was still out front where I'd left it earlier. Lucky me, the cousin on duty hadn't had a chance to wash the yellow convertible and stow it in the cavernous garage.

"Are you missing someone?" he called out, dropping his cigarette and crushing it under his shoe.

I shook my head and hoped for the best. "No. I'm just going to Makria."

"At this time of morning?"

"Keep asking questions and I'll tell Grandma you were smoking."

I hopped into my car and eased through the gates.

Grandma wouldn't be happy that I'd snuck off without a bodyguard, but things weren't as strict as they had been. My biggest concern was Xander, who would be waking up in the very near future. He knew I was after Melas, so probably the first place he'd look for me would be Melas's house, followed by the scene of his disappearance. Or maybe the other way around. Which meant I'd have to work quickly. I drove to the police station and found it manned by a young constable who was snoring through what was left of night duty.

I clicked my fingers under his nose. His head jerked up. He wiped his hand across his chin, mopping up the drool.

"Where is Detective Melas?"

"At his desk."

"Not at his desk."

Melas's chair was empty. On his desk sat the same pen and papers I'd watched him fiddle with during the night.

The constable shrugged. "What do I look like, a babysitter?"

"You look to me like a man who was sleeping on the job."

He paled. "Are you going to tell?"

"Are you going to let me go back and leave Melas a note?"

He pointed. "I know you."

"Yes, yes, everyone knows me."

"I saw you on YouTube."

"Everyone has seen me on YouTube."

"Leave your note, but do not touch anything."

Leaving a note wasn't my original plan, but under the circumstances it gave me time to peek at the paperwork on Melas's desk. The top layer was a map of the Pelion area with dozens of little red ink marks dotted around the

ALEX A. KING

mountain. The locations of the fires. There was nothing on the desk to suggest a connection between Melas and Baby Dimitri's sister Vikki.

I scribbled a note and was this close to leaving it when I changed my mind and shoved it into my pocket. I went back to the constable.

"If a big, quiet guy comes here looking for me you didn't see me, okay?"

"But I can see you. You are standing right here."

"Am I? Could be I'm a ghost."

"I do not believe in ghosts."

"Baboulas? Do you believe in her?"

He shuddered. "Please do not tell Baboulas."

"As long as you don't tell the big, quiet guy I was here you won't be on her radar."

"Okay, okay, I will not say a word."

I turned to leave, then remembered something. "Where were you six hours ago?"

"Bathroom," he said. "My wife cooked *revithia*."

Revithia. Chickpeas. No wonder he was in the bathroom.

"I'm sorry."

"Not as sorry as I am," he said mournfully.

———

GRANDMA CALLED as I got back into my car.

"Did you do a bad thing?" she asked me.

"I did not have sexual relations with that woman," I told her.

She didn't laugh. "Xander is looking for you."

"I bet he is," I muttered. "I'm busy. I don't suppose you can call him off?"

"Xander can be like a dog with a bone."

"Am I the bone in this story? I am, aren't I? Can't you … I don't know, send him away for a day or two or something?"

"What are you doing, Katerina?"

"Looking for Melas."

"Probably he is at his mother's house. I will help with Xander as long as I can send Elias with you."

"Fine," I said. "Have him meet me at Makria. I just need to know Melas is okay."

"What is going on, Katerina?"

"I don't know, but I know I don't like it."

"Xander will not be a problem. Go now."

"Wait—how is Tomas?"

"He is busy studying at my kitchen table."

"Studying?"

"He is researching an obscure type of safe. Apparently there is a lock out there that has confounded him."

"I'll be back later."

"Try not to get killed, eh? I do not feel like another war just now."

Chapter 16

Elias was waiting for me in Makria. I found him in the village square, ordering two coffees to go from a kafeneio that understood caffeine addicts and their needs. Did Elias know me or what?

"I love you," I said.

He grinned. "I am just happy not to be at the morgue today."

The morgue. Crap. I slapped my forehead and quickly dialed the morgue's number. Nobody answered, probably because I wasn't there to pick up.

The sun was hauling its carcass over the horizon. Makria's people were bustling around the village, taking care of the morning's errands and chores. A thick curl of smoke rose from the bakery's chimney. Tomas Melas was hard at work. Our first stop was the bakery, where I bought two hot loaves from the human barrel with his son's smile.

He handed me two loaves wrapped in paper. "For you, free."

"One is for your wife."

"In that case, only one is free." He shook with laughter at his own joke.

I accepted the loaves and gave one to Elias. "Wait here," I told him when we reached the Melas's yard.

"And now I am even happier than I was."

"I hate you," I said.

His grin spread. "Women, you are always fickle."

I thought about what Tomas had told me. There was no way I was going to mention it to either of the men unless they brought it up first. If Elias and Stavros found happiness together, good for them.

"I don't want to go in there alone, but I think I have to."

He patted my shoulder. "Better you than me."

Not wanting to break protocol, I called out to Kyria Mela from outside her gate. She let me call her name three times before she stuck her head out the window.

"Katerina? What do you want?"

I held up the loaf. "I brought bread."

"Where is Hera? She always brings the bread." Her helmet head vanished, and she appeared in the doorway, flipping her hand at me. "Come, come, bring it here."

Into the yard I went, quaking in my shoes.

"What is new?" she demanded.

"Besides this bread?"

"I want news, not jokes."

"I've got a new job."

"At the morgue? I heard. I also heard two bodies were stolen, including that woman." Her nose wrinkled like she'd stepped in dog poop. "You know, yes?"

"Know what?"

Kyria Mela shook her finger at me. "Never play the fool with me." She tapped her temple with that same finger. "I know. I see what you are thinking. Nikos told you that the boy, Tomas, is his son. Just because she became pregnant while they were together, does not mean he was the father."

Wait—she knew? Of course she did. Kyria Mela knew everything.

"It puts him in the running," I said.

"Have you ever seen Pamplona in Spain, where the bulls run through the streets and *vlakes* let the bulls chase them?"

"Not in person."

"This thing with my son and that woman is like that."

My head tilted. "I don't understand."

"That woman's mouni was like the bulls charging through the streets, and my son was one of the vlakes who got trampled. But he was not the only one. He was not even the first or the last. I know you think that is my grandson, but that boy is not my blood."

I said nothing. Silence was so much smarter, under the circumstances.

"Come." She grabbed my arm. "I want to show you something."

"Will it involve knives and fingernail-pulling?"

"Do you want it to?"

Horror slathered itself all over my face. I felt my skin creep into position. Kyria Mela snorted. "Photographs. I want to show you photographs."

"Do I want to see photographs?"

"Yes," she said darkly, "you want to see these photographs."

Into the spider's lair I went. This wasn't my first time. Kyria Mela keeps her house an almost clinically OCD level of clean, which isn't surprising, given what I knew about her personality. Dust probably shook its head at the front door and went to rest in a neighbor's house instead. The palette is neutral and light. The furniture is tasteful in an old-fashioned, mothballs-live-here way. Kyria Mela was watching me assess her place.

"Nobody brings dirt into my home. Nobody."

"Not even your grandchildren?"

Her face dissolved into smiles. "They are different. They can bring anything they want in here—even *kaka*. Come."

She led me to a room I'd been in before: her parlor or display room. Many Greek homes had one like it, a room for company only. All her fancy things were on parade here. Paintings. Knick-knacks. Embroidered pillows.

I could suffocate to death in a room like this.

On the floor the pretty Oriental rug was hiding a secret. Underneath was a hidey-hole big enough to hold a grown man, and a box of Kyria Mela's old torture implements. She was keeping them for one of those rainy days where she needed to torture someone. Today wasn't a rainy day. Not yet.

"What do you see?" she asked me.

"A very nice room that could use some air?"

"With air comes dust." She gestured toward the heavy table that was weighted down with photographs. The Melas clan was portrayed in mismatched frames. Silver. Gold. Glass. Kyria Mela didn't let anything as plebeian as wood frame her precious family. "Keep looking."

I scanned the photographs. The whole family was depicted one photo at a time, from its origins on Kyria Mela's wedding day to a recent photo of some chubby cheeked kids who were obviously from this gene pool.

"I don't see it."

"That is because there is nothing to see."

"I should let you know right now that I'm really bad at riddles."

She sighed like I had the IQ of a zucchini. "Does anyone in my family look like that boy?"

I looked again. "No."

"Do you know why that is?"

"Because the Makris genes are rock and the Melas genes are scissors?"

She tapped me on the forehead with her knuckle. "No. Because that little boy is not a Melas. He is someone's son, but he does not belong to my Nikos."

"So you're saying someone else is the father?"

"Very clever. Give the woman a *koulouraki*."

I waited before going on, just in case there really was a *koulouraki*. Turning down cookies wasn't my style—even a potentially poison cookie from Melas's mother. Kyria Mela used my patch of silence to jump in with her own theories.

"Of course Nikos has a good heart and he is not a suspicious man, so he believes Tomas is his son." She waited with an expectant look on her face.

"I can neither confirm nor deny that's what he thinks."

Being the middleman wasn't my idea of fun. Bad things happen to middlemen and messengers.

She tapped me on the forehead again. "You are showing my son loyalty and that is a good thing, but he is not standing here right now and I have a kitchen full of knives—sharp knives."

Yikes. "Okay. Whose son do you think Tomas is?"

Shrug. "Could be anybody. The woman had a reputation." She eyed me carefully. This was the part where I was supposed to show her mine, and then she'd show me hers. I really wanted to see hers first. "What do you know?" She barked the last part and pointed her finger. Very intimidating.

"She used to be a stripper?" I blurted.

"A-ha! I knew it was something like that."

Aww damn it. Kyria Mela was a sorceress. A dark one. Not evil, but definitely shady.

"I have been watching her since she began to sniff, sniff, sniff around my son. I thought to myself: 'Why is this married woman skulking around my young, smart, and very, very handsome son when she has her own husband?' And do you know what I discovered?"

I opened my mouth. It wasn't necessary.

"I will tell you. Men. An army of men. Old men, young men, Greek men, foreign men. All the men."

"Turks?"

"No. She had one standard."

"Anyone you know?"

"Everyone. Those poor children. Only the Virgin Mary knows whose sons they are. But none of them is a Melas, guaranteed."

"Why are you telling me all this?"

"So you can tell my son the truth."

Was I offended or shocked? Hard to say. "Wait—what? You want me to be the bearer of bad news?"

"Of course. Better for him to be angry at you than me. I am his mama." She patted me on the head. "Good girl." Her face clouded over. She pulled a phone out of her apron pocket and glanced at the screen. An anachronistic moment. Greek villagers of a certain age looked oddball when they fiddled with their phones.

"Where is that boy? I told him to call his mama," she said. "He always calls me in the morning."

Here came the icky feeling again, the wrongness, the memory of Melas vanishing out the police building door with Baby Dimitri's kinky sister.

"Did you call him?"

She looked at me like I'd sprouted a second head. "For

what? He said he would call me. If he loves his mama he will call."

"Maybe he's busy."

"He is never too busy."

Bold words. But I wasn't fooled. Behind them stood a worried mother. Melas wasn't exactly a mama's boy—not in his mind, anyway—but he was an honorable man, one of the good guys. If he'd promised to call and he hadn't, there was a reason.

"I have to go," I said.

"Go, go, and if you see my son tell him to call his mama."

———

THERE'S a point in every whodunit where the detective—amateur or not—gathers enough puzzle pieces for the picture to make sense. I was no detective, and I had a brain full of puzzle pieces, most of them double sided and from different puzzles. I couldn't make out the picture on the front of the box, mostly because there was no box. If there had been a box, I would have chosen to scoot past the dismembered gangster's wife and the strangled bookkeeper. Something pretty with flowers would have been my choice. Maybe a palace with lush gardens. Ooh, maybe a nice scene of Greece. Santorini. Delphi. Places I'd never been but planned to one mythical 'someday'.

I wandered back to Makria's parking lot. It was almost empty now. With tourist season over, the tour buses were fewer. The Beetle was hanging out with the black compact Elias was driving and Kyria Mela's brown Peugeot.

I called Melas's phone. It rang until his voicemail grabbed the wheel and told me to leave a message.

"Home?" Elias said.

"No. Let's drive."

He saluted me and followed the Beetle out onto the mountain's main road.

Puzzle pieces bounced around my head like popcorn. I pecked through the kernels Kyria Mela had flicked at me. She didn't think Tomas was a Melas, and to be honest I wasn't all that surprised. It seemed to me like Litsa had been a tourist destination for a lot of guys in the area. Any one of them could have left behind a boy-shaped souvenir. And now I was stuck with the task of delivering the bad news to Melas. Hopefully he didn't believe in shooting the messenger.

So who was Tomas's birth father?

Maybe that was the key. Why else would anyone try to snatch Tomas after his mother's murder? Find the father, find the murderer and the motive.

In the meantime, I wanted to know what business Baby Dimitri's sister had with Melas.

Maybe she didn't have business per se. Maybe it was something else.

Like a tip.

———

BABY DIMITRI WAS STILL in his robe. For a moment he reminded me of Dad's next-door neighbor. The difference between Baby Dimitri and the elderly retired judge was that Baby Dimitri's perfectly creased pants were zipped up and I couldn't see his penis.

He wasn't happy to see me. He was even less happy when I started talking.

"Why you come here to step on my balls, eh?"

I tried not to look offended but I couldn't help myself.

"I haven't said anything interesting yet! You don't even know why I'm here."

He scoffed at that. "You have one dead woman, she goes missing, so you come here—and why? Because she fell on my shop."

"You said she was our problem, that we should take the body and go. That tells me you know more than you're telling me."

"Maybe I did, maybe not. Who can say?"

I raised my hand. "I was there. I can say."

"Probably you misunderstood. Greek is your second language, yes?"

Greek was my second language, but thanks to my mom's gentle prodding and my time in Greece, my second language was almost as sharp as my first.

"I heard what I heard."

"Whatever you are trying to say, say it to my face."

Challenge accepted. "You knew the body was Litsa's before we identified her."

He slammed the door. I hammered on the wood.

"You told me to say it to your face."

"I was wrong. It would be better if you say it to the door."

With one hand I whipped out my lock picks. With the other I retrieved my phone, opened YouTube, and began hunting for a video that would show me how to crack the Godfather of the Night's door. It wasn't much, as doors went. Frankly, I'd expected more. Something with a growling dog behind it.

"I'm surprised you don't have a guard dog," I said to the door.

"I had two mastiffs once. They kept licking the lotion off my skin. Everywhere I went, lick, lick, lick. Finally I got tired off all the licking and I had them killed."

A gasp punched its way out of my throat. Before I could nail him to a cross as a dog murderer, he laughed.

"Relax, Katerina Makris-with-an-s, I sent them some-place where they could lick, lick, lick, all they wanted. Did you know dogs like honey?"

My eye twitched. "They do?"

"They will lick honey off anything. Anything."

Of all the things I didn't want to know, I really didn't want to know about dogs and things they'd lick. My imagination was already unspooling horror reels in my head.

"Enough about the dogs." I popped the lock and flung the door open. Surprise skittered across the older man's face, but he recovered fast.

"You really are a Makris."

"Did you ever doubt it? Tell me how you knew it was Litsa before we did. Did you kill her?"

"No! I have never killed anybody." He made a face. "Okay, maybe that is an exaggeration, but I did not kill Litsa. Look, Litsa and I had a history, okay? The kind of history where I would know her anywhere, even if she were chopped into pieces and thrown out of a plane."

"Were you sleeping with her?"

"She worked in my club. Do you know how often I saw her naked? All the time."

"So why did you say she was our problem?"

He held his hands together in a V and used the hand-made letter to punctuate his words. "Because she is a Makris! Ask your grandmother. If there is a death in a family, that makes it your family's business before it is anyone else's. You think I want to get on your grandmother's wrong side?"

"Are you afraid of my little old grandmother?"

"Everybody with a brain is afraid of your grandmother, even me."

"I thought you were a tough guy."

Two palms up. "Me? You forget I am just a shoe salesman."

"I bet you'll be glad when they fix your roof and you can go back to hanging out, watching the world pass by."

He made a face and paired with it a shrug. "Eh. I am getting too old for that. Maybe my idiot nephew can leave school and take over the shop for me. If he turns up."

I said nothing about Donk and his current status as a refugee in the Family dungeon. Baby Dimitri was still on my list of dodgy characters who may or may not have killed Litsa. Even if he didn't do the chainsawing himself, he knew more than he was letting on.

"While I'm here …"

He rolled his eyes at the ceiling. "*Panayia mou!* What now?"

"Why would your sister want with Detective Melas?"

His face shuttered. "The police? Why?"

"Just curious."

"Curiosity is a dangerous thing. Careful where you point it, eh?"

I changed the subject. "Is Laki still out of town? I'm surprised he's not enjoying all these fires. Is it envy keeping him away?"

He opened the door long enough to thunk me on the forehead. "For a clever woman you are an idiot. Now get out of here before people start to talk."

"They already talk about me."

"Not you—me. I do not want you to ruin my reputation."

I trotted back to my car, then a question popped into my head. I went back to the house and knocked again.

"What now, eh? What now?"

"One last thing, I promise."

"Go ahead, ask your question."

"Laki's father died."

"Yes. Now *yiasou*."

He shut the door.

"That wasn't a question!"

"Okay, okay."

"What did he inherit?"

"For an idiot sometimes you are smart. Will you go now or do I have to call the guards?"

"I'm going, I'm going. But you're wrong about something. There wasn't just one dead woman. There were two."

"What does that have to do with me? Nothing."

"Her name was Voula," I said.

"Her and maybe hundreds of thousands of other Greek women."

"This one worked for a law firm."

His face was a tile of Greek marble, smacked several times with a sledgehammer. "Never heard of her."

Chapter 17

Katerina Makris, smartest idiot on the planet. Or most idiotic smart person. No point being offended; this was Greece, where people said what was on their minds … except when they didn't. Greece is a country full of contradictions. Probably it wanted Germany to think it was crazy so it wouldn't expect its money back. I figured Greece had staved off centuries of enemies that same way, flashing its wisdom one minute, knocking back hemlock and frothing at the mouth the next.

My self-esteem was rock solid. Or at least the outer crust was stable. At times in my life I'd been complacent and maybe even lazy (thanks, streaming television), but I was confident my IQ was in triple figures.

What my intellect told me was that Baby Dimitri had just handed me a chunk of mental gold. But before I could melt it down into something useful I had somewhere else to be.

Vikki and Donk occupied a boxy white modern villa in a rundown neighborhood. Like Baby Dimitri's place, good taste had come to their place to die … unless you were shooting porn. Lucky for Vikki (not so much for Donk) she was. Last time I was here there had been souvlaki delivery mopeds parked out front. Today, the wide driveway was empty.

I rang the doorbell and waited.

And waited.

And waited some more.

Then I did a Greek thing: I pressed my ear to the door and listened.

Somebody on the street snickered. Two somebodies. A couple of kids who should have been in school, working toward a future that didn't involve slinging olives in a factory. They were maybe Donk's age, that era of boyhood where the hormones drive the machine more often than the brain. The kid on the left was bouncing a basketball. The other one had a skateboard tucked under one arm. They were dressed like they'd just rolled out of whatever 'hood produced entitled white kids who didn't believe in things like education and good manners.

"What's so funny?"

"We are going to see your ..." The kid with the ball dropped it long enough to grab his non-existent pecs and jiggle them.

Charming child. He was going places with those manners, like politics.

"What makes you think that?"

He shrugged. "Every woman who comes here ends up in one of Kyria Vikki's movies."

"Every woman?"

"All of them."

Huh. How about that. "Not me. I'm not interested in her movies."

They snickered some more. Boys. What these brats needed was a reality check. I pulled out my phone and swiped to the picture of Voula I'd taken in the morgue. I waved it under their noses.

"Have you seen this woman here?"

They peered at the screen. "What's wrong with her?"

"She's dead."

"In the picture?"

Nod. "Do you know her?"

They turned bloodless white under their summer tans.

"We saw her."

"Here?"

"Here and in a movie."

Interesting. My cousin Yiannis told Voula had never been in one of Vikki's movies. Someone was lying and I didn't think it was these kids.

Is she really dead in that picture?" Basketball asked.

"She's really dead. Someone strangled her with the strap of a handbag."

The kid with the skateboard gagged, then he projectile vomited onto the cracked sidewalk. Whatever bravado they possessed had vanished.

Aw damn it, here came my empathy.

"Can I buy you guys an ice cream? Chocolate? Some of those little plastic wrapped cakes?"

The smirks returned. So much for my empathy.

"You could take off your clothes."

Ugh. I was about to deliver a cutting and possibly psyche-scaring remark when Elias stepped up onto the sidewalk behind them. He grabbed their heads and banged them together like a pair of coconuts. Not hard enough for NFL level damage but with enough force to make them twitchy every time they saw a woman naked for the next few weeks.

"Show some respect," Elias said as the boys rubbed their goose eggs. "Did you find anything, boss?"

"Nobody home. You're Greek so you probably know lots of Greek stuff, right?"

Elias watched the teenage boys scram. Three houses down the road they rediscovered their bravado and regained their swagger.

"I know less than I did when I was their age."

Didn't we all? The cruelest thing about getting older was that I was suddenly realizing I was a dumbass. "I need information about a bequest. Laki's father died. I want to know what his father left him."

His eyebrows went hiking into the wilds of his hairline. "Laki had a father?"

It was a reasonable question. Laki was older than old dirt. His father must have been a dinosaur.

"Until a few days ago. He left something to his son and I want to know what."

"You think it is something to do with the murders?"

"No, but I think it has everything to do with the fires."

Elias thought about it a moment. "Easy. Money talks. Find out who his father's lawyer was and pay the lawyer."

White envelope crime. Greece ran on stationary filled with cash.

"How do we find out who his lawyer was?"

Elias unclipped his phone and sent a text message. Less than thirty seconds later he had a name for me.

"Pavlos Makris."

"Are we related?"

"He is family but he is not Family."

Fantastic.

———

PAVLOS MAKRIS. What could I say about the man? He was an anthropomorphized grease stain in a cheap suit.

His law office was located in a shed at the bottom of his garden, next to the chicken coop. He belonged to the straight branch of the Makris family tree, the same branch that produced Kyria Dora, the local fortune teller. His smile was as slicked on as his hair. Both looked like they were about to flake.

"No," he said.

"No?"

"I cannot just give you that kind of information."

Elias stepped over a chicken, pecking at a mound of cracked corn. "Want me to hurt him?"

The slimy lawyer winced. "You cannot intimidate me. I am an officer of the law."

Elias reached into his pocket.

Pavlos's hands shot into the air above his head. "Okay, okay, I will tell you anything you want to know. Please do not kill me."

"I was getting breath mints," Elias said, hand emerging with a rectangular green box. "Some people are so paranoid."

The lawyer groaned. "I take it back."

"Too late," I said. "You can't take it back. You could get disbarred for lack of integrity."

"Really?"

No, not really. But he clearly thought otherwise. I was starting to suspect he'd scored his diploma in a cereal box.

"So what did Kyrios Lakis inherit from his father? Money? Guns? Bomb-making supplies?"

"One moment." He rifled around on his desk. When that didn't pan out, he moved his investigation to the squat filing cabinet next to the milk crate that was holding a chicken and some tufts of of hay. That was a no-go, too. He picked up the crate, made a satisfied sound, and grabbed a manila folder that was stashed underneath. He hugged his prize against his chest. "If you want what is in this folder it will cost you."

No problem. I'd come prepared. I waved an envelope under his nose. Nestled inside was a short stack of twenty-euro bills. The real deal.

Pavlos scoffed but his eyes didn't leave the envelope. They followed as I swished it back and forth. "You think I want money? I do not want money."

"Please don't tell me you want sex."

"I want to work for Baboulas."

Huh. I didn't see that coming. "You want to work for Grandma? Why?"

"Because a business as big as hers, she needs a lawyer."

"She has good lawyers."

"Are you saying I am not a good lawyer?"

My eye twitched. I tried not to glance at the chickens, at the crate, at the corrugated iron roof overhead.

"No …"

"Then what are you saying?"

"That there's no job opening."

"How do you know if you have not asked her?"

He was going to make me call Grandma, wasn't he? Fabulous. I tapped Grandma's name in my Contacts list. She answered in a huff and wanted to know where I was.

"I'm not dead, that's the important part. Say, I found you a new lawyer."

"A new lawyer? Is there something wrong with my old lawyers?"

"Not that I know of."

There was a pause. Then: "You are with Pavlos, yes?"

My gaze cut to the shack's ceiling and its dark corners. The only eyes up there were arachnid. "How did you know?"

"He has been trying to convince me to hire him for

years. The man is a *touvlo*. I would not give him a job as a lawyer if he was the last lawyer on the planet."

She'd just called him a brick. I couldn't disagree. "It's like that, huh?"

"Worse. What do you need with him?"

"Information."

"What information?"

I told her and she laughed. "For that you went to Pavlos? I will tell you for free. Laki's father left him an airplane. He was a pilot."

The envelope vanished back into my bag. I tilted my head toward the garden.

"Time to go," I told Elias.

Pavlos was crestfallen. "But what about my job?"

"Maybe next time," I told him.

"Everything is gone this week. First my receptionist takes time off without asking, and now this."

The neurons in my brain twitched. "You can afford a receptionist?"

"She is terrible. She keeps filing my paperwork in the filing cabinet, then I cannot find anything."

"Sounds like a monster."

"And worse, she always tries to tell me about the law, like I don't know. She went to college, yes, but only one of us went to law school."

Those twitches in my brain morphed into flashing lights. "Was she a paralegal?"

"That is what she called herself," he said, moping his forehead with a handkerchief.

"Was her name Voula?"

He perked up. "Why? Do you know her?"

I gave him the bad news and I gave it to him straight.

He let out a gut-shaking sigh. "Now I will have to find a new receptionist."

"Cheer up," I said. "Half the country is looking for jobs."

———

I WAS GOING NOWHERE–FAST. Mostly because I was waiting on a couple of donkeys to cross the road. They wanted to get to the other side but they were taking the slow, scenic route. They should have listened to the chicken. Chickens were stupid but they knew time wasn't something they had in abundance.

Meanwhile, my brain took a few minutes to do some mental yoga, which is the only kind of yoga I do.

Laki had two things: an airplane and a penchant for making fires. Problem was, the gold-toothed henchman was a lot of things but he didn't strike me as the kind of guy who'd kill and dismember Litsa, murder Voula, and make Melas and Hera vanish off the face of the planet.

Except he was a henchman or something like one, wasn't he? Murderer and abduction were textbook henchman moves.

How did everything tie together, and how was Baby Dimitri's sister involved? She was a pornographer with a penchant for a certain type of actress, but that wasn't illegal, was it?

First thing's first, find Laki's plane.

I didn't have Laki's location or his plane's.

What I did have were questions, insatiable curiosity, and—I hoped—six out of nine lives left.

My phone rang. Nobody was there. That's how I knew it was Xander—that and caller ID.

"Katerina can't come to the phone right now," I said. "She ran away to join the circus." As soon as I ended the call, my phone buzzed again.

This time it was Gus.

"Please tell me you did not quit."

"I didn't quit. I'm just taking a mental health day. I called, I swear, but you didn't pick up."

"I never do," he said. "These days it is just people wanting to leave bodies. Now I am like a shaky little dog, frightened of the phone, frightened of the elevator. I remember when I used to have time off. I had a life. Now there are only dead people."

"Tomorrow morning I'll be back, and I won't let anybody leave so much as a severed finger."

"You are the best receptionist a man could have. I have been trying to contact Detective Melas but he is not answering."

Melas was still incommunicado. My worry ratcheted up another notch. "So you're calling me? I don't know where he is."

"They say you and he are going to have sex. There is even a bet, did you know?"

"I know," I said dryly. That rat bastard Takis was supposed to drop it. I really needed to get around to wringing his neck. "Please tell me you didn't place a bet."

"I could use the money," he said. "I could leave the morgue and find somewhere else to work—somewhere with sunlight."

———

THE DONKEYS MOVED ON, leaving several brown piles in the street. Ten minutes later I pulled into a parking place outside Marks & Spencer in downtown Volos. I needed black clothes if I was going to do this mourning thing. Aunt Rita was thoughtful and generous but our taste diverged above the ankle. Her style worked for her but I was more low maintenance. Or no maintenance. I guess Aunt Rita had more fun dressing for womanhood than I did.

Elias looked at the department store like it was a tragedy about to happen.

"You can wait here if you want," I told him.

His face lit up. "Really?" It fell again. "But Baboulas …"

"I won't tell her if you don't."

"I will be right there." He pointed to the street corner where he'd have a view of both doors.

In I went. For people in financial trouble, Greeks were flocking to the British store. I paused by the store directory to locate women's clothing, then, sidestepping a cluster of teenage girls, hurried over to the nearest black women's' clothing. It was my lucky day; the change of seasons meant that black was back in a big way.

I found my size, snatched a couple of black sweaters off the shelf, and ventured off to find bottoms to go with them. I grabbed several pairs of black pants off the rack, turned to find a dressing room, and walked smack into a pair of overdeveloped chests. The chests were attached to pair of balaclava-covered heads.

The Balaclava Boys.

"Oh, come on," I said. "You can't wear those in here. And besides, I already know what you look like."

"Really?" Big Balaclava asked. "What do we look like?"

"Like Detective Melas. That's the only reason Hera keeps you around, because you're bad copies of her ex boyfriend."

Small Balaclava pulled out a gun. It was compact and mean looking.

"You can't bring that in here either."

"We're NIS. We can do anything."

Big Balaclava elbowed him in the ribs. "Now we have to kill her. We weren't supposed to kill her."

"Why not?" I asked. "You already killed Litsa and Voula."

"That was not us. All we did was take the body."

"If you didn't kill them, what do you want with me?"

"We don't know. We are following orders, that is all."

A pair of rocket scientists.

The door was behind them. All I had to do was make it to the door, then Elias would be there with his gun. Mentally, I face-palmed. Why hadn't I insisted he come with me?

"Let's go," Big Balaclava said. "We are parked out back." He waved the gun toward the back of the store. Great. Elias had a blind spot. These guys could zip off into the sunset with me trussed up in the back of their van and no one might know I was missing for hours.

"I don't want to," I said. "If you're not going to kill me then it's pointless trying to take me. I'll kick and scream."

"That does not mean we can't hurt you. In fact, our orders say we can hurt you."

"It would be best if we did hurt her at least a bit," Small Balaclava said. He shoved his gun against my lower back and pushed. My bladder tensed, letting me know I could pee on them if they tried to get weird.

They marched me toward the back door.

"You," a voice said behind us. It was the gravely sound of a throat that had done more than its share of yelling. "And you."

Big Balaclava turned around. "What?"

A little old woman was standing behind us—okay, in front of us now. Widow. Knee-high stockings. She looked out of time and place in the modern department store. Her finger was pointed at Big Balaclava's face.

"That. Where can I find one?"

"What?"

Moron. "She means your balaclava," I told him.

"My mother made it," he said.

The woman sniffed and turned on her heel.

"Crazy old woman," he muttered.

The woman whipped around, and with both hands snatched both balaclavas off their heads. Then she bolted out of the store on bow legs.

"*Gamo tis mana's sou's kachika*! Now we have to blindfold you," Big Balaclava said.

He wanted to make sweet love to my mother's goat. I didn't have the heart to tell him she never had a goat, just Dad and me. "What's the point?"

"The point is that our boss will put a foot up my *kolos* if I don't."

"I'll close my eyes."

"Okay, that could work."

"The boss won't like it," Small Balaclava said.

"Who is your boss? It's Hera, isn't it?"

"It is definitely not Hera, but if it was we would not tell you."

"It's totally Hera. Who else would use a pair of Melas lookalikes to do their dirty work."

And they were adequate lookalikes. Between them, Tomas and Irini had captured the men well on paper. I might even be fooled if I had a traumatic brain injury.

"It's not dirty work," Big Balaclava complained.

The other guy did a hand wobble. "Kidnapping is a bit dirty. But your family will get you back as soon as they give us the boy."

"You mean Tomas? What do you want with Tomas?"

Big smacked Small. "*Vlakas!* What is wrong with you?"

"Ow!"

They tried to steer me past the cash registers but a cashier with power brows gave them a look that said their balls would be forfeit if we tried to enter the Employees Only zone.

"I hate shopping," Small Balaclava said.

They changed directions. We were headed for the side exit.

"We can't go that way," I told them.

"Sure we can," the big guy said. "We just walk right out."

I shrugged. "Fine. Let's do it."

My arms were full of merchandise, all of it security tagged and unpaid for. The moment we passed by the sensors they lit up like a tree at Christmas. Obnoxious beeping pierced the air. The Melas lookalikes stood there blinking, stuck on stupid. Not me. I was a criminal's grand-daughter, damn it. My DNA knew what to do. I flung the clothing in their faces and ran for the corner, where Elias was waiting.

"Run," I yelled.

Like a good bodyguard, Elias waited until I was safely past him before following me back to our cars. I jumped into the Beetle, fired up the engine, and got the hell out of Dodge.

I called Grandma on the way.

"Those Melas clones tried to grab me while I was shop-ping. They're after Tomas and they're NIS."

"No problem," she said darkly. "I will take care of them."

A sigh of relief escaped me. "Thanks."

"The store called me. Xander will go to the store to collect your things and pay for them."

"Xander," I said faintly. I'd have to remember to have

the clothes searched and x-rayed before I put them on. Revenge might bite.

————

WITH XANDER out of the way, it was safe to go back to the compound. Flaunting my presence didn't seem smart, so I took the covert route through the dungeon. I really needed to speak to Donk.

"He is not here," Monobrow told me, "but he left his sock behind if you want a souvenir."

Eww. No thanks.

"The other day he said Litsa went to see his mother. I don't suppose he mentioned it to you?"

Evasive: "Maybe he did. Maybe not."

I sighed. "Can I get an IOU on the *loukoumia*?"

He wagged a finger at me. "This is a one-time offer. What do you want to know?"

"When did Litsa go to see Donk's mother, and why?"

"Two days before her body fell through that old *malaka's* roof. Why, I do not know. Either the boy did not know or he did not say."

Now I really wanted to know if Litsa came home from that meeting. Instead of rolling the footage, I took the easy route. I called Grandma. She had a way of being one step ahead of everyone so she'd know if Litsa made it back home or not.

"No," Grandma said. "Nobody saw her after she left that morning, not even my electronic eyes. Why?"

"Do you know where she was going?"

"No."

"I do."

She waited. It was good to know something Grandma didn't. So sue me for gloating a teensy bit.

"Vikki. Baby Dimitri's half-sister. That's where Litsa went."

There was a long stretch of silence. The kind of silence with knives in it, and possibly guns. "Vikki," Grandma said finally. "Interesting."

"That's it? Interesting?"

"What more do you want from me, eh? Stay away from Vikki. She is trouble."

The last thing I needed was another job offer, but I had no intention of staying away from Vikki. Everyone missing —Melas, Litsa, Voula—was connected to her.

But first I wanted to solve the problem I could solve. I made a vague, non-committal promise to Grandma, ended the call, pressed Marika's name in my contacts list.

"Marika," I whispered into my phone when she answered. "You want to come on an adventure?"

"That depends. What kind of adventure? Is it to the morgue? Because I have already seen that."

"Not the morgue."

"Then yes. The boy still cannot get into the safe and I am getting bored. Why are you whispering?"

"Xander is looking for me."

She laughed. "If Xander was looking for you he would have found you by now."

That hurt my feelings just a teensy bit. "Maybe I'm better at hiding than he is at seeking."

"I do not think so. Where are you? Let me get my supplies and I will meet you."

I told her where to find me, and ten minutes later she showed up with her bulging shoulder bag and a big grin.

"I feel like a real spy," she said. "Maybe Baboulas will let me become a spy. A spy's work is less dangerous than a bodyguard's."

"Marika, have you *ever* seen a James Bond movie?"

"Takis will not have them on in the house. He says they get everything wrong, especially the part where women love spies. As your bodyguard it was constant danger and intrigue. How could being a spy be worse?"

We walked back to the Beetle, which was hidden from view of the road behind a haystack.

"Where are we going?"

"To the airport."

Marika clapped her hands. "A real adventure!"

I didn't break her heart just yet by telling her that we were looking for a plane not a flight.

We sped toward the outskirts of Volos. Elias was behind us.

"You want a snack?" Marika said. "Because I could use a snack."

"What have you got?"

"I have this chocolate cake but you cannot have that. Those are Baby's favorite."

"Do you have anything that isn't Baby's favorite?"

"No."

"Thanks," I said, "but I've eaten."

"I do not suppose we are stopping for souvlaki again," she said hopefully.

"I thought you had a bag full of snacks."

"Snacks are not a meal."

"Meal after. I'll even buy. In the meantime, I'm trying to figure out a mystery."

"What mystery?"

I told her everything I knew, except the part where Tomas was maybe, probably, although possibly not Melas's son. No part of that was my secret to share, and even though Grandma wasn't supreme evil after all, I wasn't convinced Melas wouldn't wind up as the crunchy filling in a speed bump.

"A mystery! I love mysteries almost as much as I love romances. Who is the father if it is not George?"

"I don't know." I gnawed on my lip as I drove. "Could be anyone."

"Now you are thinking like a TV detective," Marika said. "You know what we need? A lie. A big lie."

I didn't like this sound of that. "What kind of lie?"

"I don't know, but if this works maybe Baboulas will promote me to spy."

My mind crunched the data. Laki. A plane. Baby Dimitri's sister. Two dead women. A missing cop. A missing NIS agent. Melas lookalikes who had tried to abduct Tomas.

Why on earth would Hera take Tomas?

A penny dropped. Not a shiny new penny, but one crusty with age. What if I wasn't the only woman Melas had trusted with his secret? What if Hera believed Tomas was his?

But even if she had known, that wouldn't explain why Litsa and Voulas' bodies had been stolen, or why she'd make two attempts to snatch Tomas.

Ugh. Think, Kat. Think.

We drove out to the small domestic airport outside Volos. Laki wasn't Grandma; he didn't have his own runway. There were a limited number of places to hide a plane in the Volos area, and even fewer where he'd be able to take off and land with any frequency, so the airport was my first stop. It had a series of hangars, any one of them perfect for stowing Laki's inheritance.

I pulled into the airport's smallish parking lot and found a pair of spaces together. Elias slid in alongside the Beetle.

"I'm walking," I said. "You two stay here. If I'm not back in an hour, call Grandma."

Marika heaved herself out of the passenger seat. "How can I be a spy if I sit around and wait while you have all the fun? I am coming with you."

Elias looked like he wasn't happy with my plan either. "We all go or none of us go."

"Good," Marika said. She thrust her bag at him. "You can carry this for me. My back hurts because of the baby."

"I am a bodyguard," Elias said, "not a baggage handler."

"Nobody is just one thing in life," she told him. "Look at me. I am a wife, a mother, a bodyguard, and also a spy."

Elias almost choked on his tongue.

"Okay," I said, organizing my pockets. I had Dad's old slingshot in my back pocket. In my other back pocket I had Hera's super-duper stun gun. In the front, marbles that were a gift from Baby Dimitri. In the absence of pebbles and stones they were the perfect ammo for the slingshot. "Let's do this, and let's do it quietly."

"What are we looking for?" Marika wanted to know.

"I don't know, but I'll know it when I see it," I said.

The airport was smallish but it was still a lengthy hike to the hangars. Greece's financial woes were working in our favor. Austerity around here meant keeping non-essential lights off. Only the runway and terminal were lit up. The hangars and their surroundings were the kind of dark that is good at hiding secrets. This night thing was really working for us.

Marika was sweating. "Are we there yet? My feet hurt."

"Spies do not complain about their feet," Elias told her. He adjusted her bag. What was in that thing anyway? Rocks? Guns? It wouldn't be the first time she'd hauled a full arsenal to the party.

We sidled up to the first hangar, crept along its flank until we reached the corner where the side met the front. I peeked around. No cars parked out front. The doors were open. No shenanigans were afoot--not in this hangar anyway. I confirmed my suspicions, then motioned Elias and Marika to the next hangar. The next two had nothing to hide either. Planes were parked inside but they were the property of legitimate local businesses, or so my search engine told me.

The next hangar was empty. No plane. No nothing.

Two more to go.

Marika complained all the way to the next structure. Elias' face was stone, if the stone had set in the I'm-going-to-strangle-her position.

"Spies have to be quiet," I told her.

"I am not a spy yet. This is my apprenticeship."

I looked at her. "Uh …"

Elias opened his mouth to speak. Marika shut him down hard and fast.

"If you speak I will show you what is in my bag," she said.

"What's in your bag?" I asked her. "Besides snacks."

"Spy things," she said mysteriously.

Several cars were parked out front of this steel hulk. My belly flip-flopped. One of them belonged to Detective Nikos Melas. Melas was around here somewhere, probably inside this hangar. Score.

The massive sliding doors were pulled shut. The padlock hung from the lock like a dislocated joint. There was nobody about that I could see. Didn't mean they weren't inside though.

"Wait there," I told Elias and Marika.

"Good idea," Marika said. "That way if you are captured I can rescue you."

Elias rolled his eyes. He followed me around the corner,

ignoring my instructions. Sometimes it was like talking into a void.

There was a narrow gap between the giant doors, enough for a sliver of light to leak out and enough for a nosey poke Greek-American to press her eye to the slit.

Eureka.

Airplane.

And not a commercial aircraft. Not that I could tell, anyway. Smaller than Grandma's private jet. White. That's all I could see.

Inside there was light, coming from one of the far corners. Someone was here, or the plane was afraid of the dark.

I motioned for Elias to go back. We scooted around the corner.

Marika had disappeared.

Chapter 18

"We did bring Marika with us, didn't we?"

Elias held up Marika's big shoulder bag. "Would I be carrying this otherwise?"

He had a point. "So where did she go?"

"Probably to find food."

That wasn't a stretch. Marika liked food at the best of times. Pregnant, she was the culinary equivalent of a vacuum cleaner.

"Did you hear anything?"

"Nothing, boss."

"Me either."

We looked around. No sign of Marika. No bread-crumbs leading to a bakery or other eatery. I walked to the back of the building and peered around the corner. She wasn't there either. There was a regular sized door. I jiggled the handle. Locked.

"She's just gone," I said, turning around.

Elias had vanished. Marika's bag was on the ground.

"Are you kidding me? Where the hell is everyone?"

No answer.

I walked back to the front corner. The doors were still shut. The parking area was devoid of human life. I needed to think, so I flattened my back against the wall and closed my eyes. Probably now was a good time to call Grandma and have her send what passed for a cavalry in our family. That would mean Takis and Xander. Xander was, no doubt, furious at me for zapping him, and Takis would be livid because Marika had tagged along with me. I'd tried telling him nobody puts Marika in the corner, but he seemed to think women should be seen and not heard unless they're calling their men for lunch. Except Grandma. But she was less woman, more mythological figure. She used men like Takis as toothpicks.

No, there was no time. Whatever was happening was happening now.

Time to get Marika's spy supplies out.

I crouched down on the cracked concrete and opened the big bag. The top layer consisted of snacks. *Tsokofreta* bars—or as I knew them, chocolate wafers of sadness. Wafers were popular in Greece. I didn't get it; Greeks were happy people, so why eat wafers? Oooh, now here was something promising: ION chocolate, the kind with almonds. My new favorite. I ripped into the foil and broke off a row of nut-speckled chocolate. Creamy. Melt-on-my-tongue goodness. Europeans knew how to do chocolate. Lately the major brands back home were more waxy than milky.

As I stood up, a woman stepped in to view. Short geometric hairdo in violent red. Smokey eye shadow. Lashings of red lipstick that made her look like she'd been punched in the mouth and left for dead. She was in her thirties but her thirty miles of road saw mostly rush hour traffic. She had a gun and a cigarette, and one of those things was pointed at me.

"Are you going to make me choose?" I asked Vikki, pornographer, Donk's mother, and Baby Dimitri's half-sister.

Her face tried crumpling but the Botox had a death grip on her muscles. "Fuck the Virgin Mary, what are you talking about?"

"Gun. Cigarette. You know, both those things will kill a person, but one is slow and one is a whole lot faster."

"Do you know how much cigarettes cost? Bullets are cheaper."

"So you're going to shoot me?"

"Only if you keep talking."

"That's a problem," I said. "When I get nervous my mouth has a tendency to run faster."

She had a gun and I had nothing except the chocolate bar in my hand. Call me crazy but I really didn't want to throw chocolate at her. What kind of psychopath wastes good chocolate? I should have grabbed the wafer. I could have attacked her with the wafer.

I pitched the chocolate bar at her anyway. It struck her on the breast and bounced off. She threw the gun at me and clocked me on the nose. Pain shot through my head. Tears flooded my eyes, spilled over the edges, skated down my cheeks. The gun bounced off and landed several feet away.

Only one of us went diving for it.

Me.

Proud of myself for thinking and moving fast, despite the searing pain in my nose, I pointed the gun at Vikki.

"Where are Marika and Elias?"

For someone on the wrong end of a gun she was awfully smirky. "Your fat friend and the *pousti*? They are inside."

Indignation rose in me. How dare she make judgments

about my friends? And they were friends, even Elias. More than that, their safety was my responsibility.

"You know he's gay?"

"When it comes to human sexuality, I know everything."

"What do you want with them?"

"Nothing. I want you."

"You can't have me."

"Everybody can be had for a price, and if not, there are other ways. I made you an offer and you turned me down, so now I have to try those other ways."

Thoughts danced through my head. None of them were pretty. They involved fire and pain and screaming.

"Couldn't you be like a normal pornographer? They find lookalikes and exploit them instead."

"No. I offer authenticity. That is my brand. It is you or nobody, and I cannot give my customers nobody. They love variety, especially when that variety is someone notorious."

Notorious? Hardly. Grandma's reputation must have rubbed off on me. It wasn't earned.

"What about Voula?"

"Voula." She scoffed. "Voula was nobody."

I felt around in the dark and swung, hoping to hit the information piñata. "So why kill her?"

"I have a small but wealthy group of clients who pay big money for a certain kind of movie."

Bile lurched up my throat. She was talking about snuff movies. Movies where there's no happy ending, only death —real death. "You killed her for money?"

"How else is a woman supposed to survive in the world? I have to make money or perish. I have a son to raise, his future to think of."

"Does Donk know about this?"

"Yiorgos does not care about my business. All that

matters to him is that he has the latest phone and designer underpants. Children do not think about the future and the things parents have to do to secure that future for them."

Black spots kaleidoscoped in front of my eyes. The gun felt shaky in my hand. My palms were sweating.

"And Litsa? You killed Litsa too, didn't you?"

"She was the only Makris I could buy, and she was enthusiastic about performing until she realized what kind of movie we were making."

A sob lodged in my throat. For a moment I couldn't breathe. I leaned against the hangar's steel flank and tried to suck air.

Vikki reached for the gun. "Here, let me take that from you."

Not a chance. I squeezed the trigger.

Nothing happened.

"You do not have to die," Litsa said, "at least not at first. I can make money—big money—while you are alive. All you have to do is work for me."

Why didn't I stop to call Grandma or the police? Where was Melas when I needed him? Where was Melas when he needed me?

"What did you do to Detective Melas? Where is he?"

"What makes you think I did anything to the detective?"

"A little bird told me."

"A little bird, eh?" She dug her fingers into mine, trying to pry the gun from my hand. The useless, broken gun. "Give me the gun. It is a prop, but even a fake gun costs money. Your policeman is fine. Maybe you two can be in my movie, eh? My newest stars."

Relief washed over me. If Melas was alive then all I needed to do was find him and figure out a plan. My fingers let go of the prop. "*21 Hump Street*," I said. "*My Big Fat Greek Porno.*"

Vikki grabbed my chin. "Not just a pretty face. Have you thought about implants? Take her inside," she said to someone I couldn't see.

A couple of goons materialized. Pretty boys with bare chests and low-slung jeans.

"Should we pat her down first?"

"If she had a weapon would she have hit me with a chocolate bar?"

The goons swapped glances like they couldn't figure out if it was a trick question or not.

Vikki rolled her eyes. She wasn't impressed with the help any more than I was.

"Good henchmen are so hard to find," she told me.

"That's why Grandma recruits from inside the family," I said. "They're not all smart but they're competent."

"Just take her inside," she purred.

Her muscle-bound flunkies each grabbed one of my arms and steered me around the front to the towering doors. Cold sweat bubbled out of my pores. My throat tightened. Fear was having its way with me, and there wasn't a thing I could do about it.

Near the parked cars, something moved. Something or someone. A tiny movement that nobody else noticed. I tried to get a better look but the goons jerked me around until I was facing the hangar's entrance.

The doors slid open enough for us all to enter, then they closed with a metallic *clang*. In front of me was the plane I'd spotted through the narrow gap. At the back of the hangar, lights had been set up. I didn't know much about the movie business, and everything I knew making porn came from the twenty times or so times that I'd watched Boogie Nights, but to my inexperienced eye it looked like Vikki had outfitted the hangar to serve as a porn set. Leather couches (easy to wipe down, I supposed), round bed, an office setting (desk, chair, filing cabinet), and a dungeon setting, cobbled together by someone with a limited imagination but plenty of time to watch *Fifty Shades of Grey*.

I found Marika and Elias next, sitting on another leather couch. Marika had an expression like a sack full of wet cats. You couldn't tell it from Elias's face but he was plotting murder. On the outside he was calm, collected, and ready to rip out a heart. Both of them were gagged with ball gags that I hoped were clean. I flipped a wave at them. They didn't wave back on account of the handcuffs.

Sitting in two armchairs (gee, Vikki really liked leather) were a pair of oiled-up young guys who looked like they'd been hired for their stamina, not their acting skills. They were both playing with their phones, expressions bored.

"Katerina Makris-with-an-s!"

It was Laki. He poked his head out of the plane and waved. Laki was old, gaunt, and had gold tombstones where some of his original teeth had been. The rest of the spaces were empty.

"Light any good fires lately?" I asked him.

He grinned. "I cannot complain. I have cheese, I have bread, and I can make fire any time I like, from the air."

One mystery solved. A million more to go.

"The police aren't too happy about that."

"Why? If they want my bread and cheese all they have to do is ask." He winked at me and eased down the plane's steps. For a guy who was born when a woman showing her ankles was a sin he was awfully spry.

"Laki!" Vikki barked. "Get back in the plane."

Laki shook his head. "No respect that one. Her brother is the world's biggest *kolotripas*, but he knows respect."

A *kolos* is a butt and a *tripas* is a hole. I couldn't disagree with his assessment of Baby Dimitri's character, even though I liked the old mobster.

"Why are you helping her?"

"What makes you think I have a choice, eh?"

I swung around to Vikki. "Baby Dimitri is going to kill you."

"Not if I kill him first," she said.

"Why would you kill him? Isn't he your money tree? Your other money tree, I mean."

Her laugh was bitter and wrathful. Someone around here was the proverbial woman scorned, and it wasn't me.

From his shirt pocket Laki pulled out a soft packet of tobacco and rolling papers. "Ask this one how much she gets if Dimitri dies."

"*Skasmos*, old man," Vikki said.

"I'm going to guess nothing," I said.

Laki nodded as he rolled. He licked the paper's edge and sealed it shut. "Nothing."

"Close your mouth, you old *vlakas*, or I will kill you."

Laki laughed. "She always says that. 'Laki, I am going to kill you.' 'Laki, I wish you were dead.' 'Laki, I will feed you to the dogs.' But here I am. Why? Who knows? Not me. I just make fire and fly my plane."

Now I was curious—and eager to keep the conversation going. The more talking they did, the less killing Vikki would have time for.

"Who gets his money now?"

"The boy," Laki said, lighting the cigarette balanced on his lip.

"Donk?" That wasn't bad. After all, Donk was Baby Dimitri's nephew. It made sense that he'd inherit. As far as I knew, Baby Dimitri didn't have kids of his own.

"Yiorgos?" Laki laughed around the damp edges of his cigarette. "No. The other boy."

Vikki whacked Laki in the head with her fake gun. Without making a sound, Laki toppled over. His lit cigarette rolled away. Vikki crushed it with her leather sole. Beating up old men—she was a monster.

And that gave me my opening. I yanked Hera's stun gun out of my back pocket, shoved it up against Vikki's neck.

ZAP.

She sagged to the ground. Her flunkies—the two who had escorted me inside, plus the two from the chairs, waiting on their close-ups—converged on me. They were unarmed and over-endowed.

"Are those real?" I asked them. "Or do you stuff them? Because I read an article once where male underwear models stuff their underwear with white bread because you can mold it really easily around … you know."

They dropped their pants.

Huh. No bread, white or otherwise.

"I don't suppose you've seen a policeman around here?"

They pulled up their pants. One of them pointed to the plane.

"Are you guys going to stop me?" I sidled over to where Marika was making furious noises around the ball gag.

"That depends," one of the guys said, "on whether we get paid or not."

I waggled my fingers at them. "Keys?"

The same guy tossed me the handcuff keys. A moment later I'd sprung Marika and Elias. Elias got busy cuffing Vikki, who was still out cold. When he was done he called the Makris Family Danger Hotline. Now I had to find Melas. I hoped like crazy he was okay.

"You'll get paid," I said. "I'll make sure of it. Find a piece of paper, write down your names and phone numbers, we'll work something out." They made faces like that was acceptable, then went hunting for paper.

Marika jumped up. "Where is my bag?"

"Outside."

"You left it outside?"

"I was busy being captured."

"Me, too," she said. "Elias, go get the bag. I need a snack."

He shot me a look.

"Please get it," I said. "We'll never hear the end of it if you don't."

"So Takis tells me," he muttered.

Marika bristled. "What did my soon-to-be-dead husband say about me?"

"Nothing." Elias took off.

"I will wait here." Marika gripped the back of the couch. "I feel weak. Go on without me."

"Take care of Laki," I told her. "He's old, and I don't want him to die on me."

I jogged up the plane's steps. It was smaller than Grandma's plane, and not nearly as plush. I spotted Melas immediately at the back of the plane, tied up near the bathroom. It wasn't all bad: he had location going for him.

His eyes lit up when he saw me. I loosened the gag and yanked it out of his mouth.

"Katerina?"

"In the flesh. You okay?"

He looked fine—tired, disheveled, but okay. Melas's restraints were all cable ties. I knelt down beside him and began hacking with the multitool that lived in my bag.

"Relax, I am immortal."

I snorted. "How did Vikki convince you to leave the police station?"

"She told me she knew who started the fires."

"Laki."

"Laki," he said. "How did you figure it out?"

"Laki's father died recently and left Laki his airplane. It wasn't a leap to put the plane and Laki's favorite hobby together."

When the last cable tie popped open, Melas rubbed his wrists and ankles, then he gathered me into his arms.

"Who is with you?"

"Marika and Elias."

"What are the odds Marika will not burst in here, looking for peanuts?"

I thought about Marika's snack supply. It should keep her satiated for at least ten minutes. "Slim to none."

"That's too bad. I had plans."

"Since when?"

"Since you charged in here."

"You make plans fast."

"I am a spontaneous kind of man."

His hand was traveling up my thigh and his lips were on my neck. The hand stopped before it reached my goodie box. I wasn't sure how to feel about that. My emotions were battling my hormones, and my hormones were the only ones with any real conviction. They wanted what they wanted, and right now they wanted Melas.

"Katerina?" Marika called out. "I have a very important question."

Melas tensed.

"What?" I asked.

"Are we stopping to eat on the way home? Being held prisoner has made the baby hungry."

Melas raised his eyebrows. "The baby."

I stifled a laugh.

"Sure, we can eat," I yelled back.

There was scraping of metal against concrete. The doors were opening. That had to be Grandma's rescue team. Boy, they worked fast. I slid out of Melas's grip, grabbed his hands, and pulled him up.

"Uh oh," Marika said from outside the plane. "Here is trouble."

Melas and I exchanged looks.

"We tied Vikki up," I said. "It can't be her."

"Stay here. I will go first," he said.

Like that was going to happen. Melas should know by now that I wasn't an obedience school graduate. I followed him out of the plane, jerking to a halt when I reached the second step.

Hera had decided to show up for the party. She looked like she'd wrestled a tornado and lost. Her skimpy sheath dress, what there was of it, was shredded in strategic places. Her hair was bedhead. Her makeup was I-banged-the-whole-band. She looked so much sexier than me.

I looked down at my wilted shirt and jeans, whose stretch had decided to take an extended relaxation break. At least my boots were nice.

"Hera, what is going on?" Melas said.

Hera's hand fluttered to her torn neckline. "Nikos. Thank the Virgin Mary you are here." Her other hand was behind her back, holding something.

Someone.

She jerked her hand around. It was fastened around Tomas's wrist.

My heart stopped. It had been doing that a lot lately.

Tomas grinned and waved. "Thea Katerina!"

I couldn't return his grin. I tried but it wasn't happening. "Don't you dare hurt him," I said through gritted teeth.

"Hurt him?" Hera slapped a wounded expression on her face. "I rescued him."

Melas schlepped down the rest of the steps. I was right behind him.

"Rescued him from what?" Melas wanted to know.

"That woman, of course." She pointed to Vikki, who wasn't in a position to defend herself, what with the cuffs and gag. "She was going to kill him like she killed his poor mama."

"Is that true?" I asked Tomas. "Did she rescue you?"

He lifted his chin up then tilted it down. "I was trying to follow you, Thea Katerina, but this crazy lady grabbed me and made me go with her."

I made a disgusted sound and marched over to Hera. Slapping her seemed like a good idea, but I had an even better one. I pulled out her stun gun and gave her a zap. The batteries were fading so she only got a half dose, but it was enough for her to stagger backwards and release Tomas's wrist.

"That is mine," she said, between chattering teeth.

"Was yours, and now it's mine."

Zap.

"Ow," she wailed. "Make her stop, Nikos. I did this for you."

Melas looked unconvinced. "You did what for me, Hera? You abducted a child. Do you have any idea how much trouble you could be in?"

"I saved him."

"Did not," Tomas said.

"Why did this one say she did it for the detective?" Marika said. She was at the end of a *tsokefreta* wafer bar and was already ripping into the plastic around a chocolate cake with her free hand. She waved it under Laki's nose, and when he didn't respond she shrugged and took a bite of the confection.

Uh oh. "Because she's crazy," I said, trying to steer the conversation in a less dangerous direction. Just because Tomas probably wasn't Melas's son, didn't mean his life wouldn't be in danger if certain people knew there was a chance he could have been. "What did you do with the bodies, Hera? That's what I want to know."

"What bodies?"

"The ones you had your lackeys steal from the morgue —the lackeys who look like Melas."

"You think I stole corpses? Why would an NIS agent— allegedly—steal bodies?"

She'd come out of the NIS closet to me but she was still playing the "allegedly" card in front of everyone else.

"Just a hunch: because you're crazy and evil."

"I am not crazy!" she yelled. "I was busy being kidnapped in the woods by Baby Dimitri's crazy sister! And somehow I lost my bag and my phone. Do you have any idea how much that bag cost?"

Oh boy, I couldn't wait to give her the bad news, that Dad had sliced the leather to pieces.

"By 'woods' she means 'private property.' Grandma's private property," I explained. "Where I come from that's trespassing."

"We are not where you're from," Hera snapped.

"What kidnappers?" Melas wanted to know.

"The ones who were chasing me. That is how I wound up looking like this! I have been locked up for days in a bathroom!"

Vikki rolled off the couch. She hit the ground hard, made a pained noise, then began rolling across the hangar, toward the rear door I'd noticed earlier.

"Heh," Marika said, polishing off the cake. "She reminds me of a souvlaki."

"Everything reminds you of a souvlaki," Elias muttered.

"You said Hera was fine," I said Melas.

He shrugged. "She is fine."

"Why would Vikki lock you up?" I asked Hera.

Hera marched across to the human tumbleweed, seized Vikki by the hair, hauled her over to where we were standing. "She accused me of having sex with her brother."

I laughed. "Why would *anyone* have sex with Baby Dimitri?"

Suddenly everyone was laughing.

At me.

My eyes narrowed. "What?"

"Baby Dimitri is rich, powerful, and a criminal. Women love rich, powerful criminals," Marika told me. "Plus he sells shoes."

"Women love shoes," Hera said.

"I wouldn't touch him for all the shoes in Europe," I said.

"And that is why I like you," Melas said.

Hera shot me look that more steel in it than a claymore's blade. "Ha! You spend a lot of time with Baby Dimitri. I hear you have even been to his house—twice."

"Yes, and I waited outside both times because he wouldn't let me in! Anyway, you can talk. How are those Melas lookalikes working for you Hera? Take them to his house lately?"

Melas set himself in stone, legs apart, arms folded. He didn't look like a man in a merciful mood. "Why, Hera?"

Tears bubbled over the NIS agent's lower lashes and poured prettily down her cheeks.

"Do you practice that in the mirror?" I asked.

"Sometimes," she said. She turned to Melas and amped up the waterworks. "I only did it because I love you."

Melas wasn't having it. He unclipped his phone and tried to make a call. "*Ai sto dialo*, the battery is dead."

I handed him my phone. He walked a short distance away, talking animated and low. Sounded to me like he was calling for backup.

There was the sound of tires rolling across blacktop outside, then car doors slammed. Takis and Dad were in the building. No Xander.

Dad's face was deceptively relaxed. His eyes though were telling a different story. "You okay?" he asked. Then he bear-hugged the stuffing out of me.

"I'm fine," I said against his jacket. "But somebody needs to check on Laki."

"Laki is my responsibility," said a different voice.

Baby Dimitri had entered the building. He'd lost the robe and found some clean, freshly pressed clothes and a dollop of Brylcreem. It was autumn but Baby Dimitri was always Florida in summer. He'd come alone and he'd brought a gun the size of a weightlifter's arm. He pointed it at his half-sister.

"Somebody put her in my car."

Melas tucked my phone back into my bag. "Vikki is ours. She's responsible for two homicides. Kyrios Laki is ours, too."

Takis and Marika had Laki up on his feet again. He greeted his pal with a gold flecked grin. "Dimitri, is that you?"

Baby Dimitri's voice softened. "Of course it is me, *malakas*. What are you doing here?"

Laki looked around, confused. "Where am I?"

"Wow, Vikki must have really hit him hard. You should

get him to the hospital for a cat scan," I said.

Chin up-down. "There is nothing wrong with him," Baby Dimitri said.

"But—"

"Is that Katerina Makri? She looks different," Laki said. He winked at me and flashed his dentistry.

Baby Dimitri's gaze was level with mine. "That is Katerina, but she had a little work done on her face."

It took me a moment to understand what was going on. Laki had some form of dementia. He'd mistaken me for Grandma. Poor guy.

"*Katalaves?*" the godfather said to Melas. *Do you understand?*

Melas nodded. When it came to the fires he wouldn't get his man. "But we're taking Vikki."

"Dimitri, no," Vikki protested. "I am your sister."

Baby Dimitri didn't look at her, didn't speak. He walked off into the sunset with his pyromaniac pal.

———

MELAS DROVE me back to my car.

His eyes were on the horizon, beyond me. They were clouded over and someplace that wasn't exactly here. Slumped shoulders completed the desolate picture.

"There is something bothering me," he said.

"What's that?"

"At first I thought it was a coincidence. When I was at work, the texts you sent, sounded to me like you knew I was at my desk."

My heart stopped for a moment. Xander had been right, damn it. Melas knew.

I could have lied but that wasn't me. Not about something like this. Melas was a good guy, he deserved better.

"I knew."

"The police station is bugged, yes?"

I did a little hand-tilting thing that meant so-so. "Visual only. No audio."

He blew out a long sigh and shoved his hand through his hair. Then he fixed his steady gaze on me. "How long have you known about the cameras?"

"Since my first week here."

"And you did not tell me Baboulas was watching us?"

"No."

"I guess I do not have to ask why."

My heart was leaden in my chest. "You were just a good-looking man then, a policeman who enjoyed flirting with me. And I had only just learned I had family besides my father."

"And now?"

"You're more."

"But you still chose not to tell me my workplace is bugged."

"I know."

"What am I supposed to say?"

Words weren't exactly falling out of my mouth either. We stood there, hands in pockets, looking over each other's shoulders. The whole thing made me hate clothing manufacturers even more, because they're incapable of putting decent pockets in women's clothing. So I was stuck only being able to shove my hands in finger-deep.

"Why did you tell me Hera was fine?"

"Because I wanted her to be. She is crazy but I still care about her."

"I don't understand."

"Understand what?"

"How you can care about someone who staged the abduction of a little boy just to impress you when she 'rescued' him. Whether Tomas was your son or not, that's just sick."

I have to go," Melas said.

"Where?"

"Look on your cameras. I am sure they will tell you."

He got back into his car, drove away.

———

I WENT DRIVING, found myself a mostly deserted beach, where the only life form around was an elderly bartender with a large menu. I ordered a Shirley Temple, then another. Sometime later I went looking for a public restroom, otherwise known as a bush.

It had been that kind of summer, and now fall was shaping up to be more of the same.

———

GRANDMA WAS in the kitchen when I slouched back to her shack, hours later. She was pouring hot syrup over cold *kataifi*, baklava's hirsute cousin. Outside, Xander was playing a game with Tomas and Dad. There were cards involved, and toothpicks. Tomas was cleaning house.

"Either the syrup has to be hot and the pastry cold, or the syrup has to be cold and the pastry hot. That way the pastry stays crispy," she explained.

"Is it ready to eat yet?"

Wordlessly, she grabbed a plate and dumped a piece of *kataifi* on top, then she spooned extra syrup on top, until it was swimming. I all but snatched it out of her hands, then hunkered down at the table, shoveling sugar into my face.

"Man?"

"Melas," I said around the pastry.

"Nikos. He is almost a man."

My head jerked up. "Almost?"

"His mama is too attached to him and he allows it." She pulled the phone out of her pocket. "Where is Rita? Nobody tells me anything."

I ducked my head down and hid my smile. "He found out about the camera at the police station."

Grandma made a sour face. "Then he would *hezo* if he found out about the camera in his bedroom."

I choked. Coughed. "What?"

"Relax, Katerina, I am joking. Do you want me to have him moved to another city?"

"You can do that?" Who was I kidding, of course she could.

"I can send him anywhere in the world. Maybe a small island where the people throw their garbage into the ocean and wipe their *kolos* with their hands. Can you imagine Nikos living somewhere like that? I can."

I laughed. Her mouth curved upwards and her wrinkles developed new wrinkles.

"Laugh. It is good for you. But seriously, let me know if you want me to send him away."

The last bite of *kataifi* vanished off my plate. Would Grandma mind if I licked the ceramic?

"He was already upset. I think the camera thing was just syrup on the *baklava*."

"Too much? He should try being a woman sometime. We can bleed for a week without dying."

"Aunt Rita can't."

"She would if she could, and that is what matters. Why was Nikos upset? Because he found out Tomas is not his son?"

My mouth fell open.

"Close your mouth," Grandma said. "You look like

a fish."

"How did you know?"

"Everybody talks, and sooner or later they talk in places where I have ears. Also, anybody with eyes can see who that boy's father is."

"Who?"

"What fun would it be if I gave you all the answers?"

"I don't like fun," I said.

She patted me on the arm. "Not everybody in this family is blood. Look at Xander."

I looked at Xander through the window. Nice view. I liked looking at Xander—Xander who hadn't yet taken his revenge on me for the zapping I'd given him. I liked looking at Melas too, and now I'd screwed things up royally. But if someone granted me a do-over I still wouldn't tell him about the cameras. It had everything to do with integrity. Grandma had trusted me with her private subterranean sanctum. She'd opened her home, her family, and her world to me. There's no way I'd throw that back in her face, not even for Melas. As a cop he should have understood that integrity is everything.

Grandma slid another mound of *kataifi* in front of me. This time, I picked at the dessert. The first piece was for eating my feelings. This one was for quiet contemplation while I processed Grandma's acceptance that Tomas wasn't blood. Not everybody from her generation, especially in Greece, was that progressive.

While I was doing that, Gus called.

"Please tell me you will be at work tomorrow," he said. "Two new bodies came in today while I was in the bathroom. At this rate I will have to start advertising for cannibals."

"I'll be there. Those bodies are as good as gone."

"If you do this I will love you forever. Before I forget,

the tests came back from our stolen woman, the one with the handbag. She was pregnant." There was a ding in the background that I recognized as the elevator opening. "*Gamo tin mana sou*," Gus swore. "Get that out of here or my receptionist will shove it right up the hole in your *poutsa!*"

I winced. There were some places foreign objects just shouldn't go.

"Promise me you will be here tomorrow," Gus said. "If you do not, I will be buried in bodies."

I crossed my heart but didn't hope to die because Gus would never forgive me if mine was one of the bodies clogging up his morgue, then I ended the call.

So Voula had been pregnant. Interesting. And tragic.

"I need some money," I told Grandma. "Probably a lot."

"Okay."

"Aren't you going to ask me what for?"

"No."

"Really?"

"Whatever you want the money for, I know it is something good."

"How big is the graveyard in Makria?"

"Why?"

"I want to put some people in it."

"I will talk to Father Harry."

"Thank you."

Grandma carried a piece of *kataifi* to the table and sat it down next to my dead grandfather's olive oil can. She picked up a fork and stuck it into the dessert.

"You are a good girl, Katerina."

"I don't feel good. Mostly I feel useless."

"All the best people do. That is why they push themselves to be better."

———

I WENT to see a man about a boy. The man in question didn't look happy to see me. His roof was still rubble but today he was out of his house and at the scene of the crime, watching the contractors clean up the mess. Baby Dimitri was in his usual chair; only today it was facing the store instead of the beach. He had two other chairs. He offered me one, but I turned it down. Standing gave me the upper hand, or so Grandma said. It was one of her tricks.

Grandma had said anyone with a pair of eyes could see who Tomas's birthfather was. There was little resemblance now, but she had known him all her life.

"It's you, isn't it? You're Tomas's father."

The aging gangster didn't deny it. "I suppose you will go running to Baboulas now."

"She already knows."

"And I am still alive? Either it is a miracle or her sheep have escaped."

"So you and Litsa, huh? For how long?"

"From the time she first walked into my club, and until the day she walked out. After that, I was something she did between men."

"It didn't bother you that she was married?"

Shrug. "Why? It did not bother her."

"And Voula?"

"Voula was a nice woman who brought paperwork to Laki from her lawyer's office, and that is how I met her. Nice women are not for me—not for long, anyway. Nice women want things. Families. Homes. Husbands who do not sit in front of their shoe and souvenir shops, enjoying foreign breasts."

"Before that she was a stripper. I figured that's how you knew her."

"She was not one of mine."

"Did you know she was pregnant?"

"Not until after I had sent her away. She came to my house to tell me, but Laki and Vikki were there, so I pretended that I did not believe her. I said only the Virgin Mary, Christos, and God knew who the father was. Do you think I am a monster, Katerina Makris-with-an-s?"

"Does it matter what I think?"

"Every man needs someone to hear his confession."

Being Baby Dimitri's confessor didn't thrill me. "Vikki threw Litsa out of the plane as a warning, didn't she? She didn't want any secret children around, grabbing her inheritance, and she wanted you to know it."

"My sister has entitlement issues. Everything I have worked for, she believes it is hers." He spat on the ground, politely missing my boots. "Nothing will be hers when I die, and I do not intend to die for a long time."

"Who gets it?"

He grinned. "You would like to know, yes?"

"Donk? Tomas?"

"I have secrets, Katerina Makris-with-an-s. Greece has been kind enough to allow me to keep a few. Having money helps."

"Wow, owning a shoe and souvenir shop must be more lucrative than I thought."

He winked. "Let it be our secret, eh?"

I wasn't done connecting dots. "That must be why Voula made the movie for your sister, because Vikki threatened to tell Yiannis she was pregnant with your child. What I don't understand though is who took the bodies from the morgue." I chewed on the edge of my nail. Then it came to me. "That was you too, wasn't it?"

Two palms up. "Maybe I did. I cannot say."

"What did you do with them?"

"Litsa will be returned to your family. Voula is on her way to her family."

"It's my understanding that they won't be able to afford a burial."

"I have taken care of it."

"Why did you use the Melas lookalikes?"

He shrugged. "Why not?"

"How did you convince them to help?"

"I have friends in places."

"High places?"

"They do not have to be high to be useful. Remember that." His attention slid away from me to a point further down the sidewalk. "Here comes my favorite *malakas*," he called out. "*Re, malaka*, what are you doing?"

Hours after the hangar ordeal, Laki was still wearing the same shabby outfit. He shambled along the sidewalk, grin lighting up the rock formation that was his face.

"Look, it is my hero," he said to me. "I have a present for you."

"You're welcome, but I didn't really do anything."

The gold-toothed pyromaniac lowered himself into the seat next to Baby Dimitri's and crossed his legs. Socks with sandals. Why was I not surprised?

"All women like presents," Laki said.

"It is true. Women love presents." Baby Dimitri's lip curled up. "You smell like a goat," he said to his pal.

"I always smell like a goat."

"Today you smell like the back end of a dead goat."

Laki laughed. Here was a guy who didn't seem all that traumatized by his ordeal. He didn't even have an egg on his head where Vikki clocked him. "Hey, Katerina, do you like your car?"

My eyes narrowed. "Why?"

From his pocket he withdrew his tobacco pouch and began to roll. "No reason."

The Beetle technically belonged to Grandma, but she'd bought it for me. It wasn't the red Jeep I'd left at home, but it was a nice consolation prize, and it was new, unlike my Jeep, which was easing into geriatric territory. That Jeep and I had been places together. But then so had the bright yellow Beetle and I. I was growing to love the zippy little drop-top.

The same zippy little drop-top that currently had a wide curl of smoke spiraling out of its passenger seat.

I yelped.

"Do not worry," Laki said, beaming from ear to wrinkled ear. "I have a gift for you, remember?"

THANK you for reading *Night Crime*, the sixth of Kat Makris' adventures!

Want to be notified when my next book is released? Sign up for my mailing list: http://eepurl.com/ZSeuL. Or like my Facebook page at: https://www.facebook.com/alexkingbooks.

ALL REVIEWS ARE APPRECIATED. You may help another reader fall in love ... or avoid a terrible mistake.

ALL MY BEST,
Alex A. King

Also by Alex A. King

Disorganized Crime (Kat Makris #1)

Trueish Crime (Kat Makris #2)

Doing Crime (Kat Makris #3)

In Crime (Kat Makris #4)

Outta Crime (Kat Makris #5)

Seven Days of Friday (Women of Greece #1)

One and Only Sunday (Women of Greece #2)

Freedom the Impossible (Women of Greece #3)

Light is the Shadow (Women of Greece #4)

No Peace in Crazy (Women of Greece #5)

Summer of the Red Hotel (Women of Greece #6)

Family Ghouls (Greek Ghouls #1)

Pride and All This Prejudice

9 781986 840774